Tales fr

The Grand Castle Hotel

To Graemer and Heather
With thanks
John

John Orr

Acknowledgements

I would like to thank Mrs Elaine Quigley for typing the stories and always with unfailing good humour.

Special thanks to my wife Betty, who edited, proof read and corrected my appalling grammar. Without Betty nothing would ever have happened. Thanks also to Patrick Luskin who allowed me to quote from his book 'A Voyage of Discovery' (2003) and for his anecdotes from the Lough.

Dedicated to

My family

The Grand Castle Hotel

Contents

(j)   A Cold Room
(k)   Miss Mary Martin
(l)   A Band of Brothers
(m)   The Snatch
(n)   The Walking Sticks
(o)   The Perfect Man
(p)   Births, Marriage and Deaths
(q)   Johnathan Charles Montgomery IV
(r)   Lady Mary Fitzwilliam-Howard

Part 3   Staff

(a)   Mrs Hughes
(b)   Helen
(c)   Sean and Billy
(d)   Charlotte and Simone
(e)   Pierre's Pickle
(f)   Wee Hughie
(g)   The Mysterious Michael
(h)   Jane
(i)   The Laundress's Lapse
(j)   The Managing Director

Prologue

Everyone has a favourite place in all the world; or if they don't they ought to.

My outstanding favourite is Ashford Castle, Lough Corrib and the wild beauty of Connemara.

Ashford Castle has a long and chequered history, originally built on a Monastic site on the Mayo/Galway border by the de Burgo family in 1226.

The de Burgo's/Burke family retained ownership of this special place until 1589 when they lost it following fierce fighting with Sir Richard Bingham, Lord President of Connaught who took possession and added a fortified enclave.

In either 1670 or 1678 Dominic Browne obtained the estate by Royal Charter and in 1715 the estate of Ashford was established as a Hunting Lodge in the seventeenth century French Chateau Style.

In 1892 the estate was bought by Benjamin Lee Guinness who added two large Victorian extensions and extended the estate to 26,000 acres planting thousands of trees in the process. Following the death of Benjamin, his son Lord Ardilaun extended the Castle further in the neogothic style. Lord Ardilaun's love of the area was such that he derived his title form Ardilaun Island on Lough Corrib.

Lord Ardilaun developed the woodlands and gardens and rebuilt the entire west wing of the castle, connecting the early eighteen century part in the East with two de Burgo towers in the west. Finally Lord Ardilaun added battlements to the entire castle. Lord Ardilaun's influence extended into Lough Corrib where he introduced steamboats especially the 'Lady Eglinton' to ply between villages on Upper Lough Corrib and Galway city.

On the death of Lord Ardilaun the estate passed to his nephew Ernest Guinness who sold it to the Irish Nation in 1989.

1940's	The Castle was opened as hotel by Noel Huggard
1970	Castle bought by John Mulcahy who restored it and doubled its size
1970's	Golf Course built and opened
1985	Castle bought by US Investors including famous Rugby Player Tony O'Reilly
2007	Castle sold to Gerry Barrett for £50m

2011	Receivership
October 2012	Put up for sale
May 2013	Castle bought by Red Carnation Group for £20m
January 2014	Red Carnation Group acquired Lisloughrey Lodge

Ashford Castle has had many famous guests, none more so than John Ford, John Wayne and Maureen O'Hara when the film 'The Quiet Man' was shot there in 1951.

Other VIP's include King George V and Queen Mary, Prince Edward Earl of Wessex, Ronald Reagan President USA, Ted Kennedy Senator USA, Oscar Wilde, John Lennon, George Harrison, Brad Pitt, Pierce Brosnan and Prince Rainier III and Princess Grace of Monaco.

At twenty seven miles long and ten miles wide Lough Corrib with a surface area of sixty eight square miles is the second largest Lough in Ireland. Its average depth is twenty one feet with the deepest point being measured at a depth of one hundred and sixty feet. Lough Corrib lies mainly in County Galway with only the north east corner in County Mayo.

Folklore has it that Lough Corrib has three hundred and sixty five islands contained within it; however the Creator of Charts indicates a much more accurate one thousand three hundred and twenty seven islands within its waters.

The islands are rich in wildlife supporting otters, mink, stoats and frogs while an abundance of bird life exists. Most famous of the islands on Lough Corrib is Inchagoil situated midway between Cong and Galway City where evidence of an early Monastic settlement is still visible to the naked eye.

The first canal in Ireland, known as the Friar's Cut allowed boats to sail from Lough Corrib to Galway City in the twelfth century. However, there may have been even earlier passage as Viking boats and battle-axes dated from the tenth century have been discovered in the bed of the Lough. These 'dug out' canoes are forty feet long and well preserved. Ashford Castle sits on the banks of Lough Corrib.

Connemara

What can one say about Connemara that has not already been said. Connemara is a district in the west of Ireland with boundaries that are not well defined. Some define it to be the land contained by Killary Harbour, the Maam Valley and Lough Corrib, a line from there to the sea at Barna and the Atlantic Ocean. Others draw the eastern boundary line from Killary Harbour to Kilkieran Bay in the West of County Galway.

I say, it does not matter a jot how you define it, Connemara is quite simply the most beautiful place on earth.

Until now everything that I have written is fact, or facts as I understand them. While the wild beauty of the West of Ireland has inspired my wild imaginings, everything from here forward is entirely fictitious --- the outpourings from a fevered mind!

Part 1

The Henrys

To most people a hotel is simply a place to lay their head on their way to or from somewhere else. Usually a hearty breakfast is an indulgence but often that is as far as the guest's thoughts travel.

For more discerning guests the standard of personal service and the quality of the food takes on a new meaning. For the tiny minority a 'hotel stay' is almost a spiritual experience.

In reality a hotel is much more than somewhere to sleep; it is a microcosm of a much greater universe.

The Grand Castle Hotel is more complex than most. Situated on the banks of a vast lough (lake) the Hotel is exactly as it is described in the brochure: A Castle of nearly one thousand years duration it oozes romance, mystery, style, elegance and hints of a violent past. The Castle is to be found in possibly the most picturesque and rugged part of Ireland, sitting in its own estate of many thousands of acres.

Services provided by the Hotel include beauty parlours, spas, swimming pools, hairdressers, tennis, croquet, an eighteen hole golf course, horse riding, falconry, archery, sailing, boating and many water sports, designer shops, chauffeur driven limousines and doctors and counsellors when needed by distressed residents.

This story of the Grand Castle Hotel begins with nine stories about HENRYS, for no particular reason other than the fact that some of them are 'writ large' in the Hotel's history.

The Grand Castle Hotel

Henry Comes to Stay

Henry sneaked into the Grand Castle Hotel amidst the chaos of change arising from new ownership. Moving from single ownership to become the 'diamond' in a worldwide chain of hotels many millions were being spent to achieve six or seven star status.

Only the very best was good enough for the 'Castle' so anything that wasn't dumped was stored in back rooms pending final decisions following the upgrade.

For several days Henry slunk around, seeking to find the perfect living arrangements. For several days prior to moving in, Henry had watched the comings and goings with the intense observation of a C.I.A. agent. Now Henry was convinced that he could remain undetected in the grandeur of the Castle for at least a year, but only with careful planning and secretive living.

Henry watched from the shadows as Directors yelled at Managers, Managers roared at Housekeepers and Supervisors and the Workers suffered.

Wallpaper was ripped from walls, bedroom furniture dismantled and linens stored. Following four days of careful observation Henry found his suite. A cavernous room to the rear of the Castle had become the general storage area for unused mattresses, pillows, linen, soft furnishings, chairs and settees. It was now filled to capacity and required only minimal adjustments to turn it into a comfortable home. Conveniently Henry's new accommodation was only a few metres from the kitchen and vitally had an escape route if Henry's presence was detected.

"Perfect", Henry thought as he made himself comfortable. Well past midnight and everything in the Castle was quiet and still as Henry slipped quietly into the kitchen almost stunned by the amount of food available to him. Henry delicately sampled some Beluga Caviar, then some delicious Foie-Gras. Taking just enough to ensure that Chef would not detect the theft; Henry started to stockpile his larder that very night.

Over the course of several weeks Henry laboured diligently to improve the ambience of his new home. By night he raided the kitchens and slipped silently outside for a 'breath of air'. There was no doubt, Henry enjoyed this luxurious lifestyle so he made the decision to spend the entire winter here and (perhaps) move on in the springtime. Everything seemed 'set fair' for a season of mellow fruitfulness, then disaster struck.

Helen, the General Manager was enjoying her morning coffee from a delicate porcelain cup when the text arrived from Eva informing her that she would be with her in a few hours.

Eva the new Proprietress and Chief Executive was known for her fastidiousness; no item was too tiny for her scrutiny and strong men quavered in her presence.
Helen was confident that she ran a 'good ship' but decided on one last 'spot check' before the 'big boss' arrived.

Managers, Heads of Departments, Housekeepers and Supervisors were summoned and instructed to examine every room in the Castle. All must be perfect.

In keeping with usual protocol the General Manager's wishes were 'passed down the line' to the people who would effect her orders.

Henry was relaxing into a mid-morning snooze when he heard his front door being opened, followed by a high pitched scream. Immediately alert, Henry listened closely to the clip-clop of high heels running at top speed.

Some minutes later he heard the door being opened, ever so slightly.

"My God" the Supervisor shrieked "we have an infestation of rodents, there are droppings everywhere". The Supervisor added "this place stinks, we must inform the Housekeeper". Together they informed the Housekeeper who informed the Manager, who brought their discovery to the General Manager.

The news made Helen quite faint, she could see an immediate end to her 'grace and favour' apartment, her beloved Audi TT and the other perks that 'went' with being General Manager.

However, Helen was made of stern stuff; she would not relinquish her post without a fight. She gazed at the assembled staff from behind her giant oak desk "get every Porter, Groundsman and all other available Staff, together with vans, tractors and trailers to the back of the Castle" she instructed the Manager. "When you have vacated everything drive completely off the estate and set everything on fire. You remain until there is nothing left to identify it with the Castle", her eyes were pleading as she stared at her Manager.

The Manager could feel his 'knees go weak' realising that his job, with all his perks could soon perish. "Right, let's go" he ushered the assembled Staff out of the office.

Helen rang Pest Control, trying frantically to prevent the panic from rising in her voice. The Environmental Officer was most facilitating, especially as she offered him and his wife free accommodation for a weekend if the Pest Control Officer could come immediately.

The Officer arrived on site in ten minutes, then it with the turn of the painters, the cleaners and decorators.

All of this panic passed unnoticed to Henry; long before the Pest Control Man arrived he had slipped quietly out through his escape route. By the time the painting started, Henry was resting peacefully across the way from Pat Collins bar. Rumour had it that the bar cuisine was at least as good as the fare provided in the Castle, so all he had to do was wait until he could locate a suitable entranceway.

The Grand Castle Hotel

The Henrys

Eva literally stopped Hank in his tracks the first time he saw her. On impulse Thomas (Hank) Henry flew from his headquarters in Switzerland to view his latest potential acquisition, a famous but run down hotel in London.

Hank stepped out of the revolving doors and cast a critical eye over his new purchase. In one sweeping glance he took in the faded paint, the worn furniture, the absence of someone to greet him and, worst of all the smell and taste of decay and lack of leadership.

As he stepped further into his property his eyes fell on the most beautiful woman he had ever seen. Almost as tall as himself the elegant slim blonde lady reflected everything he would want for the hotel; grace, warmth, that mysterious something that set it apart from all others.

The young lady spoke, her voice was low, her words eloquent and, with one sentence Hank knew this was a girl of 'excellent breeding'. But what was she doing here in this dump of a place; she belonged in some stately home attended by a retinue of servants.

The young lady's words tinkled like music in Hank's ears "I'm afraid the hotel is not open for clients". She murmured, "Not much of a hotel then, if it doesn't have clients!" Hank smiled.

"No indeed, sir, not much of anything, I'm afraid the new owner will have to spend millions of pounds to make this a proper hotel!" the blonde lady replied.

"So it has a new owner?" Hank asked "Do you think he has been taken for a fool?"

"Oh no, this could be a perfect place with the right leadership" the young lady extended her hand "my name is Eva and I represent the liquidators. I was awaiting the new owners when you walked in!"

"Sorry to upset your plans! Hank laughed "but as a poor ignorant outsider I would love to know what the hotel would need to make it successful. By the way, my name is Hank!" He shoved out his hand and Eva shook it delicately.

Hank added "you are very young to hold such an important job". Eva's colour rose. "I am twenty three, I have a degree in Economics and a Masters in Management" her voice took on a sharp edge.

Hank raised his arms, palms outward "Sorry, I've often been told that I am totally lacking in tact and diplomacy".

It was Eva's turn to laugh "I'm sorry, when people look at me they see a blonde bimbo and assume I slept my way up the management ladder".

Hank protested "I assure you that I thought nothing of the sort, in my own awkward way I thought I was complimenting you".

"Perhaps we should start again" Eva laughed "You asked what I would do if I owned this hotel" ... then she told him.

Finishing her dreams, Eva looked at her watch and announced that the buyer was an hour late and she could wait no longer.

Anxious to continue to have her company Hank suggested lunch at a little restaurant just up the street. Eva could leave a note on the revolving door announcing that she would be back in an hour.

Eva hesitated for just a moment. It was not her habit to dine with complete strangers but what harm could befall her in broad daylight; besides Hank seemed to be such an interesting man.

"Ok" Eva scribbled a quick note and together they left for the restaurant. Eva liked Hank's old fashioned manners as he walked on the outside of the street, held the restaurant door open for her and moved her chair into place for her.

Throughout lunch Eva talked for England while Hank listened, enraptured. Their waiter was certain that Hank must be incredibly rich to have such a stunning consort; in the waiter's mind 'Hank was punching way above his weight'.

In truth Hank was as plain as Eva was beautiful, but over lunch Eva discovered something that no other woman had seen; she just had to see him again.

So she told him so, subtly and with finesse and suddenly Hank had a date that night with the most beautiful woman in London. "My God" Eva leapt up "we've been here for two hours, I must fly, what will the buyer think?"

"He will probably think he's the luckiest man in London when he sees you. But he is not; I am, for it is me who is taking you to dinner tonight!"

"Hank, I must fly" Eva gasped, but Hank insisted on escorting her back to the hotel.

"Oh thank God" Eva trilled as they neared the hotel, "there is no one here". She unlocked the revolving doors turned around and kissed Hank on the cheek "I'll see you at eight" she whispered.

When Eva entered the revolving door she immediately spotted that Hank had followed her. Laughing she announced that he must go as the buyer might turn up.

"He has" Hank chortled "Please to meet you, I am Thomas Henry, the new owner".

Icicles descended as Eva's voice changed to ice cold "That is despicable, you have been making fun of me, that is contemptible!"

"On the contrary" Hank replied "I have been having a wonderful time with a beautiful woman with whom I will be dining this evening. Perhaps we should get down to business!"

During the guided tour Eva's 'icicles' melted and by the time they had returned to the foyer the warmth had returned between them.

With a cheerful wave Hank indicated that he was looking forward to dinner.

While it was not strictly necessary for Hank to be present throughout the negotiations for the Sale of the Hotel he continued to be ever present. On completion he made Eva an offer she could not refuse, a six figure annual salary to become his Special Advisor in Hotels and Catering.

It was obvious to all that Hank had fallen hard for the beautiful Eva. What was harder to follow was the fact that his feelings appeared to be reciprocated.

Despite meaningful glances, accidental touches and brushing off non-existent fluff from each other's clothes there was no sign of real romance. Then Hank announced a celebration banquet in his new dilapidated hotel. Either by accident or design Eva drank too much Dom Perignon Champagne and announced to Hank that she loved him.

Six weeks later they were married, despite Hank's reservations, and only after long discussions about age differences, differences in appearances and outlook. At forty years of age Hank believed he was much too old for Eva; at twenty three years of age Eva believed they were perfect together. Hank insisted on one stipulation prior to celebrating their marriage; in the event of a potential break-up they would stand face to face to tell the other partner that their life together was over. Hank insisted that there must be no 'Dear John' letters, texted goodbyes, nor emails. Eva agreed readily, declaring that she would never be the one that ended their marriage.

Despite numerous offers, flirty comments and downright demands for sex Eva remained resolutely faithful. She had eyes only for Hank; as far as she was concerned he was the love of her life. Hank simply adored his wife!

For five years they worked happily together expanding their business, travelling the world together revelling in each other's company. The only 'blip' was when Eva learned that she could not conceive because of a physiological abnormality. Eva suggested that they could have Hank's baby with a surrogate mother but Hank was adamant "if he could not have a child with Eva there would be no child"! He was totally fulfilled with his wife.

Five years on Hank handed the business over to Eva. He had been developing an IT wing to the Company and he now felt that it required his total attention. So Eva became Proprietress and Chief Executive for Hotels and Catering.

She and Hank continued to roam the world, but no longer together. "Ah well" Hank thought "maybe the joy of the homecomings make up for the absences". In reality neither Eva nor Hank believed this to be true.

From a base of six hotels the Group had grown to more than forty and Eva was presently pursuing interests in Central and Eastern Asia. Leaving home with a heavy heart knowing she would not see Hank for more than six weeks, she had thrown her arms around his neck, declaring "You know, I love you even more than I did all those years ago". Gruffly Hank responded "me to"; then she was gone.

In India Eva was feted everywhere she went, new hotels mean building contracts, new jobs, wealth to the local economy and in many cases the countries needed that wealth. Eva was appalled by the condition under which people lived but realised she could do little about it, the more she travelled the greater was her distress.

Eva stood with tears streaming down her face in a shanty town near Mumbai. Raw sewage trickled down the stream between the tin houses, the stream from which women drew their water, washed themselves, their children and their clothes. As she stood Eva heard a low moan emanating from beneath a tin shelter. When she investigated she discovered a young girl not much older than fourteen who had just given birth to a baby girl. The mother was haemorrhaging badly so Eva immediately rang for help. Despite her pleas no medic, nurse nor ambulance would venture in to the stench of the shanty town. Running back to her limo Eva grabbed a shawl and called for her driver to follow her. Very reluctantly the driver followed and together they extracted mother and child and raced with them to the hospital.

At the hospital the doctor's eyes told their own story as Eva held the mother's hand as she lay dying on the trolley. With the last of her strength the mother pointed to her daughter and cried "take", then expired.

"What will happen to the child?" Eva asked.

"Who knows?" responded the doctor perhaps she will die, or maybe she will be sold to bad men, no matter what, her outlook is bad".

"Could I adopt her?" Eva asked.

"Not officially" the doctor responded.

"What can I do?" Eva groaned in despair.

"Take her" the doctor responded "she is not registered, she does not exist".

Eva looked at the tiny infant, so helpless and immediately swore to herself that this child would have an amazing life. With the doctor's co-operation she simply wrapped the child in some sheets and walked from the hospital.

Now she had the tricky problem of getting 'Harriet' out of the country and into Britain. There would be difficulties at both ends.

Back in the hotel Eva bathed her daughter, organised clothing and arranged to meet with the Cultural Attaché. She would build at least one hotel, possibly two but she needed help to bring her daughter home.

The Attaché was a man of the world "big problem" he muttered, "cost much".

"How much?" Eva demanded.

"Ten thousand English pounds 'in cash'" replied the Attaché.

Forty eight hours later Harriet was legally adopted by Eva and Thomas Henry and free to leave the country. Passports were provided for the child and a nanny, then it was time to bring Hank 'up to speed'.

Eva tried to control her breathing when she spoke to Hank that night. "I have something to tell you" she announced "a surprise, but I cannot tell you over the phone!"

Hank could detect the excitement in her voice, the same excitement that he had heard when Eva had first met him. His heart sank "just tell me" he asked.

"I can't" Eva responded all too aware that their conversation may be listened to, by others, I will tell you when I see you".

Eva rang again at the stopover in New York but, once again, she was just as evasive 'she would' tell him when she saw him.

'Face to face' that was what they had agreed and now she was going to tell him face to face. Hank's heart broke!

Hank cancelled all his engagements and drove home. At home he gave all the staff the day off, telling them he would not need them until tomorrow, then he retreated to his office. Hank closed the curtains, switched on his desk light and booted up his computer. It was the work if only a few minutes to find a suicide site. Hank read for several hours then drove to the pharmacy where he purchased several items including vials of potassium. Hank drove to the vets where he purchased syringes and vitamins for his dogs.

Back home he filled his syringe with potassium; the site had told him that i/v injections would cause a massive and fatal heart attack in seconds. He re-read where to find a suitable vein and how to bring it to the surface. But first he had to say goodbye! He decided that his note must be brief, without recriminations and must acknowledge the love he had enjoyed. Several drafts later he settled on

Dearest Eva

I know we always said that we would 'do it' face to face but I am not strong as I once thought.

I cannot bear to hear the words telling me that you have found someone else. All I can say is that you are my one and only true love and I cannot bear the thought of life without you.

My final hope is that your new partner will bring as much love to you as you gave to me.

Love forever

Hank

Finding the vein was easier than he had thought and injecting the potassium was painless. He just had time to withdraw the needle before the crushing pain crashed in, ending his life.

Eva burst in with the joyous yelp "I'm home!" Seeing no sign of Hank, she rushed with their baby to his study. "Surprise, surprise" she belted holding out Harriet, just before noticing him slumped over the piece of paper on his desk.

The Honourable Henrietta

The Honourable Henrietta Elizabeth Grace Spenser-Perceval had lived for twenty years in the smallest guest room in the Castle when the new owners took over. Known to all as Ettie, the Honourable Henrietta lived in splendid penury, just about getting by on her state pension, a tiny inheritance from her late father and occasional presents from her brother, the Earl. For the past ten years Ettie had been selling off her share of the family silver to make ends meet; now she was left with only a silver salver, four crystal brandy balloons, a silver napkin ring and her grandmother's cameo brooch.

During her twenty year tenure the previous owner had never once raised Ettie's rent, enjoying instead the presence of a British Noble (no matter how minor) here in his Irish Castle.

Ettie was gloriously unaware that she was a charity case, accepting little gifts of fruit, scones, biscuits and other goodies on the assumption that this was how the Grand Castle Hotel treated all its guests.

The new tariffs came like a bolt from the blue, the 'suits' having decided that there should be parity of costs across the entire chain. Helen, the General Manager felt certain that Eva, the Proprietress, knew nothing about the changes, but she valued her position too much to raise a fuss.

'Permanent' residents received notification of the new tariffs along with their usual monthly bill. The hotel management 'recognised the contributions made by long term residents, but fully understood their position if they decided to relocate elsewhere'. In truth 'the Management' did not want 'permanent residents', short term 'stays' was where the profits lay.

Ettie took the news with typical British stoicism; of course she must move, but how and where?

For more than ten years Ettie had 'gardened' around the grounds with Charles the Head Gardener and today was no different.

Ettie and Charles had been re-potting in the potting shed for more than an hour when Charles raised his concerns. "You are troubled, Your Ladyship!" Charles claimed. For ten years Ettie had been telling Charles to call her by her first name and additionally, she was not a 'Ladyship'. She had explained constantly that she was 'the Honourable Ettie Spenser-Perceval- but preferred the simple epithet 'Ettie'.

But Charles was having none of it! He always 'knew his place'. Since beginning work in the Castle grounds more than fifty years ago he had never once put a foot wrong. Ettie was gentry and he was a common man and 'that was that'.

Other staff smiled knowingly at the Darby and Joan relationship between the gentle elderly lady and the head gardener, assuming there was more to the relationship than a love of flowers.

In truth Ettie contributed greatly to the magnificent gardens. Having been raised in a Castle with a team of servants and gardeners Ettie had spent most of her youth working and playing with the children of the staff. Her father, the Earl was thirty years older than her mother and her half-brother was more like a father than a brother. So Ettie's life was largely open air and gardening.

For the first time Ettie did not correct Charles use of 'her Ladyship' and then he knew there was something seriously wrong.

"Whatever is the matter Your Ladyship?" he iterated.

In a small voice Ettie explained that she would have to leave the Castle. She simply could not afford the new tariff. Ettie added that she had very little money and would so miss the beautiful scenery and the quiet serenity of the Castle Grounds. She did not add that she would also miss Charles terribly. Not only was Charles her oldest and closest friend, he was also her only friend. In 'moments of silliness' Ettie thought they were like an old married couple; but that was ridiculous Charles was only sixty six and she was in her late seventies.

Charles could barely breathe, the news had 'knocked the stuffing' out of him. If he gave it any thought at all, he just assumed that 'her Ladyship' would always be around for him. "Oh, my word" he gasped "what are we doing to do?"

Ettie smiled "You are going to continue to keep the gardens beautiful and perhaps I can come to see you sometime". Charles nodded as the scalding tears flooded his eyes.

Ettie's parting was painful for her and the staff. Several staff commented that all of Ettie's possessions were contained in one suitcase; more than one cleaner, porter and gardener wished they could offer her lodgings but they all lived in 'tied' cottages. There was not a dry eye in the Castle as Charles motored over the bridge with Ettie waving furiously as she drove out of their lives.

Ettie had been gone for a little more than three weeks when an official looking letter arrived for her to the Castle. Helen asked around but no one knew where Ettie had gone. Eventually Helen realised that, if anyone knew, it would be Charles.

Of course, Charles knew where 'her Ladyship' was living. She simply could not let her go and had persuaded her to move into his little terraced house in the village. Charles asked about the nature of the General Manager's enquiry and was informed about the letter. Charles extended his hand and offered to deliver the letter on her return home.

Whether from kindness or more likely 'nosiness' Helen said "No, I'm going into the village, I shall drop it off myself". Charles nodded and recommenced digging in the flower beds.

Driving into the village, Helen allowed herself a smile as she recalled the 'rough and tumble' of Charles' home on the one occasion that she had seen it. Charles had had a severe bout of flu and Helen had brought him sustenance from the Castle. The ground floor consisted of a living room to the front and a kitchen and scullery behind. Up the narrow staircase were two tiny bedrooms and an even tinier bathroom. Charles' bedroom was so small under the sloped roof that Helen could only stand upright in the centre of the room. Helen remembered books and newspapers scattered throughout the property, the stale smell of pipe tobacco, hobnailed boots and unwashed clothing. The overall ambience was one of dust, cobwebs and stale air! 'God help poor Ettie!' she thought.

Helen knocked at the door and was welcomed inward by a glowing Ettie. The little house was gleaming and Ettie proudly showed Helen over the property, commenting all the while on the hard work that Charles had put into it. There was no mention made of Ettie's efforts. Finally Helen was shown into the back yard that Charles had converted into a garden; the rich perfume of a host of flowers filled the air as Ettie excitedly pointed to the Pergola that Charles had made for her.

Helen could barely believe the change in Ettie, who looked twenty years younger that she had less than one month ago. Then she remembered the letter.

Ettie's face dropped as she read from the contents "Oh dear, Oh dear!" she sighed "my brother has died".

Helen offered her condolences but Ettie brushed then aside "I hardly knew him" Ettie whispered "I have not seen him for twenty five years".

Then she read on ... "Oh no! No! No!" her voice was anguished. "What, what is the matter?" Helen cried.

"My brother has left me five million pounds" Ettie replied.

Helen clapped her hands "Wow you can move back into the Castle".

The look of shock on Ettie's face was palpable "does Charles know about this letter?" she asked.

"Yes" replied Helen "I had to find out where you were living".

"Promise me you will never tell him about this" Ettie cried.

"Of course" Helen readily responded "but why not?"

Ettie looked at Helen as though she were silly. "Charles is a proud man; if he hears about this he will insist on me buying a large house, probably with servants".

"What is wrong with that?" Helen asked.

"Then I would have to give up all of this" Ettie responded.

Helen nodded "Your secret is safe with me" she whispered, kissed Ettie on the cheek and returned to her car.

Helen could not keep the smile of her face 'ALL THIS' included Charles, maybe even was only Charles. Her grin grew wider at the realisation that an elderly lady had found something much more precious than money.

Harry the Great

Old Harry had ridden his last trail. If the blood-flecked saliva left room for doubt, the look on the vet's face said it all. Harry's days of galloping over sand dunes, cantering towards the on-coming tide or trekking in the hills was over.

Head lowered and shivering on a short rein Harry listened miserably as the vet uttered his diagnosis; it would be a waste of money to buy more antibiotics or steroids. Harry knew his time was up but perhaps the human creatures would treat him kindly for the time that was left to him. In his mind's eye Harry pictured himself in luxuriant pasture, rolling in clovers and daisies in a warm spring day. That would be a nice reward for the twenty five years of faithful service that he had given to the guests of the Grand Castle Hotel. Patiently he had endured kicks in his flanks, wicked jerks of his reins and downright cruelty from riders – just because they could do it.

In return for a bed of clean dry straw, a bale of hay and access to running water Harry had given his life in the service of humans. Not once had he shied, reared or kicked out at hooligan riders, instead bearing insult and praise with equal fortitude.

For twenty of those twenty five years he had been Harry the Great, the mighty leader of the stables.   At seventeen hands he towered above his companions and was at once schoolmaster, leader and lighting fast, then age caught up and he was simply 'Old Harry'. For five more years Harry patiently plodded around carrying overweight school teachers and obese Americans who thought they were John Wayne.

Now he stood, miserably waiting to hear his fate!

Over the years Harry had seen many old horses arrive at this point. He had watched in horror as the human creatures tethered the frightened animals to a post and watch as the vet fired a metal bolt into the poor horse's head. The 'thank you' for years of loyalty – a metal spike in the brain.

Harry frequently pondered about the morality of these human creatures! Where was their decency? Where was their belief in fair play? Where was their sense of justice? Where was their honour? Harry finally concluded that these human creatures were born with a lack of nobility. While he still had his strength Harry should have made a run for it, instead he reasoned that if he worked extra hard he would be rewarded with glorious retirement. Yet year after year he saw the bolt being fired into old horse's brains, then the poor animals cut into pieces to provide foodstuff for the hunting dogs.

Every day Harry was praised by the stable lads, at night he was often slipped an extra helping of oats and didn't they tell him he was the best horse ever. No! They could not turn him into dog food! Harry was special; he would escape the terrible bolt.

Now all was quiet in the yard, the Head Lad had given instructions to leave Harry in the paddock and give him an extra helping of oats.

Gratefully Harry lowered his magnificent head into the bucket of restoring oats. He 'just knew' that after a good feed he would be good as new. Well maybe not as good as new but good enough to live a few years in quiet contentment. In his mind's eyes Harry envisaged himself in the west paddock by the banks of the lough; long days spent chewing contentedly, sleeping in peace under the stars, listening to bird song morning and evening. Harry's reverie was interrupted by the heavy tramp of the Head Lad. The Lad neither spoke nor looked at Harry, instead simply hanging the contraptions that contained the dreaded bolt on top of the five barred gate.

The Lad turned and hurried off. Harry's dreams ended! In years to come and Harry's story is retold, experts will claim that the Lads fed too many oats to Harry and his blood got fired up. Others may say the Lads slipped large dosages of steroids into the feed.

Regardless of cause Harry was not going to 'go down' without a fight. He raised his mighty head, whinnied loudly and took off. Soon his canter had become a gallop as Harry raced to the top of the field. He stood for just a moment. He looked over towards the awesome Castle, then to the stables, then he took off.

Like the wind Harry careered downhill determined to show 'them' what he could still do. With a mighty lunge he soared high into the air easily clearing the tall hedge. In mid-air everything seemed to go into slow motion for Harry. From his great height he saw a bright yellow Porsche sports car racing frantically on the wrong side of the road. In horse talk Harry tried to yell "You are on the wrong side" but it was all too little too late!

Both driver and Harry died instantly as Harry crashed landed on the car. For Harry at least, it was perhaps a better death than a bolt fired into his brain!

Henri pays a Visit

"Madame" the cultured French accent resonated through the foyer of the Grand Castle Hotel. "Do I look like someone who would remain as a guest in the second best room in your establishment?" The would be guest continued "I am Henri the Comte de Orly, direct descendant of the Kings of France; I will rest in the Presidential Suite".

The Receptionist pressed the hidden button, summoning Helen the General Manager. "What seems to be the problem, Sir?" Helen asked the now irate client.

"The problem Madame is that this person failed to recognise me and insulted my station by offering the second best suite. I am the Comte de Orly, I do not 'do' second best!"

"I am sorry, My Lord" the General Manager replied "but the Presidential Suite is presently occupied".

"That is what I tried to tell him" the Receptionist interjected. The Comte gave her a look that let her know that her position was beneath contempt. "Remove the interloper!" instructed the Comte.

The Presidential Suite was presently occupied by Eva the Proprietress and Chief Executive and Helen was certain that Eva would move for no-one. The glacial Eva took orders from no-one and she certainly would not facilitate this rude Frenchman.

Just then Eva glided into the reception area. The Comte immediately detected the aura of power and spoke directly to the Chief Executive. "Madame, I am Henri Le Comte de Orly and I have decided to honour the hotel with my presence. These people tell me I must be happy with the second best Suite but I demand the Presidential Suite!"

Helen could barely contain her excitement as she waited for Eva's famous classical put down. To Helen's great surprise Eva turned the Register towards herself then instructed the General Manager to make their esteemed guest comfortable in the Presidential Suite. Helen tried to splutter "but Madam, you occupy the Presidential Suite" but before the words formed Eva instructed that the present resident should be provided with an excellent Suite, free of charge.

As Helen stood flabbergasted, Eva turned to the new guest and assured him that it was an honour to have him in this hotel and she would do everything she could to make his stay a happy one. In the meantime perhaps the Comte would care to have coffee or a drink in Eva's office until the room was prepared. The Comte accepted in that romantic French accent.

Helen stood rooted to the spot, what was Eva thinking about, letting this nasty man into her special Suite? Did Eva see something that she had missed or was she attracted by the cultured French accent? Helen simply could not tell!

In his Suite the Comte carefully distributed his wares throughout his quarters; suits from Saville Row and the very best Parisian tailors, shoes from John Lobbs, Cartier watch left carelessly by the bath and several folders arranged along the worktop of the giant desk. The Comte was confident that by tomorrow the entire staff would know about him and his achievements.

The Comte dined simply then enjoyed an excellent sleep in the Emperor sized bed. Following a superb breakfast the Comte informed the Receptionist that he would be out all day on business not returning until eight o'clock for dinner. "That ought to be enough time to allow staff to 'go through' his curriculum vitae' and spread the news upwards" thought the Comte.

The Chambermaid was not easily impressed, she had 'done American and Irish Presidents, Ambassadors and the rich and famous of Britain but even she was shocked as she 'tidied' the Comte's many folders. Here was the Comte advising Putin about his quarters in Moscow and on his country estate, on another he was being congratulated on the restoration of the Palace of Versailles. On and on the list went of the Comte bringing culture to the rich and famous across the world. But, one folder 'stood out' from all the rest, here was La Comte being congratulated by the Sheik in completion of the seven star hotel in Dubai. The Chambermaid could barely breathe as she read the glowing tributes to the Sheik's honoured friend, "wait 'til Housekeeper heard this" there was enough potential gossip here to keep the hotel 'going' for a week. Then she discovered 'the Ribbon' and the glossy photo of the French President presenting Le Comte with the Legion of Honour for his unfailing work in promoting French culture worldwide.

The Chambermaid could wait no longer, breathlessly she ran to inform her friend the Housekeeper. The Housekeeper told the Manager, the Manager told the General Manager and Helen told Eva. Over the course of the afternoon, the General Manager, the Manager and the Housekeeper all felt it necessary to inspect the Presidential Suite to ensure it was up to the required standard.

Invited for afternoon tea in Eva's office (a surprise in itself) Helen recounted the Comte's achievements.

Eva smiled inwardly!

Claude Dupont returned to his luxurious Suite in time to have a shower, change his clothing and look around before dinner. With a smile of satisfaction Claude noticed the 'tidying' that had occurred. By now the entire locality would be aware of the famous Comte who was living amongst them. Claude whistled to himself as he showered, remembering five years sharing a cell in a grim Parisian prison with the most famous 'conman' in all of France.

Claude had put those five years to good use; first he had developed his own speech patterns to reflect those of his famous cell mate, then he 'sat at the Master's feet' learning all that he could about human weaknesses and greed. Together Claude and the celebrity prisoner spent endless hours in the prison library imbibing everything they could learn about art, sculpture, finance and world affairs. More importantly Claude learned about the importance of clothing and how to wear it, how to walk, stand still and detect the most subtle of subliminal messages. Not only was he was willing student. Claude was astute in the extreme. Incarcerated for burglary, house breaking and common theft Claude's star cell mate initially looked upon him with disdain. People such as Claude were brutes, ham fisted criminals who were no better than the beasts in the field. The conman, on the other hand was an artist, combining intelligence, finesse, culture, charm and an attention to detail that was denied to mere mortals.

Claude learned well and following four years of tuition was ready to put his newly acquired skills to the test. As Claude and the celebrity exited the prison gates the star imparted two final pieces of advice. One, Claude must never attempt to combine his new career with his old calling and two, he must never 'work' France, that was the celebrity's domain and he would brook no competition. On parting from his cell mate, Claude ceased to exist and Le Comte was born.

Le Comte spent a successful season in London and despite a couple of near shaves, he had finished the time 'well ahead'. Without spending a penny of his own money he had acquired a very fetching yellow Porsche Carrera, never paid for a single night's accommodation and received several thousands of pounds for sharing his skills. Advice on the World Financial Markets, Bloodstock, Market forces and potential political upsets provided lucrative incomes but now it was time to move on. A couple of 'hustles' had proved to be particularly successful and now the Comte decided that he needed a holiday. Having scoured through several quality newspapers, journals and top of the market advertisements he decided a stay in the Grand Castle Hotel in Ireland would suit his taste. But first to work!

Several phone calls to an old friend in Paris, coupled with the exchange of twenty thousand euros resulted in Le Comte receiving the magnificent Portfolio of his business successes. A further five thousand bought the Legion of Honour and a flattering photograph and write-up about Henri, Le Comte de Orly with the President of France completed Henri's needs.

The Comte was enjoying a simple starter in the grand dining room when Eva stepped in. The Maitre d's head jerked back in surprise. Madam never ate with the guests, preferring instead to dine at her desk or in her apartment.

"May I join you?" Eva's low husky tones interrupted the Comte's thoughts.

"I would rather you did not" the Comte responded "I am not well disposed towards anyone in this hotel".

"I'm sorry" responded Eva "May I ask why not?"

"Madame, today when I was away on business your staff interfered with my portfolio" the Comte affected a hurt tone.

"I regret I must take the blame" Eva accepted. "I have a rule that the client's room must be returned to pristine condition every day. I want clients to believe that we provide the highest possible standard!"

"Madame, my life revolves around standards and right now I know that your entire staff will be familiar with me and with my business. Can you deny it?" Henri demanded.

"I'm afraid I cannot" Eva responded "but let me come to the point, I would wish to hire your services".

"Pah" Henri spat and "you could not afford me, Putin paid five hundred thousand pounds for my services, the Sheik paid twenty thousand pounds".

If Eva was perturbed she did not show it. "I want to make the Castle the cornerstone of my business and I am prepared to allow you to stay free of charge for as long as you wish and I shall pay you one hundred thousand pounds for your advice and guidance".

A look of disdain crossed Henri's face "A mere pittance" he shrugged "what possible reason would I have for such an undertaking".

Eva went on to describe how part of the Castle had been built in French Baronial style but, with subsequent extensions and developments the 'Frenchness' got lost. Perhaps the Comte might use his experience to restore the Castle to its previous grandeur?

Henri noted the 'vast experience', so she too had read his C.V. or been told about it. At first he looked pensive, then he clapped his hands. "Ah, the challenge, I will do it. Now please, may I finish my meal?"

Henri approached Eva's office with a mixture of Gothic arrogance and due deference for the Proprietress. Over coffee, provided in the most delicate porcelain, Eva asked if Henri had given their idea any further thought.

"Oui, Madame" Henri began then blushed "sorry, yes madam, have you thought of a name, a motif, a motto for your 'baby'?"

This was not the sort of response that Eva had expected from a 'cultural' expert. "No" she replied, hesitantly.

"Perhaps the Red Rose Group? Or Red Carnation 'no-no' there is one of them, what about the White Rose?"

Henri detected the slightest of disapproval in Eva's eyes, he immediately jumped to his feet, rushed to Eva's desk and clasped her cheeks. "Of course Madam, you are so right, the White Rose is not for us; angelic yes but not passionate. Yes madam your idea is the right one, no name, just a simple motif with the flowering white lily. Genius Madame! Genius!"

Eva smiled weakly, totally unaware that she had spoken, but Henri was adding "let us place the motif on our letterhead". Hurrying to the main office Eva and Henri issued their instructions for the new motif.

The General Manager could not discern any real difference in impact with the new addition but wisely kept her thoughts to herself; Eva and the Frenchman were ecstatic!

Three weeks into his tenure and Henri came up with his best idea so far. His continuing presence in the Presidential Suite was losing the hotel more than twenty thousand pounds each week. He was adamant, he would move to the apartments to the rear of the Castle, they were quieter and he could prepare his ideas in greater silence. Much to Eva's surprise the Comte chose a modest, single bedroom apartment at the outer edge of the Castle insisting that it was perfect for his needs. He moved in immediately, reckoning that he could have a further month's 'holiday' before making his escape.

To provide Eva with confidence Henri inspected all the rooms in the Castle, paying close attention to the 'baronial' section. Though he knew nothing about architecture or hotel furnishings Henri did recognise quality when he saw it.

The Patek Phiillipe watch lay temptingly on the dressing table and Claude the small time thief knew that he must have it.

Checking quickly around and forgetting his cell mate's warning Henri quickly pocketed the watch, then he noticed an eighteen carat gold pen. It too joined the watch in his pocket. Whistling cheerfully he continued with his rounds. Much later as Henri crossed the foyer

Helen called urgently for his attention "A valuable watch and a pen has been stolen, do you think I should tell Eva?"

Henri paused for just a second, "No she is very busy at the moment working on the proposed renovations. I will deal with it!"

In the victim's room Henri attempted to console the distressed pair. With his most persuasive of French inflections he assured the clients that their loss would be covered by the hotel's insurance. Unfortunately, the heavy tariff placed on hotels by insurers meant that the victims would probably only receive around two thousand euros. With bewitching Gallic charm, Henri added "if Sir was to claim the items were lost at home he could claim up to twenty thousand pounds without the bother caused by police". Henri saw the light of greed switch on in the victim's eyes. "No, no" the victim protested, "we do not need the police". Henri could 'read the maths'; pen and watch could be replaced for ten thousand pounds and then a ten thousand pound bonus.

For Henri a new 'business' was born. Without bothering Eva, while assuring Helen he was 'on the case' a Cartier, two Rolexes, a Breitling and several valuable brooches and a matching pair of rings now nestled in Henri's suitcase, and all without involving those troublesome policemen.

Then Eva sent for him! Initially Henri prepared to bolt, but then he decided to brazen it out. Eva was beside herself with a mixture of delight and terror. One of their best customers was coming to stay for a month and he always travelled with some of his art collection. This time he was bringing his Bacon, a Picasso and a Matisse and Eva quaked at the security implications.

"Do not worry" purred Henri "I know a very good private protection company. I believe we would need at least four guards, though they are very expensive" Eva nodded "that is not a problem, the customer always pays". She smiled broadly "How did I ever manage without you, you are so good".

"Thank you Madame, now I will organise security".

The VIP was welcomed with all the accord normally provided for a visiting President. Henri smiled indulgently when Eva introduced him as her Special Advisor and Security Expert.

Together he and Eva showed the VIP to the room next door to their Suite where a deck of cameras, focussed in on the wall of the VIP's lounge. "As Sir can see, your art will be under surveillance twenty four hours each day without interfering with your privacy. There will be a guard outside your door and we have the normal hotel security for your protection".

"I hope I can afford all this" laughed the VIP.

"Indeed" murmured Henri.

Two armed guards stood by the door as a workman, supervised by Eva and Henri mounted the artwork on the wall. The VIP expressed himself well pleased and Henri assured him that he would personally inspect the guard every two to four hours". As usual the VIP and his partner enjoyed the simple pleasures of the area, being neither demanding nor troublesome.

On the morning of the third day of his stay the VIP requested a driver to take himself and his wife into the city. They did not require an evening meal but would appreciate 'something' left for a late supper. Henri assured him of his very best attention!

Early evening and Henri is standing in the VIP suite, he has arranged several bouquets of flowers, left a selection of fruit and placed plated snacks in the fridge.

Then Henri looked at the Matisse, then the Picasso and finally the Bacon; he was enraptured. So enraptured that Claude Dupont went next door and ordered the security guard to switch off the cameras then he called his 'man at the door'. "Cover the paintings with a sheet and bring them to my apartment. I will distract the receptionist". While his cohorts relocated the paintings Henri rushed to Helen's office telling her that he had to rush into the city. He had just received notification that material he needed had arrived. Henri then added "if Madame asks, tells her I shall return first thing in the morning". Then he made his way to reception, keeping the receptionist's attentions until he saw the 'guards' rounding the corner of his apartment.

Henri rushed to his apartment, grabbed his suitcase and threw it into the back of the Porsche. Next he held the bonnet open to allow the priceless artwork to be placed carefully inside, ten thousand pounds changed hands and the guards sped off.

Henri drove out of the castle at his usual gently pace, waving to the concierge as he did so. In his mind's eye he had already sold his holdings to a 'fence' he knew in Paris for at least ten million pounds. Unconsciously as his excitement mounted his foot pressed down on the accelerator. He thought a few weeks in Monaco would be nice and maybe a month or two in the Maldives, his heart raced, as did the Porsche. In his excitement Henri forgot that he was no longer in France, not for moment did it strike him that he was driving at one hundred kilometres per hour on the wrong side of the road.

Then a great horse fell from the skies; Henri died instantly.

The Garda Commissioner wore his most solemn face as he shared coffee with Eva in her office. Solemnly he announced that the real Comte de Orly was most hopeful that this unfortunate incident would not make the newspapers. In addition to the artwork the Garda had found several valuable watches, jewellery and pens which had not been reported as stolen. Silently he slid the haul over towards Eva, "perhaps you might return these to their rightful owners!"

"Of course" said Eva "and what might I do to reward you, Officer?"

The Commissioner's shock was a joy. "Madam, I do hope you are not trying to silence the police force?"

"Of course not!" Eva responded.

"In that case" the Commissioner boomed, rising from his chair "a silver perpetual trophy to be donated by the hotel to be played for among the Garda football teams" he hesitated "and perhaps five hundred euros to the victorious team?"
The Commissioner noticed the tiny change of atmosphere, "perhaps two hundred!"

Eva nodded, almost imperceptibly.

Happy Huaary

Sandra had spotted a bargain mid-week break to the Grand Castle Hotel and impulsively made the booking. Normally the two nursing sisters from a large Dublin hospital would never consider such grandeur, but the Castle was offering reduced prices and four nights for the price of three. How could two impulsive outgoing women resist, besides they had not been able to go to Benidorm this year.
Jean and Sandra did what Jean and Sandra always did So! Why not a little bonus treat!

Who knows, with a little luck they might even 'snare' a rich husband. According to the 'girls' they were each aged thirty two, which meant they must have been twelve years old when they first met in the Preliminary Training School twenty years ago.

Jean hailed from Kenmore in County Kerry, while Sandra grew up in Waterford City but since that first fateful meeting they had grown closer than sisters. With the passage of years hospital food, red wine and junk food the 'girls' now weighed more than twelve stones, had the same streaked blonde hair and forty E busts. Though changed considerably since their student days the girls refused to believe that their best days were behind them. Maybe the Junior Housemen and Registrars looked for younger models, but Jean and Sandra still held hopes that Mr Right was just around the corner, and what better place to find him than the Grand Castle Hotel!

The Castle was everything they had hoped for, luxury on a grand scale, opulence beyond belief, service fit for a queen and the rugged splendour of Connemara, what more could two girls hope for? Well, maybe two interesting and interested men!

The girls were in their third day having explored Joyce's country, the Quiet Man experience and horse riding around the estate, they now sought further adventure!

As Jean bounced on the super comfortable bed she announced to Sandra that she would love to try something adventurous. She told Sandra how she had adored Percy French when she was little and she knew that he was besotted with the 'Twelve Pins' a stunning mountain range in Connemara. "Let's go walking in the Pins and let's climb Ben Baun" Sandra was becoming increasingly excited at the thought of all the exertion. As super-busy ward sisters both she and Sandra were capable of the most arduous trek – or so she thought.

Sandra checked the atlas "Ben Baun is only two thousand, nine hundred and thirty two feet" she laughed "a dawdle for athletes like us".

Impulsive as ever, the girls set off in glorious sunshine stopping frequently by the roadside to 'capture' the rugged beauty on camera. The afternoon sped bye, then they were in 'the Pins'. Ben Baun looked a helluva lot higher when they stood at its base, but nothing daunted our heroines. Off they set in that peculiar 'nurse walk' head down, butt out. Soon their breathing quickened and the heat began to leave the day. No problem, they would soon make the top.

Light was fading as they made the summit with both agreeing that the view was worth the effort. Then Sandra mentioned that she wished they had brought some food from the hotel. Jean shivered and added "and some warm clothing". Here at the pinnacle of Ben Baun flimsy blouses, shorts and plimsoles suddenly seemed inappropriate and the temperature was dropping. "Best get a move on" they uttered in harmony.

They had descended less than fifty metres when the mist began to roll in. The mist thickened to a freezing fog and soon the girls were shivering violently. Within minutes it was impossible to see anything before them. "We'd better hold hands" Jean announced "otherwise we will lose each other".

Every cautious step brought new dangers. All that was required was one stumble at the wrong moment and catastrophe would ensue. "Maybe it would be best to shelter in these rocks!" Jean announced "walking is becoming much too dangerous". Sandra acquiesced, suggesting that they should "cuddle up" for heat. Despite the 'cuddling up' the freezing fog chilled to the bone, then Sandra noticed that Jean had stopped shivering; she reached across and felt Jean's tummy and found it freezing cold. Both nurses realised that shivering stopping as temperature dropped hailed the onset of hypothermia, then death.

Sandra announced "Jean if we stay here we shall die, if we continue down the mountain we might die. It's not much of a choice, but we must move!"

Just then a childish Scottish accent spoke out of the mists. "Never fear ladies I will get you down safely".

The shock of the voice coming out of nowhere reduced both nurses to silence. "Take my hand" the boy instructed "Now take your friend's hand" he added "we will be safe in no time".

The boy led the two friends with a sure footedness that astonished them. The girls could discern no path, see no dips, chasm or streams yet the boy strode out confidently and they followed. The fog thickened yet the boy showed no fear and his confidence transferred to Jean and Sandra.

After what seemed like hours the boy stopped and pointed at a laneway "Follow that" he instructed "you will find your car at the end of it, it's about two hundred yards. Now I must go to find my father!"

The boy turned. Realising that they had failed to thank him for saving their lives the girls turned to thank him but, he had faded into the fog.

When they turned back towards the lane a large black cat leapt from the stone wall and preceded them all the way to the car, its tail serving as a beacon and its meows encouraging them onward.

The Castle was just awakening when two tired hungry guests turned up in reception. One look from the Receptionist convinced the ladies that they needed to provide some explanation. "We were caught in fog on Ben Baun" Sandra volunteered "but a kind little Scottish boy guided us down" Jean added.

"That would be Happy Haaary" explained the Receptionist "he and his father were guests here and the boy was such a happy chap with a lovely Scottish burr that he was known to all as Happy Haaary". She reached beneath her desk and extracted a newspaper dated 1910 and handed it to the girls. Haaary and his father had been guests at the Castle more than one hundred years ago, when they spent their days hill walking in 'The Pins'. On the penultimate day of the holiday Haaary and his father had also been caught in the most horrendous fog. Next day Haaary's father's body was found at the bottom of a steep incline, but Haaary was never found. The hairs stood erect on the necks of both Jean and Sandra as they looked at the grainy old photos of Haaary; their Saviour.

Then they became aware that the Receptionist was speaking again "there have been at least a dozen reports of Haaary saving climbers over the years. Then he vanishes into the mist" externally looking for his father!

The girls felt the hot tears well up in their eyes as the Receptionist concluded "there was a legend that Haaary's cat pined away and died after the loss of Haaary".

"A black cat?" the girls asked in unison.

Hen's Hen Party

Hen's hen party was in full swing in the bar in the village just outside the walls of the Grand Castle Hotel. By all accounts, theirs was the 'in' place to be, with the best food, friendliest staff and the greatest variety of drinks on offer in the area.

A stag night was happening elsewhere but, for tonight, the girls had no interest in where the boys were, or what they were doing.

Tonight belonged to the girls and they were determined to make the best of it. The group had been knocking back 'shots' since six o'clock and already some were beginning to fade. The wall clock 'struck' ten as the heavy drinkers 'settled in', with the weaklings nodding off.

No one was certain why Hen was called Hen. Some thought it was a shortened form of some fancy name while others thought it derived from Hen's Scottish mother who called all females 'Hen'. Regardless of the name Hen was the 'queen of the pack'. Despite being a slim five foot three Hen had 'hollow legs' and could drink the strongest man under the table. Five, four, three, two, one squealed the bridesmaid and another sound of shots hit the target. By midnight Hen and Julie were the 'last men standing'. Fourteen 'faders' snored soundly around them, oblivious to the country music being beaten out by a local four piece band. "Bottoms up" slurred Julie. As Hen raised her glass she glimpsed a tall stranger in their midst. At least six feet ball, with unfashionably long hair, the new arrival grinned lasciviously towards Hen.

"Tell him to buzz off" slurred Julie as she joined her friends in oblivion.

"What do you want?" Hen demanded.

"Fancy a dance?" the newcomer asked.

"Can you not see this is a girlie party?" protested Hen.

The stranger looked around "It seems the party's over and guests are asleep" he grinned "so how about that dance?"

On the tiny part of the floor allocated for dancing he held her a little bit too tightly. She was very tired though so Hen rested her cheek against his broad chest. When the 'set' finished it seemed to make sense to stay on the floor waiting for the next round.

If Hen noticed that he was holding her hand she made no comment. As the last waltz played they swayed rhythmically together, lost in the moment. Then it was over.

"What are you going to do with the girls?" her new companion asked. "Except for Julie, they are all staying here. Julie and I have rooms booked in the Castle."

"Rooms?" the man asked.

"Yes" Hen replied "one for the bridesmaid and one for the bride, Me!"

With an apparent lack of guile Hen's dancing partner asked if she would need transport to convey her unconscious friend back to the Castle. Then he offered to provide that transport and Hen thought it would be churlish to refuse. With some difficulty they got Julie into the car, then out of it and into her room.

Gallantly Hen's new helper offered to escort her to her room, "just to protect her from 'marauding Vikings'" he laughed.

Finally finding the room, Hen stumbled inside and her escort stepped inside to hold her and prevent her from falling. Probably due to the heat in the room Hen's world began to swim and she felt herself sliding towards the floor. She had only the vaguest awareness of her Sir Galahad picking her up and carrying her to the bedroom.

Gently her knight in shining armour drew back the duvet removed Hen's shoes and outer clothing. Not so gallantly perhaps he too quickly shed his clothes and slipped into bed beside the semi naked Hen.

Hen woke with a raging headache. Desperately squinting her eyes to keep out the sunlight she stumbled into the gracious en-suite. Several minutes of fumbling then Hen located her stock of paracetamol, downing four of them in one go. Squinting to ease the pain from her throbbing head she found toothbrush, paste and a water source.

It was only when she had completed her teeth clean that she became aware of a water gushing in the shower. "Oh my God" she thought "I've left it running all night. I could have flooded the entire Castle". Then 'He' stepped out of the shower.

"What are you doing here?" Hen hissed.

"It seems I am taking a shower" he grinned widely; "How do you feel this morning?"

"Awful" Hen muttered" "I don't remember coming home, and anyway, what are you doing here?"

Her 'guest' laughed. "You don't remember me putting you to bed, then?"

"Oh God, oh God" Hen groaned "We didn't ..." she left the question hanging.
"No we didn't!" Sir Galahad replied "but it was a nice bonus for me on the night before your wedding!"

Several "Oh God's" later the seriousness of their position filtered into Hen's head. You must leave now, before Julie or my mother arrives here.

"All in good time" he claimed "I thought I would have breakfast with you!"

"No you won't" Hen cried now thoroughly alarmed "Get dressed and get out".

"Ok, ok, just for you, but I will always remember this night that we spent together".

If Hen's head had 'thumped' less she might have blushed.

Instead she pushed him towards the door as he attempted to get dressed. Hen opened the door by the tiniest fraction and peeked out. "It's all clear" she whispered "Go!"

"I have to tie my shoelaces" he insisted.

Hen's panic zoomed, someone was bound to come. "Go, go!" she demanded and eventually he stumbled into the corridor.

Her guest had taken only two steps down the hallway when Hen hissed "Wait!"

He turned to face her. "Make sure the best man has the rings before I arrive. I don't want to be standing there in all my finery while you and the best man hunt for the rings".

Henry (Hal) Thompson

Boatman

Hal was born to the water. To all his family and friends it was known that Hal was only truly happy when he was 'on the lough'. Not surprising really as Hal was the tenth generation of his family who earned his living on the water. Early in the seventeenth century, his grandfather nine times removed had built a boat using local timbers and his own innate strength. As the youngest 'sons of the sod' he was never going to inherit the farm and he had no desire to travel and he needed to earn a living. At first he carried passengers from village to village then the local Lord opened a passageway to Galway city. Old Mister Thompson soon realised that there was money to be made from trading, so he bought a bigger boat. Business boomed and soon the family had two fine vessels that transported both people and materials to and from Galway. Prosperity continued through the eighteen and nineteenth centuries until 'An Gort Mor' (the Great Hunger).

Between the mid eighteen fifties and eighteen sixty Thompson's boats was one of very few businessmen that did not go out of production. Hal's five times removed grandfather carried thousands of tired, hungry, weak and dying emigrants to the great port in Galway City. Often barely scraping a living, the Star of the Sea carried its unhappy human cargo on the first leg of their journey to the new world.

Somehow Thompson's survived only to be 'wiped out' by the great recession of nineteen thirties. At the beginning of 1934 Hal's grandfather admitted defeat and sold his beloved Star of the Sea for a fraction of its worth. Denied the joys of the water Granda Thompson 'took to the bottle' and the family fortunes disappeared.

When the Castle opened as a hotel in the forties the new owner concluded that the great lough could be an excellent asset and decided on buying a boat to provide fishing trips for his wealthy clients. There was no question about it; one man knew the moods and the movements of the lough better than all others. Hal's father was the only man for the job! Though only a lad of eighteen years Hal's father fitted perfectly into the role of skipper augmenting his wages with tips he earned from sharing his vast knowledge with the anglers. For thirty years Skipper Thompson diligently attended to his duties, then in 1975 two momentous events occurred. At the relatively advanced age of forty eight the Skipper married twenty five year old Molly Montgomery and he became Skipper of a new forty feet craft which would double as a sightseeing vessel and could also be used to carry anglers to the many hundreds of islands on the lake.

Two years later, at the grand old age of fifty Skipper Thompson became a father and everyone agreed that Hal was the image of his Great Grandfather, Captain of the Star of the Sea. When the old Skipper decided to retire at a young sixty eight years old Hal was the natural successor. Hal's cup 'runneth over' his dream achieved; only one thing could be better than being Skipper and that was to own his own vessel --- but that was impossible.

The years rolled bye with little change on the water. When Hal was not on the water he was tinkering with his vessel, getting her ready for whatever duty the hotel General Manager had organised.

Home life was as idyllic as home life could be. Unlike his father, Hal had married young. Since their first day in primary school, just outside the estate walls, Hal was in love with Kathleen Brown. All through primary and secondary school Hal and Kathleen were inseparable and it was no surprise to anyone when they announced that they were getting married at the tender age of eighteen. Hal had just 'inherited' his father's role and believed if he was old enough to be a Skipper, he was old enough to get married. Despite gentle chiding from both sides the young couple went ahead with their marriage plans.

Almost twenty years on Hal loved his Kathleen more than ever and now they had two fine sons to carry on the Thompson name. If Hal was disappointed that neither Sean nor Ruardhi showed any interest in carrying on the family tradition he did not show it. Hal was happy that the boys were healthy, doing well at school with dreams of going on to University. Now that would be something. Hal often thought, the first Thompson's to go to Uni!

As usual for the month of July the boat was crammed with sightseers who had booked the one hour cruise. This was the part of the job that Hal loved best, meeting the clients. All had tales to tell, every trip was different with different 'selections' of people. Hal eased his vessel out of the harbour and was soon pointing out places of interest. Though not strictly part of his job Hal loved sharing his encyclopaedic knowledge of the lough and its islands with the clients. On each and every trip he invited members of the public to join him at his station, guiding the vessel through the water. Some shrieked with pleasure, other quaked with fear but all were enriched by the experience.

On this occasion a rather beautiful, slender blonde lady chose to take the wheel. "Obviously foreign" Hal thought, "Russian or Polish from the pitch of her voice". "What should I do?" she asked. Hal noticed that a threatening large man had moved to stand beside the blonde; so Hal indicated that there was room for only one. Hal added that "the gentleman could have the next turn". The 'gentleman' stood his ground. The young woman spoke icily and the 'gentleman' stepped back.

"You love the water?" the lady said.

"Yes" replied Hal "apart from my family it is my whole life".

"How fortunate you are" the young lady added "My name Is Ana". "I'm Hal" replied the Skipper.

When she had 'taken her turn' Ana stepped outside but stood close by the wheelhouse. For the remainder of the tour her eyes never left Hal and she hung on to his every word. At the end of the tour Ana made a point of shaking Hal's hand and thanking him for the pleasure he had provided. Her companion glowered as he followed her off the vessel.

Much to Hal's surprise Ana was back for the next tour, this time unaccompanied. This was indeed a surprise as the tour was not cheap and customers rarely came back a second time on the same holiday.

Ana smiled and asked if she could again 'drive' his vessel. "Of course" replied Hal, "but unfortunately it is not my vessel, I am only the Skipper".

"Oh, I thought you were the Proprietor!" Ana sought for the right word.

"No, I am not the owner, though I wish I was" Hal responded wistfully.

"You would like your own boat!" Ana suggested.

"Yes indeed" Hal replied and for some unknown reason he told her about the Thompson history on the lake.

Next day Ana was back and he told her about the Star of the Sea, the Great Hunger and his grandfather's loss of the business.

Following lunch Hal sought Ana out among the sea of faces waiting for the afternoon tour. Why he felt disappointed when he failed to see her, he could not understand. His usual banter with the clients was more subdued than usual as Hal worried that Ana might be unwell.

Next day she was back for the morning tour. "Did you miss me?" she teased.

"Why?" Hal responded "Were you not here?" Then he saw the disappointed look on her face.

"Sorry!" he said "wicked Irish humour, of course I missed you".

And I missed you 'Star of the Sea' she replied but my husband was calling from St Petersberg".

"So, you are Russian?" Hal enquired.

"Yes, I am Russian, but sometimes I wish I was Irish!"

"But Russia must be beautiful too" Hal questioned "and you have your husband?"

"Yes, Russia is the most beautiful country in the world; but I do not 'have' my husband. My husband has me! He owns me, just as he owns great ships, oil wells and many properties. I am an asset, a trophy to be brought but when he needs me. He does not love me, but he is insanely jealous if I look at another. I think he would have me killed if I loved another!"

Hal could not conceal his embarrassment "I am sorry" he said "that must be awful!"

"It is" Ana replied simply "I think you love your boat more than others love their woman!"

"No, no" Hal cried "I love my boat but it is nothing compared to the love I have for Kathleen!"

"And if you had Star of the Sea?"

"If I had one hundred Stars of the Sea I would trade them for my wife" Hal responded hotly.

Tears brimmed in Ana's eyes "Such a love" she murmured.

"I would give everything I have for such a love".

For a moment their eyes met and held and their world was filled with danger, then they broke the spell.

"I must go home tomorrow" Ana said "I would truly have liked to have met your Kathleen".

"You would like her" Hal smiled proudly.

"I think I would" Ana said solemnly.

The Hotel Manager rang to tell Hal that a client had booked the boat for the entire afternoon. There would be only one passenger. Hal felt certain as to who that client would be.

Ana arrived at the pier accompanied by her 'threatening' gentleman heavily laden with a large picnic basket. "Place it on the boat" she instructed. The towering presence remained on deck. "Now leave us!" Ana ordered. The bodyguard hesitated for a long moment then stepped onto dry land.

"You will let me drive your boat?" Ana asked.

Hal laughed "Your wish is my command, madam" he responded, bowing deeply in an exaggerated fashion. For the first time since they met Ana laughed.

41

Having steamed up the lough for thirty minutes Ana instructed that Hal should find an island on which to have a picnic.

Hal chose his favourite island with the ruins of an ancient monastery and soon had the boat moored. "The other side of the island is the best for a picnic" Hal offered "but alas, there is no landing place there. It is just a ten minute walk".

"No" Ana's sharp repose made Hal look up in surprise "we must stay always in sight."

"In sight of what?" Hal asked.

"My husband has me watched twenty fours per day, even when I am sleeping. As we sit here my large 'friend' is viewing us with long range telescopic lenses and listening in to our conversations. By now my husband knows I am on an island, having a picnic with a gorgeous young man." Hal blushed "perhaps we should go?"

Ana retorted "we are doing nothing wrong; we must enjoy the beautiful food prepared by Castle staff. Tell me more about 'Star of the Sea'" Ana pleaded "tell me of the love story between your family and the boat.

For two hours Hal talked and Ana listened entranced. Finally she whispered "it's time to go, my Star of the Sea".

Hal laughed "may I remind you that this is not the sea, this is a lough".

Almost inaudibly Ana whispered "you will always be my Star of the Sea; now we must go!"

Back at the pier Hal held Ana's hand as she stepped onto terra firma. As Hal stepped off the boat Ana impulsively stood on tip-toe and kissed him on the cheek. "Goodbye, Star of the Sea" she whispered as the long range camera caught the kiss on film.

There were no secrets between Kathleen and Hal so he recounted Ana's sad story over dinner. Being a mere man Hal did not notice the coolness that descended as he recounted his experiences of the past few days.

Several days later Hal got a call to come up to the Castle to collect an envelope. Preoccupied with some knocking noise he had detected in the boat he barely paid attention as he tore open the envelope. All the envelope contained was a key; no note, no explanation, just a key.

Muttering to himself about the time wasted walking up from the pier to reception Hal commenced the fifty yard return journey.

As he strode back towards the water a gleaming white, forty footer glided alongside Hal's vessel. A young man leapt of the boat and was collected by an affluent looking gentleman in a Jaguar "For you" the affluent man called, pointing at the newcomer.

Hal stepped on to the beauty. Attached to the wheel were papers, deeds of sale and several items all made out in Hal's name. Hal inserted the key and turned on the engine. Having spent time inside, Hal went out to 'look over' his new property. The vessel had no name, but painted on the prow was an odd shaped fish; as an expert of the water's Hal knew it was a Star of the Sea.

In great excitement Hal rushed home to tell Kathleen the great news. "Have you seen this?" Kathleen said handing him that day's newspaper. Front page headlines, a grainy photo of a young woman kissing a man and the dread news that a Russian oligarch had shot and killed his wife then turned the gun on himself. Kathleen had moved to the kitchen from where she called "Is that 'your' woman? It seems she was having an affair and was spending hundreds of thousands of Euros on her lover!"

The colour drained from Hal's face as he looked at poor dead Ana. Then the thought struck him, "what wife would believe the story he was about to tell?"

Harry Vance - The Big Tipper

Henry Albert Vance had been coming to the Grand Castle Hotel for as long as anyone could remember. Universally known as 'Wee Harry' he breezed into reception each second week in July, during holiday time in 'The North'.

Wee Harry stood five feet four inches in his sock soles; initially slim, his girth had expanded over the years until he gained his present roly-poly shape.

Always heard long before he made it into reception, Harry's hearty guffaws delighted and amused in equal measure.

Even before he signed in Harry was spraying tips to all an sundry. Ten euros to the commissionaire, another ten to the 'boy' who carried his well-travelled bag to his room.

With every passing year Harry's suitcase took on added decorations, with labels from every country in Europe. Though battered and worn by several years of hard wear the Louis Vuitton suitcase bore testimony to its quality.

The receptionist greets Harry as an old friend, accepting twenty euros with modest gratitude. "Well Harry" she asks "where have you been since last year?"

With his usual hearty laugh Harry points to labels from Monaco to Egypt. "Hardly!" he announces "and anyway there is nothing to beat this place with its brilliant staff."

The receptionist blushes and turns the register for Harry to sign. Harry's distinctive flourish is just about decipherable 'The Manor House' ----Down. The receptionist turns to the register and laughs, "Still slumming it in your big house, I see!"

Harry's booming laughter was heard all the way to his room.

Over the course of the week Harry takes in everything, he swims, samples the sauna, plays billiards and tries his hand at golf, shooting, archery laughing all the while. Tips continue to fly as Harry rewards everyone for their help.

Henry's generosity as well known by all the staff but none more so than in the grand banqueting hall where Harry breakfasts, lunches and avails himself of the splendid dinners. Harry rewards the chef, kitchen staff waiters, supervisors and the dining room manager on every visit to the 'eatery'.

Harry is so generous that it causes some staff embarrassment. Staff beg him to stop giving but Harry is unfailing; over the course of the week several thousand euros changed hands all the while accompanied by Harry's hearty laugh and a booming, "Don't worry, I can afford it!"

A special treat for Harry is the boat trip on the lake which he experiences every day. The one hundred and fifty euros weekly cost is augmented with a further thousand euros for Hal, the boatman. Harry chortles, reminding Hal to share his good fortune with the children.

Wee Harry threw himself into every form of entertainment with gusto and a singular lack of talent.

Of all the entertainment Harry loved Tuesdays and Fridays best of all. Some five years previously the general manager had persuaded a classical pianist to play for clients. Though often under-attended and unappreciated the pianist soldiered on, creating magic with the classics.

Each evening Harry sat, transfixed by the beauty of the music; then one night the pianist sked if he would like to accompany him. Much to the surprise of everyone Harry had a fine, pure tenor voice and the clients began to sit up and take notice. Diners hurried through their meals, waiters and the reception staff sidled over and Helen, the general manager, listened silently from behind the drapes. There was something mystical about Harry's voice, a lost soul searching for something; who knew what?

Helen wiped away a tear that trickled unbidden down her cheek as Harry announced his final number. Just this once he would sing an old Percy French song rather than the usual classics. Harry nodded to the pianist and the first notes floated through the room, together with the soulful words from Gortamona. The stillness was palpable as every soul felt the unutterable sense of loss of a life gone for ever. The more astute clients wondered at this previously unknown side of the bluff, hearty singer. What it his pain? What had he lost? Was it life itself?

Harry's voice carried the throng to a place of mists, time gone bye and happiness lost forever. Then it was over! The audience sat in stunned silence for an eternity, then one guest clapped and soon a thunder of applause echoed around the room.

Harry slipped quietly away, signing out next morning as arranged.

With the 'season' over Helen, the general manager allowed herself to be persuaded to have a holiday. No golden beaches and hot sun for Helen, instead she decided to have a guided tour around the 'mills of the North' in Northern Ireland.

Together with the housekeeper the 'girls' set off and much to their surprise they found themselves thoroughly enjoying the historical tour of the history of the linen mills. From tiny 'scutch' mills, to village edifices to the huge York Street mills in Belfast there was so much to learn. Today they were going to a village in Co Down, famed worldwide for the quality of the linen it has produced. Though shut for several years the mill stood intact surrounded by upwards of one hundred 'mill houses'. Little houses in terraces stood like soldiers in line until one came to the 'Green'. Far from being green these were the oldest and most run down of all the village houses. Unlike the remainder of the village comprising red brick, the 'Green' was built of rough stone and clay with ten terrace houses facing a further ten across the street. Each house had a tiny back yard which contained an outside toilet and some storage space. A single cold water tap in the scullery was the only source of water with a bare bulb in the kitchen providing the only lighting.

As Helen and her friend stood in awe, wondering about the people who occupied these primitive dwellings a coal delivery lorry drew up and stopped. A small rotund man dressed in ragged clothes, a rough cap and a leather girdle on his back clambered down from the trunk.

Helen's mouth dropped open in amazement, resisting the urge to rush forward to greet her old friend Harry.

Some instinct caused her to stop as she watched the coal man stride down to the final poorest looking house. Without looking around the man entered his home and Helen walked down towards his house. This could not be her Harry she thought, next July she would tell Harry about seeing his double.

The door of the little house was cracked for want of paint, the single window was caked with dust and the tattered curtains were tightly closed, deterring anyone from seeing inside.

Her heart sinking, Helen walked up to the main thoroughfare where she stood for several minutes lost in thought.

A middle aged man passed by wishing her the time of day.

45

"Excuse me" Helen rushed after him, "could you tell me who lives in the house at the bottom of the 'Green' on the left?" She could feel her heart thump and became aware of a great lump in her throat.

"Ah" replied the passer -by "that is poor Harry Vance." He went on to add that Harry was a recluse who only left the house to work on the coal lorry and to shop at the end of the day. Apparently he bought stale bread, old ends of meat and anything the shopkeeper could not sell. No one had ever seen him switch on the electric light nor had any of the villagers spoken to him in years. The passer by concluded, "He is both a miser and a hermit. The only time he leaves the house is when he disappears for a week during the 'Twelfth' holidays in July. Nobody knows where he goes but other than that he is always at home." Helen could not let it end like that; "Do you know why he is like that?" she begged.

"Indeed I do" was the response. "When Harry was a child he took epileptic seizures and the teacher made him sit alone; children were warned by their parents to avoid him." The passer-by had more to add, "I suppose nowadays it would be called dyslexia but in Harry's school days he was considered to be stupid and uneducable. Harry left school unable to read or write and without a friend in the world, then the coal merchant took pity on him n gave him a job!" Then he added, "He could not let Harry drive nor be close to sharp objects so he invented the job of helper on the coal lorry and Harry has been doing it for nearly fifty years."

There were tears running down Helen's cheeks, "What is life like for him now?"

"Oh, the children torment him and one bright spark put a plaque on the house naming it 'The Manor House' because it is so dirty and unkempt. If you scrape back the layers of dust you will see that it is still there!" The passer-by looked pensive, "Maybe that is why he stays in the house."

Helen thanked the passer-by and returned to her friend.

"Well?" asked the housekeeper.

"Well what?" Helen responded.

"Well was that man Harry Vance?" the housekeeper asked.

"Don't be silly" Helen replied, "of course it wasn't."

In her heart Helen knew that her Harry would return to them next July.

Harriet Smythe

Harriet had been working as a Receptionist at the Castle for only three weeks when the whispering started.

She first heard it from Night Porter, then one of the Chambermaids fluttered by with the same message. Then Harriet 'picked up' on the panic that took hold; the Housekeeper was 'sharp' with her staff, the Chef grew tetchier by the day and the Manager and General Manager stomped around like a pair demented. In her three weeks Harriet had never noticed anything wrong in the Castle Hotel, but now everyone seemed to be actually looking for faults. "How silly" Harriet thought "they would be better employed getting on with their jobs rather than fussing over nothing".

It was several days before Harriet learned about the source of all the panic. "The Wicked Witch was coming to stay and that always meant trouble" the Domestic Supervisor whispered out of the side of her mouth. Harriet had to fight to control the laughter that threatened to erupt within her. She conjured up an image from an old black and white James Cagney film where the gangster muttered just like the Domestic Supervisor. It was no good, Harriet could not stop it, the laughter burst out in a great 'guffaw'.

"Surely no guest can be that bad?" she spluttered.

"Guest, what guest?" reported her colleague "this is no guest, this is the Wicked Witch!"

Now Harriet was really bewildered "I'm sorry" she said "you will have to explain".

"The Wicked Witch" the Supervisor reiterated "Eva, the owner is on her way. The Ice Queen is terrifying".

"Surely not" said Harriet "nobody is that bad!"

"Oh! She is" the Supervisor's voice had risen to a nervous squeak.

"Maybe she will only stay for a day or two!" There was no stopping her now. "One time Eva stayed for a month and rumour has it that the sales of tranquilisers rose by a thousand per cent for ten miles around the Castle".

"How interesting" Harriet smiled "I look forward to meeting her!"

"Don't let her see you looking?" shrieked the Supervisor "for she is sure to find some fault with you!"
Harriet smiled.

Eva swept in like a Spanish Galleon in full sail. The General Manager, Manager and Housekeeper were lined up in the foyer, thin lines of perspiration visible on upper lips. Outside, Eva had strode past the Estate Manager, the Head Gardener, the Gamekeeper and the Manager of the stables as though they were invisible.

While the 'outside' staff breathed collective sighs of relief and prepared to disperse, the Senior Staff in the foyer offered up silent prayers for 'an easy ride'.

Harriet sat at her console earnestly studying the bank of computer screens as the Wicked Witch sailed in.

The General Manager stepped forward with a respectful "Welcome Madam". Eva paid no attention; instead her eye swept around the reception area finally lighting on Harriet. "I see you have a new staff member" Eva addressed the General Manager.

"How the hell does she do it?" the General Manager wondered "the Witch never missed a thing!" "Yes madam" she replied "would you like to meet her?"

"Of course not" Eva retorted empirically "Senior Staff meeting in my office in thirty minutes". Without further discourse she disappeared into the private elevator that would take her to her Presidential Suite.

Harriet looked up as the collective escape of suppressed breaths from the 'bosses' swished through the foyer.

Harriet suddenly realised that she had been holding her breath so she exhaled with a great 'swoosh'!

"Don't worry" said the Manager "She has that effect on everyone".

Yes, Harriet was just as nervous as the Senior Staff but her tension had arisen for a different reason.

As Eva had entered the foyer Harriet had whispered a secret prayer "God, please don't let her 'recognise' me, don't let her throw her arms around me and announce "Hello darling"! The deal had been quite specific, Eva would allow her beloved daughter to gain work experience in one of their hotels, prior to commencing her University degree.

She, Harriet, could work for eight weeks in any hotel of her choice but must then further her knowledge of Business, Management, Economics and Politics. As part of the deal Eva agreed that no one would be made aware of the fact that Eva was her mother. Hence the reason she had applied to the Castle in the name of Harriet Smythe; a variation of her mother's maiden name.

Harriet had been staring vacantly at the ascending elevator for some time, when her thoughts were interrupted by one of the young waiters. "That woman would scare the pants of any man" the young man claimed.

Harriet fought her impulse to retort with a hot defence of her mother "I suppose so" she managed a smile.

The young waiter took the smile as a sign that the Receptionist might be friendly "I'm Jack" he said "I'm one of the waiters". Then he added "but not for long, I'll work all the hours God gives me and save every penny for next year".

Harriet's interest was roused "What happens next year?" she asked.

"I have been accepted by a University in Dublin to study medicine, but I'm having a year out to earn some money". The waiter added "my parents cannot afford to support me, so I have to work my way through 'Uni'".

There was something about the tone of the young man's voice that Harriet found attractive. She liked this notion of self-reliance and determination to succeed, so she smiled her approval. There was simply no way that she could tell this young man that she had been privately educated in the British System and had gained A Stars in English, French, Spanish, German and Russian. Neither could she tell him that she was fluent in several other languages and would commence a business degree in an Ivy League University in America in September. Despite their obvious differences in social standing Harriet immediately took a liking to the working class Jack. Consequently when he invited her to accompany him to a Ceilidh that night she only hesitated for a moment before accepting his offer.

Jack, however, had detected the hesitation "Look" he said "don't feel you have to, I know I'm only a waiter and you probably have your sights much higher".

"It's not that" Harriet laughed "it's just that I do not know what a Ceilidh is".

Now it was Jack's turn to laugh "you accepted a date without knowing what it was! Wow!" Then, he added "it is Irish dancing with the music provided by traditional fiddlers, accordionists, flautists and just about anyone else that turns up".

"Sounds exciting" Harriet exclaimed "I am looking forward to it!"

"Pick you up at eight" Jack called as he began to return to the dining area.

Eva was less than pleased when Harriet rang her on their private line to tell her she would not be able to meet her as she had a date. Eva fought valiantly to keep the icicles out of her voice. "A date, darling?" she asked "with whom?"

"With a young man called Jack" Harriet responded "he is one of the waiters and he has asked me to a Ceilidh!" Then she explained to her mum what a Ceilidh was.

"A waiter!" Eva thought "is that what I spent a fortune on a private education?" but instead she said 'that's nice darling, I hope you have a lovely time!"

And she did have a lovely time. So lovely in fact that Jack asked if she would like to go to a Fleadh in Letterkenny in Donegal.

Harriet stared blankly at him "What is a Flay and where is Letterkenny?" she asked.

Jack spelled out F L E A D H and said Flah and told her Letterkenny was a three hour bus trip away. He and some friends were travelling by bus on Friday morning and returning on Sunday night, there would Irish dancing, pipers, violinists, singers, poets – in fact, everything you could ever want, including twenty hour drinking".

The thought of continuous drinking horrified Harriet and how people liked that awful 'black stuff' she would never know. Now a nice glass of claret, that was different!

"Yes, she would try to get her rota changed and would go to Donegal with him".

The bus was packed with excited music lovers, or was it excited drinkers? Harriet never knew which. But she did know that she had the most enjoyable weekend of her life. Everyone was happy, cheerful, singing, dancing, dining, drinking; she even managed to 'down' a pint of Guinness and enjoy it.

By Sunday evening the exhausted group were fit for nothing but to fall gratefully into the bus. Jack and Harriet managed to capture the back seats, with more leg room. Just prior to falling asleep Jack whispered to Harriet "I think I am in love with you!"

The announcement coming as it did out of the blue was enough to almost sober Harriet up. Almost, but not quite, soon she too had joined the choir of snores on the long journey home.

Slightly rejuvenated by his three hour sleep, Jack escorted Harriet back to her shared apartment. As Harriet fumbled to put the key in the lock Jack, suddenly proclaimed "You know how I said I thought I loved you?"

Harriet nodded. Jack added "I was wrong, I know I love you!!"

50

Flippantly Harriet whispered "that's nice", kissed him on the cheek and slipped indoors.

Harriet wasn't Eva's daughter for nothing, her 'logical head; told her that people did not fall in love over the course of a weekend. No, perhaps it was lust or maybe infatuation but definitely not love. He was very nice though and it was nice to be treated like a lady. Doubtless Jack was much nicer than the 'chinless wonders' in her social set who considered that 'sex' was their right with any girl they turned their attention to. Jack stood up when Harriet entered the room, opened doors for her, offered his seat to others on public transport and walked on the outside of the pavement. Modern woman might well 'poo-poo' such 'old worlde' behaviour but Harriet loved the feeling of being taken care of! But love! That was ridiculous; they had known each other for less than a week! Nevertheless she was smiling as she drifted off to sleep.

Harriet was glad of the long lie-in. She awoke mid- morning, showered and had a leisurely breakfast. "There is something to be said for afternoon shifts!" she thought. At two o'clock she was behind her console reading the note that Jack had left for her. "Would you like a moonlight walk, at midnight by the river?" it read.

"Why not?" she thought "it might be a good time to cool Jack's ardour".

The moonlight danced of the rippling river, there was the merest whisper of a breeze as Jacked reached for her hand. "The pathway is slippy and uneven" he claimed "I'll take care of you". Harriet glowed!

Harriet became increasingly aware of the gentle pressure of his hand, covering hers and decided that she liked the feeling. The night was clear, the river hypnotic and the company … well the company was perfect. Suddenly Harriet stumbled, but Jack caught her and drew her to him.

Jack wrapped his arms around her and lowered his head towards her, kissing her gently on the lips. "Now the groping will start" Harriet thought; but it did not. Instead Jack leaned back placed both hands on her cheeks and declared "I really do love you, I was in love with you from the moment we met!"

"Jack" Harriet gasped, somewhat breathlessly "this is impossible!"

"In just under a month I will be leaving to work and study in America and next year you will leave for Dublin and will be gone for five years".

"Harriet, I love you" Jack reiterated "if you cannot stay I will come to America with you".

"You will not!" Harriet replied firmly "besides, not once have I told you that I have feelings for you!"

51

"You don't need to tell me" Jack responded "you kissed me back when I kissed you".

"Jack, you must forget about me" Harriet insisted "I would never forgive myself if I stopped you from achieving your dream!"

"You are my dream" Jack exclaimed.

"You know what I mean!" Harriet responded "You must do medicine".

"Then come to Dublin with me" Jack pleaded.

"I cannot" Harriet's voice was low and Jack thought, sad.

"I have to go to America". She was emphatic.

"Let's just enjoy this month" Harriet said "at least we can have that!"

The days flew and then it was time for Harriet to leave. Jack insisted on driving her to the airport, having inveigled his father to loan him his car.

Every word that Jack uttered was tinged with desperation. He would write every day.

Harriet insisted that this was their final parting; no letters, no phone calls ... nothing! She would be in America for at least six years and Jack's Course would be equally protracted. The words fell from Jack's lips like honey "I love you" he claimed "I always will. When I qualify I shall come back for you".

"God only knows where I will be in six years!" Harriet responded.

"No matter where you are, I shall find you" Jack cried in desperation.

"Time to go" Harriet said, gently kissing Jack one last time. She turned and moved to 'departures'.

"I will find you" Jack called.

Harriet smiled wistfully thinking of all the female students in Dublin, of the nurses who would find him adorable. "No you won't" she thought "you will forget".

Jack stood watching long after Harriet had passed out of sight.

Part 2

Guests

The Lovely Couple

This would be the tenth visit to the Grand Castle Hotel by Peter and Helen Smyth and the General Manager was keen to make it a huge success. Apart from the fact that they shared forenames the General Manager was drawn to the warmth of feeling that the couple had for each other. Anyone who entered their company was enriched by Peter and Helen's presence. The couple were both in their thirties and, while Peter was quiet and gentle Helen was outgoing and vivacious. Despite the differences in their natures Peter and Helen 'lived for each other'. Always friendly to everybody it was obvious to all that they were happiest when they were 'alone in their own company'. Catering staff smiled to themselves as they watched Helen gaze into Peter's eyes or flick imaginary bits of fluff of his collar. Peter always remained rapt as Helen excitedly outlined plans, devised schemes for their adventures or simply engaged in small talk.

It was unfortunate that the nature of Peter's business precluded them from visiting during the high season, but they declared that the weather was irrelevant when they came each March and October. Peter was somewhat vague about the nature of his business but staff were aware that it involved some sort of advisory role; while Helen claimed that she was 'only a housewife'.

As usual it was Peter who made the booking. He would be most grateful if they could have the room they had occupied on their first visit. Peter went on to explain that it was their anniversary and he wanted it to be special for Helen.

It was customary for the Hotel to bake a cake for guests who were celebrating birthdays or anniversaries but Peter insisted that he and Helen wanted no fuss. Peter thought he knew Helen well enough to know that the attention from other guests would cause embarrassment for Helen. The Manager smiled to himself knowing the reality was that Peter would be discomfited.

Then Peter requested that a bouquet of roses be placed in the room for their arrival; he would also like a very large display delivered on the fourth day of their stay. He did not need to explain that that was the actual anniversary.

The Manager informed his Superior and Helen insisted on little specials for two of her favourite guests.

The Castle always provided a Premier Service so it took quite some thought as to how to 'upgrade' without being noticed. Cotton bathrobes were replaced by pure silk, carpet slippers from Jermyn Street in London, Belgian chocolates on the pillow and champagne chilling on ice became part of the package.

On arrival Peter and Helen greeted staff like long lost brothers and sisters, asking after parents, siblings, children or sick relatives. Peter always impressed with his encyclopaedic knowledge of family and friends of staff. Smiling staff were certain that Peter really cared for them and held them in high esteem.

As planned, Helen, the General Manager led the pair to the requested room. The guests were overcome, insisting that Helen stay and share a 'glass' with them.

As she sipped, the General Manager was again amazed as Peter asked about her mother's arthritis, her niece's school record and her own health worries. Last time that Peter and Helen visited she had been feeling tired to the point of exhaustion. It was due to Peter's insistence that she had visited her family doctor. She was very glad to tell the couple that she was fully recovered and laughingly, assured them of her very best attention.

As usual Helen 'tried' everything as Peter sat nearby quietly reading. In the course of two days Helen had used the swimming, the spa and the beauty therapy. Then she had gone horse riding and 'tried her hand' at archery.

Peter sat patiently watching her, with love filled eyes while pretending to read a book.

The loving couple were sitting in the lounge enjoying a pre- dinner drink when a loud American voice cut across their thoughts "What do you make of these Catholic Priests?" the American demanded.

Peter looked around and realised that the American was talking to him.

All the papers were filled with the Paedophile scandal that was eating like a cancer in the Catholic Church in Ireland. Victim after victim had come out of the shadows as the scandal grew. The news had 'gone viral' making headlines across the world. The images portrayed was of a corrupt Church preying on innocent children and many found it difficult to argue with that.

The loud American was not going to be silenced "Damned perverts, the lot of them" the words re-echoed around the bar. Newcomers looked on, first in bewilderment, then in various shades of agreement.

Nothing would stop the American now that he had an audience "perverts, homos, thieves and adulterers all, that's their damned priesthood".

This was Ireland and the outsider had gone too far. Embarrassed guests seated themselves with their backs to the 'loudmouth'. Privately they might criticise their priests, but they would never do it in the presence of outsiders. But the American was not to be denied. He looked directly at Peter who sat closest to him "What is your opinion, my friend?"

For the first time ever Peter would quite happily have ceased the 'friendship' but he was much too well-mannered to ignore the ill- mannered intruder. "Naturally, I condemn any exploitation of children. Abuse of children is a heinous crime and the perpetrators ought to be punished" Peter responded gently.

"How right you are my friend" the Yank added, "by the way my name is Chet!"

Peter smiled weakly "I'm Peter" and "I'm Helen", Helen added.

"Darned perverts, the lot of them" Chet's voice grew louder.

Peter had not wish to get into a dialogue with this rude man but he could not allow his universal condemnation of the Catholic Church. "I am certain that it is a tiny minority of priests who are perpetrators of such vile crimes. In my experience most Priests are good men>

"Ah, but you don't know them" Chet bellowed "they have obviously pulled the wool over your eyes".

Noticing Peter and Helen's embarrassment the barman circled round and whispered in Peter's ear.

Peter turned to the American "Excuse me" he said "I'm afraid my table is ready".

"Lucky man" the American roared "everything moves at snail's pace in this damn Country".

On their way to dinner the Head Waiter whispered "Don't worry, Sir, I have seated you well away from our American friend".

Both Helen and Peter rewarded him with smiles of gratitude ... and a discreet ten Euros note for his services.

As always the Castle provided an excellent meal, in the most exquisite of settings; the food was delicious and the service unparalleled. Smilingly the couple noticed that it was at least twenty minutes before their 'American friend' was escorted to his table.

Following their delightful meal Peter and Helen took a walk along the river, holding hands in the moonlight before retiring for the night.

Day three was spent on the water. A discreet look at the guests' programmes had enlightened Peter and Betty to the fact that Chet was spending the morning pony trekking and the afternoon having a massage. Not that the American's agenda had an effect on their plans, but it was nice to be alone ... even in a crowd!

As always Hal, the Skipper of the boat was a mine of information as they traversed the great lake. The late autumn day was blessed with glorious sunshine and a light breeze to refresh their faces. As is always the case, keenly interested passengers were rewarded by Hal at his very best.

The 'cruise' passed in a flash. Helen leapt off the boat declaring 'we will be back tomorrow'. Hal looked at Peter, quizzically, Peter nodded. When Helen said she would be back tomorrow, Helen WOULD be back tomorrow! Peter and his book spent the afternoon on the bank of the lough as Helen scuba dived, banana boated, snorkelled and wind surfed.

An interested observer might have noticed that Peter never 'took his eyes off' Helen all afternoon. If the observer was really interested he would have spotted that Peter's book was upside down!

Showered and dressed for dinner Peter and Helen set off for a pre-prandial Gin and Tonic. No doubt Helen would regale her companions with the joys she had experienced all afternoon. Equally likely was the fact that the good humoured banter would describe poor Peter as a stick-in-the mud.

Alas, fate had another plan for them. As they tasted their first sip of the refreshing drink the loud voice was back. "What do you make of this my pacifist friend?" crowed the American throwing down a copy of the day's newspaper.

"What?" Peter asked innocently.

"That!" the American roared, seemingly unable to speak in a low or moderate voice. He squeezed in beside them his large abdomen wobbling over the table. The stubby finger stabbed at the newspaper "I told you, perverts all!"

Today's story had shifted from paedophilia to homosexuality within the Clergy of the Catholic Church. Seemingly a Senior Churchman had 'come out' admitting he was in a same sex relationship.

Chet was getting into his stride "I told you see! The only reason they become Priests is to indulge their perverted lusts!"

Peter could not let this pass "I am sure you are wrong" he protested "do you really think that anyone would wish to be homosexual! They are persecuted, beaten and legislated against. I feel sorry for them, didn't Jesus say all men are born equal".

"Equal my foot" Chet's voice reached a crescendo "they are abominations; condemned to hell and the sooner the better!"

"I'm afraid we will have to agree to differ" Peter responded quietly. Once again the hapless couple were rescued by the kind Waiter.

Day four began with the promised boat trip, followed by a shopping trip to the city. As expected by Peter, Helen overspent and took much longer than other trippers. Consequently the couple had to take a taxi back to the Castle, have a quick shower, dress and go directly to the dining room.

As they stood by the entrance waiting for the Head Waiter to return and guide them to their table the loud voice rang out "Space here, Peter" roared the American pointing to the empty spaces at his table.

Probably for the first time in his life Peter had the uncharitable thought "I can understand why!"

Forcing smiles on to their faces the 'chosen' pair began to make their way across towards Chet. Peter was especially unhappy with this arrangement as he had organised a magnum of champagne for their table. As they ate, huge bouquets of flowers would be distributed about their room with a single red rose placed on Helen's pillow. All this passed through Peter's mind as he prepared for their ordeal.

Then he heard a loud groan. A look of terror fixed itself on Chet's face as he brought his fists to his chest with a final moan he fell sidewise and toppled to the floor.

By the time Peter reached the 'patient' it was obvious that he was dead or at least in the throes of death.

Dropping to his knees beside Chet, Peter scrambled to withdraw a crumpled piece of coloured cloth from his pocket. He kissed the corner of the cloth then placed it around his shoulders. Peter lowered his head to Chet's ear and whispered the words that only an ordained Priest was entitled to utter!

The Grand Castle Hotel

Derby and Joan

Everybody at the Grand Castle Hotel agreed that Ted Derby and Joan Baxter were beautiful people.

Ted might be best described as being 'bluff' of character. Leaving school at fourteen, Ted had 'served his time' as a bricklayer. By all accounts he was a very good bricklayer who was much in demand. With over ten years of experience in the trade Ted started his own business working long hours sometimes to the neglect of family life. Just as with his bricklaying skills Ted proved to be an excellent businessman building up an extensive property portfolio. At a time when he might have taken it easy, cancer robbed him off his wife. With no children and few relatives Ted worked on until he was seventy. Handing over the business to his foreman Ted took his first holiday, to the Grand Castle Hotel.

Despite only being five foot nine inches tall many described Ted as a BIG man and with a shock of grey hair, broad shoulders, and a body hardened by more than fifty years on building sites he was still a formidable figure at seventy. Though relatively 'well off' Ted never lost the rough edge to his voice that clearly placed him as working class. Not that he ever swore or cursed as Ted hated profanities it was just that he had never made any attempt to be posh in speech.

Joan Baxter was three years older than Ted and his polar opposite. Joan was raised with all the comforts of an upper middle class home. Genteel in speech and manner Joan had qualified as a teacher in an era when women mainly remained at home. Two years spent honing her skills in England, Joan returned to Northern Ireland and found a teaching post near home. Forty years in the same school saw Joan promoted to Head of Infants, then Vice Principal and finally Principal.

Contemporaries of Joan all agreed that she was an anachronism in the modern age. Joan never lost her kind and gentle ways, never raised her voice and sought the 'good' in everybody.

Outside of school Joan was a committed Methodist with strong socialist values that saw her serve diligently on the Boards of many charities and voluntary bodies. At sixty six years old she 'took to' delivering meals on wheels to the old people, and got involved in befriending the elderly.

Joan served on the Board of her Church, led Girl Guides and spent her life in good works.

When asked why she never married Joan always gave the same answer. With a smile and that gentle voice she would reply "I did not have time and nobody asked".

At her hugely well attended retirement 'do' with not a dry eye in the place Joan was presented with a voucher for a week's holiday in the Grand Castle Hotel. That was twenty years ago and Joan had returned every year since that first time.

Helen, the General Manager of the Castle sat in the Board room with all her Senior Staff. It was that time of the year again when final preparations were put in place for the High Season.

Helen glanced down the expected guest list and smiled "I see that Joan is coming and wants her usual room". Then she added "wouldn't it be lovely if she and Ted got together! " United howls of protest echoed around the table "Joan and Ted" they screeched derisively, "working class hero and gentry, never!"

Ted had been coming to stay for nearly as long as Joan but they never met. Joan loved the late spring, early summer, while Ted visited in September but nothing stopped Helen when she had 'a bee in her bonnet'. "I think I will ring Ted" Helen smiled.

'Underlings' agreed collectively that the boss had 'lost it again'.

Joan and Ted arrived at the Castle almost in tandem. As Joan was exiting her car, Ted's taxi drew up behind.

Stepping out of the taxi Ted announced "Lovely day, darling!"

Joan looked around then realised that he was speaking to her. This was not a way of address that Joan was accustomed too, so she ignored him.

Side by side they checked in together, Ted chittering all the while. Joan had to admit to herself that this man was very popular, if somewhat coarse.

For dinner Helen had instructed that Ted and Joan should be seated in a discreet corner where there was no one else to talk to. In his hearty way Ted started a conversation and despite her best efforts, Joan found herself joining in.

"Night, love" Ted roared in his best building site voice when he had finished the meal. Joan just looked at him, dumbstruck. The only people who had ever called her 'love' were her parents and certainly not in the tone that Ted adopted.

At breakfast they again found themselves placed beside each other. "Mornin love" Ted announced as Joan wafted in. "Good morning Sir" Joan responded in her best cut glass accent. "Sir, is it?" Ted roared with laughter "nobody ever called me Sir".

"Nor did anyone call me love" Joan responded, but gently.

"Touche" Ted announced "I am Ted and I see from the Register that you are Joan!"

Joan chided herself as she felt the blush spread up her neck. "How ridiculous" she thought for an eighty five year old woman.

"Pleased to meet you Ted" Joan spoke in that refined way.

"Anything planned for today Joan?" Ted asked.

"I'm just going to sit in the lounge and read" Joan responded.

"Don't be an old fuddy-duddy, come for a cruise up the lough with me, it will put a bit of colour in those pale cheeks". Joan started to protest then the voice came out of nowhere "Yes, I think I would like that".

"Good girl" Ted roared, rising from the table "I will see you down at the pier at five to eleven".

Joan was standing at the pier in her best summer frock when Ted arrived. "No, no dear, you will have to get something warmer, it gets cold out in the water". Then he roared at the Skipper "Hal, have you a spare coat for my lady friend?" Joan was about to protest that she did not need a coat and she was not his lady friend, when Hal produced a rather nice overcoat, kept for such occasions.

The cruise lasted for just one hour, but by the end of it Joan believed Ted was one of the best informed people she had ever met. By the time they stepped off the boat they were best friends. "I think we should have a limousine from the Hotel and spend the afternoon in the Twelve Pins" Ted announced.

Joan loved Connemara but injected a bit of humour "do you think we should have lunch first?" Ted roared with laughter.

Rather than a limousine the pair set out in Joan's Volkswagen.

The weather was glorious in the Twelve Pins and Joan's sides were painful laughing at Ted's stories from the building sites.

Then Ted adopted a conspiratorial tone "Let's play hookey" he suggested.

"What do you mean?" the innocent Joan asked.

"Let's drive into Clifden and have dinner there" Ted said.

Ted and Joan giggled like school children all through the meal at the thought of the Castle staff worrying about their elderly guests.

Helen, the General Manager, was waiting in reception when the absconders returned. Trying to look nonchalant she asked "did you have a nice day?"

"The best" Joan answered, kissing Ted on the cheek and announcing she would see him in the morning.

Helen smiled with delight; so did Ted.

The word have obviously spread round the dining room staff as now there was only one table in 'their' corner.

"What's on your agenda today?" Joan asked as she sampled the delicious hot croissants.

"Our agenda, old Girl!" Ted's voice was firm. "Do you fancy a shopping trip to Galway?"

Joan could think of nothing worse and told him so.

"Thank God for that" Ted responded "I was just being polite. I thought all ladies liked to shop!"

"Not me" said Joan.

"What then?" asked Ted.

"Let's just walk round the village this morning and have a lazy afternoon in the Hotel" Joan suggested.

"No, no" Ted protested "What about a spot of pony trekking?" then he laughed out loud at the look of horror on Joan's face.

The leisurely day included a 'dander' round the village, cream teas and then dinner in the Hotel. "It's early" Ted announced in his usual less than subdued voice "do you fancy a stroll along the river?"

Joan told him she would like that very much and was immediately obedient when Ted instructed that she must get a warm coat.

The night was perfect; still, an almost full moon, the heavens filled with stars as Ted took Joan's hand along the path by the river. The touch of his hand filled Joan with a warm glow

and she told him so. Or rather, she announced that it was a beautiful night and she felt so happy.
Ted looked skyward. "A lover's moon" he said.

"What on earth is a lover's moon?" Joan asked, mystified.

"Anything you want it to be" Ted's voice had taken on a husky tone. "I say old girl, I don't suppose you fancy getting married". Ted's voice was quiet, for the first time ever.

"Married" Joan gasped "to whom?"

"To me" Ted's voice was still hesitant.

But we have only known each other for three days Joan answered, trying to bring a note of reality to the situation.

"Listen, old girl" Ted began "I'm eighty two and you must be getting near that time too".

"I'm eighty five" Joan interjected.

"Exactly" Ted was not going to be deterred "we have not much time left and we like each other, don't we?"

"We do" Joan agreed.

"Then why not?" Ted asked.

"Why not indeed!" Joan announced as Ted took her in his arms.

"When do you think this happy event should occur?" Joan asked.

"Now, we can get a special licence and be married in the Hotel on Saturday. We can spend the night in the Hotel and go home on Sunday".

"Great idea, as usual" Joan agreed.

Helen, the Matchmaker was delighted with this turn of events. She would pull out all the stops and would be delighted to act as bridesmaid.

The remainder of the week passed in a flurry of activity. Helen insisted they must have a wedding in the Church belonging to the Hotel, rather than in the lounge or dining room.

When they walked in, Joan in a simple cream dress, Ted in his best suit the Church was festooned with flowers from the Castle gardens. The Registrar performed the ceremony and the Church of Ireland Vicar 'gave them' a blessing, then it was back to the Hotel for lunch.

When the speeches were finished Helen announced a small surprise present from the Hotel, pointed outside towards the pier. Hal's boat gleamed inside and out, flowers of every variety were spread along the deck, in the wheel house and a huge bouquet of red roses rested upon the 'converted' front seats for the bride and groom. Naturally Ted and Joan were the only passengers. At the largest of the islands Hal moored the boat and carried of a large hamper. Despite Joan's offer to help Hal insisted on being barman and waiter. The champagne was deliciously chilled and the strawberries magnificent.

As evening fell their waiter prepared and served their gourmet buffet dinner, returning them to the Hotel beneath twinkling stars and a lover's moon.

One final surprise awaited the newly-weds. Helen had moved all their belongings into the Honeymoon Suite. Again there were flowers everywhere and the token red rose on the pillow. Scented candles wafted a rich fragrance into the room as Helen announced 'Wallah' and produced more champagne and strawberries.

Ted insisted that Helen stay until they 'toasted' the bride one more time, then Helen slipped away, smiling.

Helen was back at her desk when the Housekeeper burst in without knocking "they are dead!" she whispered "both dead".

"Who is dead?" Helen asked but in her heart she knew.

Standing in the Honeymoon Suite with the Housekeeper Helen heard the doctor proclaim that they had 'slipped away peacefully in their sleep'.

"How sad" murmured the Housekeeper they just had twenty four hours.

Helen stared at the peaceful faces "How wonderful" she thought "to have one perfect day then slip away to a new and better place!"

The Grand Castle Hotel

The Reconciliation

His announcement came out of 'the blue'. He no longer loved her and hadn't for some considerable time. He had added that he felt miserable and believed the only answer was a divorce.

Then he continued eating the casserole that she had spent hours preparing for him.

She stared at him with a mixture of horror and disbelief. "Is there someone else?" she asked sliding onto her seat.

"No" he responded, and she believed him. She was relieved that she was now seated as she was certain that her legs would no longer support her.

"How could this be?" she wondered. She had poured all her love on to him for more than twenty years and their friends looked with envy at them in the perfect marriage.

"Not so perfect after all" she could feel her heart break.

"What do you want to do?" she asked.

"I don't know" he replied "I suppose we will put the house on the market and split the profits!" His mind had obviously turned to his financial future!

"Split how?" she asked knowing that his input to the mortgage repayments was at least four times greater than hers. Her salary as a P.A. had remained more or less static while his mushroomed as he zoomed up the career ladder.

"Fifty-fifty" he responded "after paying off the mortgage we should have a quarter of a million each!"

Now he was in full flow even here in Dublin we should each be able to afford decent apartments.

"Apartments" she thought bitterly "they had started off in an apartment twenty years ago, but then it was not good enough for him. With every promotion the houses got bigger and now they were domiciled in this five bedroom mansion.

The house had cost slightly over one million euros but he needed the sort of house that reflected his station in life. Now, it seemed, his station did not matter!

"Are you going to move out?" she asked.

Rather bitterly he replied that he could not afford to move anywhere while he had this crippling mortgage to pay.

Wryly she thought "relatively speaking I pay the same as you and this house was your idea in the first place", but, rather than face one of his volcanic rages she 'held her tongue'. Remembering her Gran's motto that 'it was bad that stopped at the teeth' she invented one of her own 'better be safe than sorry!"

"I'll move my stuff into one of the other bedrooms" he announced, before stomping off.

She cleaned up and retired to her bedroom where she cried all night. How could life treat her like this when she loved him so much? Then she realised it was not life that was cruel, it was him. Then she remembered another time when she had been equally cruel! When she first met the man who would become her husband she was living happily with her long term boyfriend. With his tilting Kerry accent, he had swept her off her feet. New to Dublin he needed someone to show him the 'scene' and she was happy to oblige. Three weeks later she took the coward's way out, leaving her partner a note. "She had fallen in love with someone else; she could not help herself. She hoped he would find someone else who would make him happy!"

Six weeks later they had been married and began what she thought of as twenty years of wedded bliss.

"What a fool" she thought staring blankly as the ceiling and sobbing until dawn.

Over the following month the atmosphere in the house was terrible. He suggested they allocate separate areas. She begged him to come with her to see a Marriage Guidance Counsellor. Sourly he agreed to her request, leaving her to make the arrangements.

Twenty minutes into the first session he jumped up saying "If I had wanted a lecture from a Jesuit Priest, I would have gone to Church". Then he stormed out.

He was sitting drumming his fingers on the steering wheel when she eventually emerged. "I knew this was a waste of time" he claimed. She desperately pointed out that there were many types of Counsellors and they might find one to suit them. Over a two month period they visited Humanistic, Freudian, Jungian, Adlerian and Behaviourist Counsellors all with the same outcome; twenty to thirty minutes in he would rise and storm off.

65

The house was 'divided' according to his wishes. Staggered meal times were agreed, preventing the necessity to meet. Then he produced his 'killer' statement "I think we should try to be civil if we 'bump into' each other".

"Civil!" she thought "I've always been civil. It's you that is rude and produces all the tension". Still, she was yet hopeful of reconciliation and willing to try anything.

Slowly tensions did abate to the point where they could speak to each other without friction. She continued to clean, launder, shop and cook for both of them. Main meals were provided for him, then reheated when it was her 'turn'. He provided 'housekeeping' allowance and somehow they 'bumbled' along. Friends must have noticed something as they stopped calling, but were too polite to ask.

Christmas was worst. It was customary to spend Christmas and Boxing Day with one set of parents and New Year's Eve and New Year with the other. They, or rather he, agreed that this Christmas should be no different. At his parents' house he promptly announced that he was tired and stressed from overwork and needed to sleep. Apart from the turkey dinner he spent almost all his time in his old bedroom. When she joined him he rolled over as far as he could go and lay 'log like' silent and sullen.

New Year with her parents was worse. When he did speak he was rude, belittling her and anyone who dared to disagree with him. She was certain her parents were relieved when they left early on New Year's Day. She wrote an immediate letter of apology blaming overwork for his boorishness. Her misery continued unabated.

With every passing day in January he became more agitated, drinking heavily at night and leaving for work at day break. He took to leaving her notes and post-its. If he did not feel any different by Easter they should 'split-up', even if the house had not been sold. They should get another Estate Agent; this one was doing nothing for them. The negativity went on and on.

She lacked sleep, lost her appetite and lost the excess weight that she had gained during their twenty years marriage. On the rare times that their paths crossed he did not seem to notice.

Her work suffered but her boss had too much respect for her input so he never criticised. The Chief Executive knew she was suffering but did not know how to approach the previously friendly outgoing P.A. She had been replaced by some 'empty vessel' who had retreated into a hell hole of misery.

February passed and March was almost through when they received an offer for the house. Twenty thousand Euros above the asking price and he smiled for the first time in nearly a year; or so she imagined.

Easter was just around the corner and she visited yet another Estate Agents premises. There seemed to be so little one could get for two hundred and fifty thousand Euros near the centre of the Capital, so she extended her search out towards the suburbs. A day spent in Harold's Cross, another in Dundrum and still she had seen nothing to 'her liking'/
As she sat in 'her' lounge she suddenly realised why nothing was suitable, this was the 'last throw' of their marriage. The moment she bought anything their marriage was over. Her sadness threatened to overcome her, but she decided that tomorrow would be 'D' day. She had arranged viewing of several properties in the Rathfarnham area and tomorrow she would make an offer for 'something'.

She was flicking through her bundle of house brochures when the lounge door knocked and he walked in. Without waiting for an offer he sat down "I've been thinking" he said "we have twenty thousand Euros more than we expected to get, perhaps we should give this one last try?"

She noticed the 'this'. Not their marriage, simply 'this'.

"I thought we might indulge ourselves at the Grand Castle Hotel for a few days!" he declared.

Her heart lurched!

"Either as a reconciliation or as a final goodbye" he did not seem to care how hurtful his words were.

She had had a year of misery and her confidence was shot, her self esteem long gone, like a beaten dog, she nodded gratefully "that would be nice" she murmured.

He made all the arrangements. When they arrived at their room in the Castle she noticed that he had arranged to have twin beds. He noticed her look. "I told the Receptionist that I had a bad back and needed a firm bed" he explained.

He did not seem to notice the sadness in her voice as she responded "well that's all right, then!" It was more of a question than a statement.

"What would you like to do?" he asked.

"Oh you mean we are going to do things together?" she said with astonishment.

"If you wish" he replied.

"That would be nice" she murmured, thinking I'm getting good at staying "that would be nice".

"Well?" he asked.

"I think a swim first" she answered.

He was already by the side of the pool when she walked out from the changing rooms. "Wow" he thought "she looks really good".

She had had to purchase an entire new wardrobe for the trip. Her twelve stone, thirty eight D figure had been replaced with a trim thirty four C bust. In her new swimsuit she looked ravishing, but a year's confidence bashing had removed all self- respect and all vanity.

He spent most of the hour lounging at the shallow end of the pool as she streaked up and down, up and down for forty lengths. Each time she surfaced, his gaze was drawn to her; her hair streaked and dripping with water, her face radiant for the first time in many months. At horse riding he smiled at her firm butt as she mounted her pony; he remembered the grace and elegance from yesteryear.

A boat ride followed. The sun turned her hair to gold and he noticed that she had some freckles across her nose; twenty years married and he had never noticed them before! He seemed to see his wife anew as the breeze on the lough played with her hair and she laughed at some remark made by the Boatman.

Then it was their final night. He suggested they would 'push the boat out' by dining in the banqueting room and trying the chef's surprises.

Again she agreed that that would be nice!

As a special surprise he had a bottle of Dom Perignon cooling in an ice bucket. He smiled as he remembered the first time they had spent a night together. No Grand Castle Hotel then, he recalled how nervous he had been about the decision that she had to make. He had paced for hours around his tiny studio apartment, praying that she would come to him. He knew she still had feelings for her partner but his dearest and deepest wish was that she loved him more. Then the bell had rung and he opened the bottle of cheap 'Asti', his first experience of champagne. There had been many magnums of increasingly better champagne as he 'moved through the ranks' but none had tasted as good as the first bottle. In this, their (probably) last night together conversation turned to reminiscences about better times, as they enjoyed this special meal.

At last the meal was over, the last of the alcohol finished; it was time to leave. Looking deeply into her eyes he confessed that he had made a mistake, he no longer wanted a divorce.

A year of misery, self- loathing, hurt and despair invaded her voice as she replied "I do!"

Big Mo or the Funeral Fling

If effort and enthusiasm made greatness big Mo should have been a star. Big Mo's endless optimism was evident in every sport he tried but unfortunately he was completely lacking in talent. Big Mo tried them all; soccer, rugby, cricket, tennis, basketball, hockey, gymnastics and table tennis resolutely resisted Mo's valiant efforts. At school the Games Master despaired until he found a role that Mo could fill. With his endless cheerfulness he 'ran the line' often to the despair of his more talented classmates. In his usual uncoordinated way Mo often failed to keep up with the play, missing blatant off-sides or giving offside where none existed. Despite the 'aggro' that Mo caused to his friends on the field of play he was instantly forgiven when the game ended. Mo was undoubtedly the most popular boy in school. With his open countenance, rosy cheeks, innocent manner and ready smile Mo made friends effortlessly.

Mo's popularity could be partly (but only partly) attributed to his willingness to share his academic brilliance with others. It has often been said that people without talent in one area are rewarded in some other way; such was the case with Mo. A genius at Maths, Chemistry and Physics, Mo was equally 'at home' with English, French, Spanish, Geography and History. Many less talented schoolmates owed their GCE 'O' Level results to Mo's patient explanations rather than instruction by the teachers.

Mo 'sailed' through University gaining a First in Chemistry followed by a Masters in Quantum Physics. Surprising to none of his friends, Mo ignored the various offers made by multi-nationals, settling for a less well paid job as a Countryside Officer.

The new job gave Mo everything he ever wanted; a healthy outdoor life, plenty of free time for leisure activities and time with his friends and of course, to get involved in sport.

For fifteen years Mo followed his chosen profession, travelled to Manchester to see 'United' and supported his mates as they kicked their way through the Amateur League. Mo had risen to the dizzy heights of Kit Man for his mates and occasionally they allowed him to train with them but only 'out of season'.

Mo's academic abilities were recognised early on and his outside life came to an end. Now Chief Accountant, Mo spent much of his life gazing out the office windows or gazing intently into hedgerows.

His new position did bring benefits in the form of money to spend. Mo indulged his love of good food and developed a taste for Single Malt Whiskey. Over the years Mo had sampled Glen Livet, Glen Morange, Scapa, Laphroaig, Balbair, Mortlach, Isle of Dura and several Isle of Islay Malts; not only that, he had built up a fine collection of the golden nectar. Mo's eureka moment happened at the Chairman's Christmas Party. Invited into the Chairman's

Private Study he was handed, what looked like a teaspoon, of fifty years old McCallan. The Chairman had stood smiling as the ambrosia slid down Mo's appreciative thirst "Oh my God" Mo whispered in reverence "this is Heaven".

The Chairman smiled in appreciation "indeed, he" whispered "and all for twenty thousand Euros a bottle".

While uncoordinated on the sports field Mo found his real talent; dozens of courses where he tasted and learned to truly appreciate the qualities of the finest whiskies led to holidays spent in Scotland. More specifically every spare moment of Mo's life was spent visiting distilleries. It was his proud boast that he could distinguish each one of the many Isle of Islay whiskies just by the nose.

In pursuit of the 'Holy Grail' of malts, big Mo travelled extensively, read everything he could about his subject while eating voraciously. As a consequence of his lifestyle Big Mo threatened to become Outsize Mo. By the time his entire football team retired aged fortyish, Mo's weight had ballooned to twenty three stone.

The 'ex team' decided, as a man, to take up golf. Naturally Mo joined in with this usual enthusiasm and his normal lack of success. In fact, his peers agreed that Big Mo got worse with every round he played.

At the end of their first year the Handicap Committee made their decisions. The best of the ex team was given a handicap of fourteen, with various others handicaps for the remainder. Big Mo's handicap was firmly fixed at twenty four. Indeed, the Chairperson of the handicap would have liked to have given Mo thirty six strokes, but rules were rules. The maximum handicap available to man was twenty four and that was that.

Perhaps a word of explanation is necessary for readers who are non-golfers, at this junction.

If the Committee decide that a Scratch Golfer (someone who plays of '0') can complete eighteen holes in seventy two shots 'par' is seventy two. Less talented golfers are given handicaps; one would be a very good golfer, two less good and so on. A beginner, with a handicap of twenty four would achieve 'par' for him or herself if she finished with a score of ninety six (seventy two + twenty four). Should a twenty four handicapper score ninety five while a Scratch Golfer scored seventy two the twenty four handicapper would win.

Big Mo and his ex -team comrades had been playing the game for six years with Mo still fixed solidly at twenty four.

Mo had spent the previous six years in his sedentary occupation with his golf as his only exercise. But now he had combined his three passions, travelling to 'sample' the fruits of distillery after distillery, enjoying gourmet (and other) food on his sojourns and enjoying a round of golf wherever he went.

Now forty six years old and twenty five stone weight Big Mo got his lucky break. Not quite the jackpot, but five numbers and one lucky star in the Euro millions provided Mo with quite a 'tidy sum'. Mo smiled to himself at his good fortune, now he would really surprise his companions with his amazing progress.

Big Mo 'googled' and found his perfect location. The Grand Castle Hotel in the West of Ireland was offering very good deals and, best of all, they had an eighteen hole golf course and a well know 'Pro' (Professional). The Pro provided a set number of lessons but was available to meet the particular needs of his students.

Big Mo booked into the Hotel for four weeks and immediately enrolled with the golf Pro for the Intensive Course for beginners. Over a most splendid meal that night, topped up with a couple of Balbair single malt Mo prepared mentally for the exciting 'journey' ahead.

On his first morning on the course the Pro was impressive with his confidence building skills; he had taught hundreds of beginners who believed they were unteachable and every one improved. Big Mo smiled in delighted anticipation!

Three and a half weeks later into his course the Pro returned Mo's money and suggested that he might 'take up' croquet. Then the Pro took a protracted holiday!

Big Mo decided not to waste he remaining three days of his holiday so returned 'Pro-less' to the course.

For some inexplicable reason Big Mo played better that day then he had ever managed in the previous six years. On the ninth green he even 'holed' a putt from eighteen feet. His companions clapped politely as Mo stepped forward to retrieve his ball. Big Mo bent over and promptly dropped down 'stone dead'.

In accordance with the terms of Big Mo's will and with the agreement of the General Manager, Big Mo's 'wake' was conducted in the Grand Castle Hotel.

The small lounge was 'taken over' by Big Mo's entourage and the coffin placed upright in the corner. The Undertaker had done a great job leaving Mo with a slight smile on his face. The hundreds of 'mourners' who attended agreed that the 'smile' was highly appropriate, for Mo was famous for his cheerfulness.

The money that Mo had organised to 'put behind the bar' ensured a great send off. The day passed with great hilarity as increasingly more bizarre Big Mo stories were told, but then it was time for only the 'hard core mourners' to remain to finish the 'funeral fling'. Sixteen ex-team mates were 'booked into' the Castle and they remained with Mo to the bitter end, enjoying the best of Mo's malts, brought specially to the Castle for the occasion.

At the stroke of midnight the Head Barman stepped into the room. "A special treat from your Special Friend" he announced opening a fifty year old bottle of Springback Special Malt. All his drinking life Mo had longed for the 'nectar from the Gods' but at fifty thousand Euros a bottle it could not simply be purchased from the local carry out! Mo's lasting regret was the fact that he had never experienced the ecstasy that was Springback.

The team mates never knew if the Castle 'stocked' such rare whiskey or whether Mo had organised some 'miracle'. And the Barman wasn't telling.

"Wait" little Joe commanded, recalling the innumerable puns about Big Mo and Little Joe, "first glass for Mo!" Little Joe stepped forward and completely filled the Waterford Crystal Glass with the precious liquid.

If anyone thought that Joe's action was a waste of good whisky they certainly did not say so. Joe stepped over to the coffin and placed the glass at Mo's feet. Then Mo was 'toasted' with the cream of whiskies.

At four am the group finally decamped. As was her custom, Helen the General Manager had remained until the last guest left. Helen smiled as Little Joe saluted the Corpse and irreverently invited Mo to 'enjoy his drink'. Together Joe and Helen quietly closed the only door to the room, with Helen locking it and retaining the key.

At ten am a clearly hung over Joe and his mates were back at Helen's office. "The Undertakers are here" Joe announced "can we take the body?"

Helen walked before the mourners and opened the locked door and stood aside to let Joe enter. Joe took a step forward then stopped; he gazed intently at Mo.

Joe was certain that Mo's smile was more noticeable then it had been yesterday. Then he shook his head "Impossible" he thought "the light is playing tricks!"

The Undertakers moved forward to do their job and together with Joe they walked across the room.

Standing immediately before the corpse Joe decided "Mo's smile IS wider!" then he looked down.

The glass stood empty at Big Mo's feet.

The blood drained from Little Joe's face but he did not lean forward to smell Big Mo's 'breath'!

The Major's Wedding

Kate was a lady with a past. Nineteenth Century Parisian society ladies might have described her as a Courtesan; the British had a less elegant word.

Kate left her West Country home with nothing but a pretty face, an impressive embonpoint, a pert bottom and a confidence that her talents would take her a long way.

Booked into a girls' hostel Kate found work in a rather nice bookshop in London. Within a month she was having an affair with the Manager who was beguiled with her large violet eyes and captivating smile. Ignoring the fact that she was only sixteen her lover 'robbed the till' and together they ran away to France. They ran out of money in Nice but Kate met a lovely surgeon and his family who were returning to England. She hitched a ride with them all the way back to London, forgetting to tell her lover who was searching the streets of Nice in a state of desperation. Desperate pleas to the Gendarme saw him arrested, firstly on suspicion of murder and later for wasting their time.

The 'kindly' surgeon felt so sorry for Kate that he felt compelled to visit her hostel to reassure himself that she had recovered from her ordeal; or recovered from the story that she had invented to elicit their sympathy. When he saw the state of the hostel the 'kindly' surgeon just had to take her out to dinner. Then he 'just had to' take her to a hotel where he discovered that she was innocent and pure. A man of his medical knowledge should have known better, but Kate was a 'very good actress'.

The surgeon suggested that he would rent an apartment for her to get her out of 'that hovel. Kate's big eyes expressed her gratitude!

Two days followed Kate's eighteenth birthday, the surgeon's wife sued for divorce naming her as a co-respondent.

Kate's Barrister was very 'dishy' and very sympathetic as she recounted her terrible upbringing, the violence of a previous boyfriend and her gratitude that the surgeon had saved her from a life of violence. She had nothing to give the 'kind' surgeon, but herself, which she did willingly. Of course she knew it was wrong and it would never happen again. Looking straight into the Barrister's eyes she asked "what would you have done if you had been in my shoes?" then added with a sob "he was so kind".

It was all the Barrister could do to stop himself from taking this poor injured flower in his arms. He did not think the surgeon was 'kind' but he would fight for Kate. In Court Kate's performance deserved an 'Oscar', in turns humble, humiliated, then sainted trying to reward her Mentor.

The Judge assured her that she was leaving his Court without a stain on her character, then he 'crucified' the surgeon.

The Barrister was touched to accept Kate's gift of a nice 'Cross' pen. Realising that the pen would have cost her several weeks' wages he invited her to dinner.

Over dinner Basil (the Barrister) assured her that he was not like other men and certainly not like the surgeon. For a start he was not married. Basil totally forgot to mention that he had three ex-wives and hefty alimony commitments. Perhaps it was true that he was not like other men, because he did not 'bed her' until the second date. However, it may also have been due to the fact that he simply kissed her on the cheek and wished her 'goodnight'.

Kate was having none of that, so she seduced him on the second date.

For three years Basil lavished her with presents, paid for expensive holidays, encouraged her to buy designer clothes (at his expense) and begged her to marry him. She resisted all his proposals! Gradually he bought her into his inner circle making the fatal mistake of introducing her to Lord Harold Cavendish a High Court Judge and his dearest friend. Lord Cavendish was a rarity amongst the legal fraternity; he had never married, was not gay, as far as one could tell and had never been touched by a breath of scandal.

At forty five Basil was His Lordship's protégé, with a seat on the bench expected in the near future. At seventy five Lord Harry was 'safe' to be introduced to Kate. Basil reckoned, not unreasonably, that if he had been celibate for seventy five years he was unlikely to change now. He invited his Lordship round to his bachelor pad to meet his stunning girlfriend. Lord Cavendish was bewitched by Kate!

His Lordship was resting in his chambers when his clerk announced that he had a visitor "A young lady who claimed to know him".

"As yes" smiled the Judge. The clerk waited for an explanation, but none was forthcoming "send her in" he asked.

Kate was flustered to be alone in his presence, and told him so. Smiling indulgently his Lordship reassured her that he was just an ordinary man and asked how he could help her.

"It's Basil" Kate responded "I'm just not sure about him. He keeps asked to marry me, but I've just discovered that he has three former wives!"

Kate turned those eyes on the Judge and, in a voice of pure innocence she whispered "I believe God meant marriage to be a one off lasting a lifetime". She turned her pitiful look on the Judge "besides I am not certain that I truly love him" she added. Her eyes filled with tears "I have prayed constantly to God for guidance, but I cannot feel His presence. He has always been there for me, but I believe that He has forsaken me because I slept with Basil!"

The Judge laid his hand on her shoulder. "Let us pray together for guidance" he suggested. Kate looked up from under her tear strewn eye lids "I believe that sex should be reserved for marriage. It's how I was brought up. It's what I truly believe, but Basil was so persuasive!"

His Lordship touched to his soul, murmured "that is also what I believe! All my life I have waited for the perfect love, offering my celibacy to God, in love".

"Then you believe that I am damned" Kate's cries called out to Heaven.

"Not at all, Kate, the sin was Basil's for forcing you!" the Judge was most understanding.

"But he did not exactly force me, more coerced, Kate sobbed. "Do you think God could forgive me?" she cried plaintively.

"Kate you now God is all forgiving, all merciful" the Judge whispered in a tender voice, taking his hands in his.

"Could you forgive me" Kate whispered then added "How I wish I had waited for someone like you".

"There is nothing for me to forgive!" His Lordship was beneficent.

"My Lord" she whispered, "Do you think someone like you could have love a fallen woman, like me?"

The Judge enveloped Kate in his arms "love is all forgiving, my dear" he whispered "but now you must tell Basil that it is over".

"You are so good" she smiled as she opened the door "I wish I had known you first".

Then she was gone, laughing inwardly all the way to her apartment. Her research had been perfect. Everything there was to know about the Judge, she knew, including the fact that he was a 'born again' Christian.

Then she rang Basil and did exactly what the Judge had said. When he answered her call, she said 'it's over' and put down the phone.

She had to wait for three days before his call came. "Would Kate like to accompany him to a Carol Service at his Church?"

Kate would and left the Church 'linked' to the Judge's arm.

Six months later they had a quiet Church wedding, the groom was seventy six, the bride twenty three. The first night of the honeymoon was spent at the Dorchester, prior to leaving for the West Indies. The happy couple never made it to the Indies as Lord Cavendish died in his sleep on the first night of his honeymoon. Some said he died from a surfeit of sex after seventy six years of celibacy, others said the sight of naked Kate killed him. The death certificate said he died from cardiac failure.

Lady Cavendish was inconsolable at the loss of the love of her life; she perked up somewhat when it was made known that she was the sole beneficiary of the Judge's will. Two days following Judge Cavendish's death her Ladyship moved into his luxury Thames side apartment, checked over his stocks and shares, bank accounts, safety deposit box and property portfolio. When the mansion in the Country was sold and everything else turned into cash, Lady Cavendish had more than two million pounds.

But life wasn't all about money. Life was about excitement, life was the next 'mark'.

For two years her Ladyship sowed her wild oats with the most unsuitable of paramours. One gigolo 'cleaned her out' for one hundred pounds another beat her senseless before stealing all her jewellery, then Kate's luck turned.

English society still loved titles and Lady Cavendish occasionally received invitations to grand galas. Usually she turned them all down, but this invitation was for a grand event in the Savoy. The cream of London Society would be there and she was curious to see who the leading figures were.

An hour into the event and Kate was regretting her impetuous decision when a foreign looking gent introduced himself "I am Prince Abdullah Ben ...." the names went on for ages ending with "from Saudi Arabia! "I am Lady Cavendish" she laughed and "I will call you Ben, you may call me Kate!"

He did call her, frequently from various parts of the world. As soon as she would receive his call she would drop everything and fly to him. She may not exactly have been a courtesan but she came close, accepting expensive presents from every part of the globe. Diamond necklaces in Paris, sapphires in London, Rolex watch in Milan, present followed present. Three months into the relationship Ben gave her a platinum card with unlimited access, which Kate used to the full. She realised the relationship was over when the platinum card was denied. He made no attempt to contact her, no effort to explain. Nothing!

For four years Kate 'burnt up' London until her reputation was so bad she simply had to decamp. She moved to Birmingham, got bored and moved to Liverpool. She pulled a few tricks in Liverpool but loathed the Scouse accent, so once again she was on the move.

For eighteen months she lived in Manchester with a mad Irishman, playing it straight for the first time in nearly twenty years. When her mad Irishman graduated she returned to Dublin with him only to discover that he was Irish nobility and her reputation had preceded her. The stern Irish Senator advised her that his twenty two year old son was bound for greatness and the shop soiled thirty five year old Lady Cavendish must play no part in his future.

Kate stood 'coolly' looking at the Senator "How much?" she asked.

"How much what?" the Senator responded.

"How much are you willing to pay to make me give him up?" Kate laughed.

"You slut" the Senator stuttered "One hundred thousand Euros".

"Not enough!" Kate was adamant though why she was doing it she did not know. Thanks to His Lordship and the Prince, her bank account was bulging. One hundred thousand Euros was chickenfeed. Maybe she just liked 'hustling'.

"Two hundred and fifty thousand Euros and that's my final offer" the Senator roared.

"Done" laughed Kate "but cash only".

"I don't have that sort of money in the house" the Senator proclaimed.

"Then meet me your bank tomorrow at ten" Kate pressed.

"I would not be seen dead with you, in my bank or anywhere else" the Senator shouted.

"That is too bad" Kate said "I will just have to ring your son this evening".

The Senator met her at the bank. Having transferred the money the Senator hissed "I hope I never lay eyes of you again, you slut".

"Lady Cavendish to you" Kate laughed.

Then she went on the circuit, raucous nights here, and orgies there, drunken soirees elsewhere, anything for a dare. One of the in-crowd suggested they should go to Galway for the races. Ever keen for a change Kate went with him and enjoyed four days of drunkenness and losing bets. Then her knight in shining armour spotted a long legged Australian teenager and took off. Kate looked at herself in the mirror; the youthful glow was gone, she was nearly thirty six years old and she needed a rest. She rang the Grand Castle Hotel.

Lady Cavendish spent five restful days recuperating from a lifetime of excesses. A combination of good food, long walks, boat trips and a day on horseback had restored some of the 'bloom' in Kate's cheeks. At first she had thought of 'turning a trick' with one of the

77

richer guests in the Hotel but then decided it was better just to have a rest. But one can only rest for so long and Kate's feet were getting itchy. She rang an old friend in Paris to enquire after the scene but made no immediate decision to go.

She spent a further day driving a hire care around the wilds of Connemara, enjoying a simple lunch of lobster in Roundstone before driving back to the Hotel. Having enjoyed a great night's sleep and a fine breakfast Kate was on her way to Reception to organise payment of her bill and seek a Porter to carry her cases down to the taxi. A taxi that she had yet to order but that was a minor problem.

As she was passing the front doorway Kate spotted a very grand Bentley draw up outside. As the car whispered to a stop Kate stood stock still to see what the car produced.

The man who stopped out of the car looked to be about sixty with short greyish hair and a military bearing. Well dressed, the man's shoes were expensive and gleaming. The man turned and the door closed with a whisper. From a distance of ten feet Kate established that there was no wedding ring and more importantly 'no smell of marriage'.

For several moments Kate stood analysing the situation. "What should she do?" she did not need the money, but what would be wrong with one last 'trick' before she retired?"

She smiled and stepped towards the front door.

Jack was raised in genteel nobility. Kindergarten was followed by several years of private education, leading to a stint at Eton.

Home for the holidays his father, the Viscount summoned Jack to his study. Indicating Jack to be seated the Viscount did not 'mince his words'. As the youngest of four sons Jack would neither inherit titles nor a large sum of money. It was time to make his own way in the world and his father suggested either the army or the Church.

Jack chose the army.

Following twenty five years of unremarkable service in the Quartermaster General's Corps, Jack achieved his 'majority' with special responsibility for shirts, socks and shoe laces.

Cuts to Service Personnel prompted by political decisions saw Jack enter 'civvy street' for the first time at forty seven years of age. The tiny pension and lump sum was unlikely to last very long the way his wife spent money. Jack was pretty certain that a Field Marshall's income would be insufficient to keep that woman in the style she sought.

Returning home from yet one more failed interview Jack popped into a bar for a 'stiffener'. Lost in a quandary as to whether he should have sherry, port or claret he inadvertently joined two young men in a 'snug'. Settling for a glass of wine Jack tried not to show an interest in his companion's animated discussions. It seemed that the technological age was set for explosion, with I.T. ruling the world. Words like microchip, CD Rom and dozens of others that had never entered Jack's sheltered environment peppered about him like bullets. Jack's look of bewilderment must have been detected by the young man, as one nudged the other and began to laugh.

"Sorry, sir" one of the young men laughed "I'm afraid we got carried away, but you see, we have just invented something that is going to make our fortune".

"Something?" Jack asked.

"I'm afraid I can't tell you unless you have fifteen thousand pounds to spare!"

Jack bundled "As a matter of fact I do have fifteen thousand pounds" he boasted.

"You do?" one of the men queried "and you would be willing to invest?"

"I might" Jack retorted feeling his anger rise at their arrogance "but first you have to explain what you have got!"

For half an hour the two young men competed with each other in their enthusiasm for whatever it was that they had invented. Jack was none the wiser as ninety nine per cent of the jargon passed him by.

Finally they concluded "we need fifteen thousand pounds to launch it".

With grave reservations but stiff upper lip Jack signed the cheque. Agreement was reached that Jack owned 30% of the Company with a seat on the Board.

When he told his wife of his investment she responded in her usual manner "bloody fool" she spat "you've been conned by a couple of conmen" Then she made the big move, she left, got divorced and set up home with a bus driver.

The big idea was an immediate success and Board meetings in one or other of his 'partner's' kitchens often descended to farce, but a tiny amount of 'interest' did trickle in.

Five years on and his partners rang requesting a meeting with him at the Savoy. 'Another con' Jack thought or else they were going to buy back his shares at a tiny fraction of what he had paid.

To Jack's great surprise his partners has rented a suite in the Savoy, one of London's finest hotels and were already there when he arrived.   Two very well dressed strangers accompanied his partners. Jack refused the drink he was offered but joined them around the table at which they were seated. The table was laden with legal documents, pamphlets and various files and portfolios. The more outgoing of his partners spoke "we were hoping to buy back your share of the company" he declared.

"Here it comes" Jack thought "Ten per cent, twelve per cent?"

One of the well- dressed strangers opened a file and placed it before Jack.

"The offer is at the bottom of the page!" his partner pointed out. Jack fainted!

When he eventually 'came round' and examined the figure he almost passed out once more.

"We believe that is a very fair offer" one of the strangers said.

"And you are?" Jack asked.

"Your Legal Representatives" the Saville Row suit replied.

"Our Legal Representatives?" Jack asked.

"Yes, sir" he replied "your company has retained us for the past two years".

"Wow" Jack managed but sought an alteration to the contract "he would accept the figure but would retain five per cent of the shares with a non-executive seat on the Board". 'What a cheek' he thought as he listened to his own words. His partners agreed to this stipulation.

Jack settled a ten million pounds trust fund on each of his three children, bought an upmarket apartment in Kensington and purchased a Bentley Continental. Using his London apartment as a base he began his travels and kept going or the following five years.

On impulse Jack enrolled a for six weeks course on Watercolour painting that was being provided by a famous Painter. The class would be based at the Grand Castle Hotel in the West of Ireland where the light was claimed to be the best in the British Islands. Jack smiled in anticipation; his latest Bentley needed a good outing and the drive from London would be 'just the thing'.

Jack googled all the best hotels North to Scotland, then the Irish hostelries on his way west. It still amazed Jack that no matter how much he spent his capital continued to grow. Yearly interest from his five per cent share was greater than all the money he had earned in his army career.

Following a splendid journey Jack drew up outside the Grand Castle Hotel. He stepped out of the car, collected his baggage and walked towards the front door.

As he came to the door a young woman stepped out careering into him. The papers that the young woman had been holding fluttered to the ground. Lowering his case Jack said "I'm sorry" and helped to collect the lady's papers. Finally the papers were recovered and restored to their owner. "I hope those papers are not important" Jack mentioned. "Just my PhD Thesis" Kate responded her voice more than a little tremulous. "Let me buy you a drink" Jack offered "you seem a little distressed".

"A little early for me" the young woman answered warmly but allowed herself to be steered into the guest's lounge.

Kate took rather longer to recover than Jack would have expected. As she delicately sipped a dry sherry Jack learned that she was English, a widow with a title she rarely used and was in Ireland to complete her PhD.

In truth Jack was delighted with the long recovery time; he found his new companion fascinating and an interesting lady. By 'fascinating' he meant that she 'hung on' to every word he uttered; she 'oohed and aahhed' as he ever so slightly embellished his army career. Jack's stories like all army personnel tales began 'when I was in' hush-hush, covert operations with the SAS, Paras and British Intelligence "all very confidential of course", Kate murmured her agreement.

Eventually Kate smiled that she must go; she was getting a 'lift' to the Burren where she was conducting 'field trials'. She did not elucidate about the nature of the trials ... all 'hush-hush' perhaps. In reality Kate spent the day on a massive 'beauty' session involving hairdressers, manicurists, the masseuse, tanning, exfoliating and professional makeover.

Having elucidated that Jack had booked a Suite and had 'ordered' dinner for seven thirty pm, Kate walked into the dining room at seven forty five pm halting inside the doorway to await the Head Waiter. In milliseconds Kate's glance 'took in the diners' around the dining room; she smiled on seeing Jack dining alone.

Some 'intuition' made Jack look up to see the vision of loveliness that had just walked in. Recognising his companion of earlier, he waved her over. Kate smiled demurely but remained on the spot until the Head Waiter guided her to Jack's table. Kate glowed as Jack innate old fashioned manners kicked in; standing to greet her, he expressed his delight at the fact that she had honoured him with her presence.

By the time the cheese board was presented Kate knew everything there was to know about him. The magnetism of those violet eyes 'loosened his tongue' as he described his divorce, his Thames side apartment, his three children, his travels and his loneliness. Jack did not even notice as Kate subtly guided his conversation to finances. He was comfortably off, an investor; he sought out young entrepreneurs and financed their inventions; 'for a share of the profits' Jack laughed.

Kate smiled, delicately.

Then Kate apologised "I'm afraid I must go, I have a meeting with my Professor that I cannot avoid" Kate the added "he is coming here to see me, but our meeting should be over in an hour".

Jack cheered inwardly. Standing up as she was taking her leave Jack wondered if she might join him for a nightcap in the guests' lounge when she was free. Smiling Kate whispered "we shall see" and slipped away.

Kate's 'meeting' involved booting up her computer and investigating the various companies that Jack had mentioned during the meal. Several small companies listed Jack as a Director but none could be described as earth shattering. Then Kate hit gold dust. Bringing up the Company where Jack had made his money she immediately spotted the five per cent holding and the role of Non-Executive Director. Then her study hit the jackpot; a complete dossier of Jack's finances.

"Oh my God" Kate gasped out loud, he was almost as rich as her Saudi Prince. Estimates of his total wealth ranged from five hundred to nine hundred million pounds.

"Oh yes" Kate exclaimed to herself "she would be having that nightcap".

She kept him waiting before rushing into the lounge at eleven forty five, slightly flustered. "I am sorry" she gasped breathlessly "have you ever noticed how things continue to stop you, when you want to be somewhere else? I thought the 'Prof' was never going to leave'.

Jack beamed, grasping the inference.

The Waiter appeared. "What would you like?" Jack asked.

"Whatever you are having" Kate responded.

"Two large brandies, please" Jack ordered.

"I do hope you are not trying to take advantage of me" Kate chuckled, her violet eyes twinkling.

"Not at all" Jack announced gallantly "two good friends enjoying a drink, that's all".

"That will do for now" Kate thought.

Kate was particularly attentive as she appeared to 'hang on' to Jack's every word. Eventually she said 'well that's that, time to retire' setting down her empty brandy balloon.

Jack 'walked' her to her room, stretched out his hand and wished her 'goodnight'. Grinning cheekily, Kate kissed him on the cheek and said "goodnight, good friend!"

Quite naturally, they breakfasted together where Kate invited Jack to join her on a walk by the river. Abandoning any idea of painting class that day, Jack was more than happy to accompany the lady with the violet eyes.

As they walked Kate grew increasingly pensive, retreating within herself. Fearing that he had given offence Jack asked "what is the matter?"

Kate literally shook herself "nothing, nothing!" she responded hesitantly then added "problems with my course!"

"Problems" Jack asked.

"Afraid so!" Kate responded "PhD's are not cheap, I've already sold my car but things are becoming increasingly difficult".

Kate then went on to explain that she had to be in Dublin at Uni for three days each week and at the Burren for field studies for a further three days. She had treated herself to a little holiday at the Castle this week but she would need to seek lodgings in a guest house nearer to the Burren. The she explained the difficulties in getting a bus from her digs to the centre of Dublin, another one to Galway and yet another one to the Burren. The journey often took an entire day, depending upon bus services. It was difficult enough during the summer but bus services were severely cut during the winter. She simply did not know that to do.

With a rueful grin Kate whispered that she would have to part with her 'good friend' after tomorrow, as the cost to stay in the Castle were beyond her. Then brightening up she announced "Well at least we have today!"

Jack was only too happy to have the company of a beautiful woman for an entire day. "What would you like to do?" Jack asked.

"How would you feel about taking me around the Burren, I could show you the marvels of nature?" Jack was more than happy to please his 'good friend' and soon the Bentley was purring its way towards the Burren.

It was only natural in the rough surreal rockery that is the Burren that Kate should take Jack's hand as they traversed its wonders. They were still holding hands as they returned to Galway for lunch.

On the way back to the Castle it was Jack's turn to be pensive as Kate sat quietly beside him, her head resting on his shoulder. By the time they had returned to the Hotel Jack had made a decision.

Over dinner Jack outlined his proposal. Kate could move into his Suite with him. Hastily and midst much blushing Jack added "there's room enough for both of us".

Kate was indignant "this was not how 'good friends' treated her, she was appalled that he should think so little of her".

Apologising profusely Jack insisted she had misinterpreted his intentions, he was offering her accommodation as a friend; he did not expect her to share his bed.

Kate was immediately contrite "I'm sorry" she cried "but too many men have tried to take advantage of me; I thought you were another one of THEM".

Jack assured her that his intentions were honourable!

"I'm sorry Jack" Kate's voice was low "I really shall miss you, but I could not possibly share your room with you".

"Let me pay for a room in the Castle for you" Jack was desperate to continue the friendship.

Kate looked deeply into Jack's eyes "Well, alright but for one weekend only. I couldn't possibly accept your charity!" Then she added "but I do love your company."

"It's done then" Jack replied. "I will organise a room for you!"

"No" Kate protested "if you did that everyone in the Hotel, would think I am a slut" her voice trailed off.

"I am sorry" Jack gasped "I didn't think" then he peeled off five crisp hundred Euro notes "Will this be enough?" he asked.

Kate nodded humbly "I will pay every penny of this back when I qualify" she promised.

Jack drove her to Galway at the end of Kate's break assuring her that he would be there to meet her on the following Friday.

Jack's week as a watercolourist was something of a disaster as two beautiful violet eyes floated into his dreaming. Following five days that felt like an eternity Jack was back in Galway waiting for the bus. In his anxiety he had been at the bus station for nearly an hour when the bus pulled in. Expectantly he watched every passenger get off the bus, his heart sinking as the passengers tailed off 'in his mind's eye'. Jack became certain that she had missed the bus. Just as he had given up hope Kate stepped off the bus, complaining that the driver had engaged her in senseless conversation. Jack had turned to get into the car when she threw her arms around him. "Impetuously" she announced "You have no idea how good it is to see you". Then she kissed him on the lips; the merest brush, but a kiss nevertheless.

"This is not the way to the Castle" Kate queried thinking Jack had taken a wrong turn.

"I know" he said "I have a surprise for you".

"I'm not sure about that" Kate reacted "I don't really like surprises".

"You will like this one" Jack assured her.

"Do tell!" she pleaded.

"Then it would not be a surprise" Jack laughed.

In a few moments they drew up in the forecourt of a Volkswagen salesroom. Standing shining outside the front door was a brand new yellow Beetle complete with sunflower on the dash. The Sales Manager approached, handing over the keys and documentation.

"For the lady" Jack insisted.

Kate was speechless.

"I think I have the answer to your problems" Jack beamed. Sitting in the passenger seat was a large envelope with Kate's name on it.

As the five thousand Euros tumbled on to the seat Jack interceded quickly.

"No conditions" he asserted, "now you can drive across every week and you can have a room at the Castle, or anywhere else for that matter. If you wish you can return the money when you can, but the car is a gift. I really want to continue our friendship".

How could Kate refuse, when Jack put it like that. Once more she placed her arms around his neck, kissed him and whispered "You are so good."

Jack felt ten feet tall!

Perhaps it was at that point that Kate decided "to play for bigger stakes".

Only God knew when she did her 'field studies' but every waking moment of her time at the Castle spent in Jack's company. For his part Jack loved the looks of surprise on her face when he presented her with yet another present. The joy of Jack's giving was matched equally by Kate's joy on receiving.

Five weeks into Jack's 'painting course' he presented Kate with a sublime diamond necklace. The jeweller assured him it was a snip at one hundred thousand Euros having previously cost half a million.

Over dinner Jack slid the box across the table. "For you" he whispered "for making me so happy".

Kate's eyes opened wide in delight. "Oh Jack" she gasped "you spoil me". Then she added "let's get out of here, so you can put it on for me!"

"Where shall we go?" Jack asked, blankly.

"Your place for mine" Kate giggled.

Like teenagers with a guilty secret they 'slunk off' to Jack's suite.

"Oh Jack, it's perfect" Kate's breathing had increased and her voice was husky.

Then she opened another button on her blouse and displayed the flawless gems between her luscious breasts. When the lovemaking was over Jack asked her to marry him.

Kate said "yes".

"Let's not wait" Kate urged "we are both single and I would love a Church wedding".

Jack was happy to agree.

With her usual flair Helen, the General Manager set the wheels in motion. Twenty rooms were set aside for Jack's guests, sadly as an 'orphan' Kate had not family members who could attend. Sadly she informed Jack that her friends in London could not afford to attend and were too proud to accept charity from Jack.

Jack's love for his wife-to-be grew in 'leaps and bounds'. Together they organised the wedding service for the little Church of Ireland Church that was close to the Castle. Once more Helen was magnificent advising on meals, dinners and timings. Jack happily faded into the background as the 'girls' got on with 'organising'.

Jack rang his children informing them of the great event; he could not keep the excitement out of his voice as he told them of the marvellous sainted woman who had agreed to be his wife. Jack's son agreed to be Best Man and suggested that his friend Tim could act a Groomsman. Schedules were very tight, his son and Tim only able to arrive on the morning of the wedding. The son offered his sincere apologies at not being able to meet the bride prior to the service, but Jack's happiness was not going to be dented.

"So long as you are at the Church at five to eleven, that's all that matters" Jack sang out.

The son and the Groomsman made it to the Church with fifteen minutes to spare. Embracing his father the son remarked that he was delighted that his father had found such happiness.

Jack smiled cheerfully as they seated themselves to the right of the altar. Several times Jack anxiously asked if his son had the rings; on each occasion his son reminded him that his father had passed over the rings when they arrived.

The organist began the wedding march, the Bride, with Helen as her bridesmaid was on her way.

The first notes from the organ struck Jack like bullets as he leapt to his feet; the bride caught the eye of the usher and smiled briefly. The usher smiled back and Kate continued her 'march' up the aisle.

The Groom, Best Man and Groomsman turned through ninety degrees to 'welcome' the bride. Jack stepped across to stand beside his bride. Kate raised her veil and the Best Man fainted.

Chaos reigned for a few moments as Jack sought to revive his son. The Minister indicated to Helen and the Bride to be seated and spoke reassuringly to the small congregation. The Minister suggested they remove the Best Man to the vestry where there was water and fresh air. In his best reassuring voice the Reverend assured everyone that the service would continue in a few minutes.

With a shrug of apology to Kate, Jack and Tim scrambled the Best Man into the vestry.

In the vestry the Son made a miraculous recovery. "That is Kate Cavendish" he hissed.

"I know" replied Jack "have you met her?"

"Met her" the son replied bitterly "I had a relationship with her in London, then she announced that she was pregnant". The son's bitterness escalated as his voice rose "she demanded money for a termination. It was only later that I learned she told the same sob story to sixteen of my friends. She had been with all of them!"

"I can't believe this" gasped Jack.

"Then believe it" his son added "she once slept with the entire first fifteen for a bet. If you don't believe me, ten of them are out there in the Church".

"Perhaps she has changed?" Jack's voice held misery.

"Changed" his son added "she was at the beck and call of a Saudi Arabian for years; she was nothing short of a whore!"

Then the son recounted a string of Kate Cavendish stories.

Jack was devastated. He knew he was not the first man to be with Kate since she was widowed, but he had deduced that there were only five or six.

Jack's back stiffened, twenty five years of army training coupled with a stiff upper lip Britishness kicked in. He would do the honourable thing; he had asked her to marry him and she had said "yes".

There was only one course of action. On wobbly legs Jack returned to the altar, but the Bride was gone.

And the Usher was nowhere to be found!

The Great Seducer

It was the biggest event in the West of Ireland since John Wayne had stayed in Ashford Castle while he 'made' The Quiet Man in 1951.

Now Stuart Clark (not his real name obviously) had chosen to stay in the Grand Castle Hotel while he was 'shooting' his latest chick flick with Carol Acosta. Industry insiders were fairly certain that the powerful drama from which the film sprang would be converted into a stage Irish farce ... much like Hollywood had done for Scotland in Whisky Galore. Rumour had it that Clark would play the scion of a Noble Irish family bent on rescuing the lovely Acosta from certain starvation on her peasant father's tiny smallholding. With more than a passing reference to the great famine of the 1840's a film supposedly based in the post Cromwellian barbarity of the 1650's sought to fuse two hundred years into a two hour film.

Purists might argue that it was sacrilegious to tell a story of English soldiery burning homesteads, raping and pillaging in the densely populated seventeenth Century East of Ireland then drop in the potato famine of the 1840's that happened mainly in the West of the Country.

But those arguments were for another day. Today was all about Stuart Clark, handsome hero of more than forty box office successes in the genre made famous by Niven, Flynn, Grant and Gable.

Stuart had kindly agreed to be photographed by local and national press, stepping off the 'Star of the Sea' onto the wharf, swinging a local child skywards in his manly arms, kissing the General Manager as she welcomed him to the Castle. Ed, his ever faithful P.R. man was on hand to pass out signed photographs of the hero. Stuart smiling seductively at a young starlet, famous while teeth flashing, Stuart gazing wistfully into the distance, famous dimple on clear display, Stuart in Africa looking suitably chastened as he walked among the 'forgotten' children. Patiently and cheerfully Stuart answered questions from the press, agreed to kiss an enthusiastic fan and explain his role in the film.

Inside, in the sanctuary of his Suite, Stuart tore of his immaculate white suit and snarled "I need a shower and change of clothing". Obviously his fans were less sanitary than he was.

Unlike the Quiet Man of fifty years previously the star of this film was the only cast member to be billeted in the Castle. Unknown to his Irish fans, Stuart's star was on the wane, with his last two films failing to make a profit. It was rumoured that Acosta was to be the real star of the film, but her scenes were all being shot in the comfort of a studio.

Since setting foot in Ireland Stuart's mood had been foul, not for him the rustic beauty of Ireland's West Coast. Stuart's natural stomping grounds were L.A., Las Vegas, New York, Paris, London or Amsterdam.

But Stuart was nothing if not an actor. Spurred on by Ed the Public Relations expert, he smiled through breakfast, lunch and dinner, 'happily' posing for snapshots with guests and staff, he signed autographs and talked enthusiastically about his latest project. Stuart was well aware of the need for a box office hit on both sides of the Atlantic, so 'talked up' his latest offering. This would be his greatest film ever, combining loss, grief, heartbreak and a great love, akin to 'Romeo and Juliet'. Stuart invited dignitaries and 'plebs' alike to come to the set to see him prepare for his role.

With one of the world's great lovers in residence attendance at the Castle multiplied. Attractive young women and some not so young, took to 'dropping in' for cream teas in the afternoon in the hope of seeing the 'hottest' lover since Valentino. Castle staff were not immune; Helen, the General Manager smiled to herself as she saw hem lines of uniforms creep up, white blouses with an extra button undone and mascara and lipstick frequently refreshed. Helen imagined the local chemist would be delighted with the increased sales of cosmetics. However, she felt unable to reprimand the young Waitresses as she found herself reapplying her own lipstick at very regular intervals.

Despite being endlessly polite and smiling, no doubt under the instructions of this P.R. the 'great Romeo' did not make a move towards seducing any of his numerous fans.

Michelle Green flicked through the Sunday papers in her Dublin apartment. Just a shade under thirty Michelle had been Ireland's 'Premier' model for more than a dozen years. Not quite in the same league as some of the world renowned Supermodels, nevertheless Michelle was known in every corner of the Island. Strutting her stuff had brought such rewards; an apartment in Killiney overlooking the bay, a series of sports cars, jewellery and money in the bank. All the International Brands had clamoured for her services driving her daily earnings towards five figure sums and Michelle lived the 'jet setting' life. Then things changed with younger and thinner models getting the commissions that Michelle had once taken for granted.

For the previous eighteen months she had seen her earnings drop to four figures and she knew there was worse to come with the arrival of the dreaded thirtieth birthday.

Then her 'salvation' arrived, on page six of the Independent, the headline covered the top of the entire page 'FAMOUS FILM STAR ARRIVES IN IRELAND'. Michelle read on, learning that Stuart Clark was staying at the Grand Castle Hotel. Taking only a few minutes to throw some clothes in a bag and set the alarm on the apartment then Michelle was on her way.

The two plus hours of the journey passed in a flash as Michelle rehearsed several scenarios; she was all too aware that 'pulling' the star would put her back in the big league. Should she be fortunate enough to become his girlfriend, for even a few months Michelle could see her earnings go stellar. Michelle smiled to herself at the thought of Naomi, Elle, Kate, Cara and Claudia in the Supermodel league. Nothing was impossible. Failing that, the 'Red Tops' would pay up to one hundred thousand Euros for a salacious tale of how the star seduced, abused and abandoned her. Either way, Michelle 'was on a winner!"

Arriving outside the Castle, Michelle spent a considerable time 'fixing on' her face, then she strutted inside where Stuart was holding court. The audience became aware of the presence of the famous model; all questions stopped, guests and staff nudged each other and the words echoed and re-echoed around the room "there's Michelle".

Stuart Clark frowned with irritation at having lost his audience "who is that?" he hissed to the P.R. man.

Ed consulted his 'Who's Who' of Irish Life "Michelle Green, she is one of the supermodels" he replied, promoting Michelle above her station. 'Fixing on' his famous smile, Stuart sauntered over to where Michelle had seated herself. Bowing deeply he declared 'Miss Green it is a pleasure to meet you'.

Michelle affected a look of puzzlement.

Stuart smiled inwardly, for this was the look that he had perfected; 'most notably in Silver Moon' where he had played a severely wounded Confederate Officer returning home following the end of the Civil War. Unveiling his famous smile "Stuart Clark" he announced and waited for the reaction.

Michelle's look remained blank; leaving the star perplexed "You may have seen some of my movies" he declared reeling off the names of ten of the most famous.

Michelle remained unimpressed "I'm afraid I never watch films' she smiled through perfect teeth.

"Perhaps you would care to join me" Stuart's voice held a note of desperation. How could someone not have heard of him, he was the most famous star in Hollywood (at least, in his head). Stuart indicated his table laden with treats "please join me" his voice had dropped to a desperate plea.

Reaching out her delicate hand, Michelle permitted the 'Star' to assist her to her feet and escort her to his table. Retrieving the chilling Cristal champagne, Stuart gallantly poured the 'bubbly' into a flute and handed it to Michelle. As he poured the champagne he was reminded of a scene in 'The Latin Lover' where he had seduced the Contessa with his easy Latin charm.

As Michelle sipped delicately occasionally nibbling on a succulent strawberry, Stuart set about telling her about himself. His forty 'titles' fell from his tongue like bullets but Michelle remained stubbornly ignorant of his stardom. He sought evermore desperately to impress, naming places he'd been, starlets he had escorted and world leaders he had met;

91

Michelle remained unimpressed. In desperation the 'Star' blurted out that he had appeared in both Hello and OK and at last Michelle brightened up. "Ah" she exclaimed "I may have seen that".

Stuart was genuinely pleased and seeing Michelle's response the P.R. man slipped away.

"I think I have a copy of the 'Hello' spread in my Suite, would you like to see it?"

Michelle smiled sweetly "I think I would" she smiled encouragingly. "First time I've been seduced by a magazine?" she thought.

Gently taking her hand Stuart led her upstairs, talking all the while. Michelle did not take in a single word, instead playing out several scenarios. Should she 'hold out' thereby increasing his desire; should she immediately succumb or should she turn it into a marathon session. One famous 'Red Top' always sought the most salacious material; that's where the 'money' was Michelle decided. Before they reached the head of the stairs Michelle had abandoned the girlfriend idea. Up close the actor was not nearly as handsome as he appeared on the silver screen, besides his makeup was applied more thickly than Michelle had ever seen ... even on a spotty Supermodel.

Michelle more or less settled on a quick session followed by a phone call to the 'Red Top' describing any 'little foibles'. It may not be 'Supermodeldom' but it would do her career no harm and one hundred thousand Euros was not to be sneezed at!

Opening the door to his Suite Stuart 'half' smiled as he had done in 'Born to Love'. "Come in" he whispered, lowering his voice to a seductive baritone.

Still holding on to her hand Stuart led her to his bedroom without uttering another word.

Michelle was mentally counting the Euros!

"What do you think?" Stuart asked sliding open the wardrobe and displaying his rich attire. "Which do you think is my colour?" the star waited expectantly.

Michelle's mouth dropped open; she snorted.

Turning on her heels she stormed out, slamming the door behind her. Stomping downstairs Michelle fumed to herself at the loss of 'her' one hundred thousand Euros. No right thinking journalist would believe her if she claimed that the hottest of the Red Hot lovers in Hollywood was a Transvestite.

The Age of Innocence

It had been planned for months. The moment the GCSE's were over Carol and Peter would take off on holiday where, together they would lose their virginity.

Carol insisted all along that it had to be special. No fumblings in the backseats of cinemas, no groping in friend's cars, no sly 'quickies' when parents were out. When they first made love the moment would be special and live with them for the rest of their lives. When they were old and grey they would look back to a lifetime of happiness together and especially remember the 'first time'!

Carol and Peter had been 'in love' since their first meeting when they were fourteen. Sharing a desk at the Comprehensive, childish games had changed to loving regard, then other stronger feelings emerged.

For nearly a year now the young couple had been fighting to control urges arising from galloping hormones and feelings that this was a love for a lifetime.

It was Carol's idea that they should wait until they were sixteen, when 'it' would be legal. Peter agreed as Carol knew about these things.

The plan required the co-operation of Carol's older sister, who was 'in' on the secret, and her boyfriend. According to the older sister the most romantic place in Ireland was at the Grand Castle Hotel in the West. The boyfriend had a car and more importantly all four were free immediately following the GCSEs!

Booking in required a little bit of subterfuge; Carol and her sister were in one room and the two boys shared another down the corridor.

Booking in passed without a hitch though, Peter and Carol both felt 'red under the collar'. Both youngsters felt that all eyes were on them, accusing them of being 'sinful'. Eyes downcast they trailed the porter to their rooms then did a quick swap.

Standing embarrassedly on either side of the bed the teenagers agreed that his was not the time. It was not simply a matter of just jumping into bed, there must be romance, love and loving embraces. Tonight after dinner would be best!

Carol and the boyfriend's laughter could only be described as 'dirty' when the young couple joined them in the bar. "Over already?" the boyfriend teased. "No it is not!" Peter replied defensibly. "If we do it, it must be special."

"Don't you mean when you do it?" the sister chuckled.
Peter and Carol blushed. Then Peter went to the bar, only to be asked to provide I.D. The barman apologies adding "I'm sorry sir, but you look to be about fourteen".

"I'm sixteen" Peter snapped showing his I.D.

"In years to come you will be glad that you look younger than your age" the barman laughed pouring a lager and a shandy.

The foursome enjoyed a sumptuous meal with Peter quaking at the coming 'bill'. He had saved his pocket money for six months but the Castle did not 'come cheaply'.

Peter's original plan had involved one night's bed followed by breakfast, then home. Carol recognised his desperation and whispered "it's alright, I can pay".

Rather than helping, Carol's assertion made Peter feel worse; "some lover he was, he could not afford to buy dinner for his girlfriend".

Carol squeezed his hand in reassurance. Keeping up a friendly banter the meal concluded with the boyfriend suggesting "a drink before bed".

Peter's heckles rose at the lascivious wink and the nudge, nudge satire. This was not what had been planned; the other boy was turning a loving moment into a farce.

Before he could refuse however, Carol had responded brightly "that would be lovely".

Seated in the bar the boyfriend continued with his 'torture', "I'm having a pint and Carol's having a gin, what do the babies want?"

Peter's irritation increased, it was true that he was not a drinker but the boyfriend was 'getting up his nose'. He toyed with the idea of ordering a double scotch just to annoy the other boy, but opted instead for a 'coke'.

"Must keep a clear head, hee- hee" the boyfriend chortled. "Ignore him" Carol whispered ordering a gin and tonic.

For more than an hour the teasing continued with every comment like a barb through Peter's heart. Carol laughed as if the boyfriend was the cleverest person in the world.

All the way back to their rooms the banter continued, but at last they were alone.

Following a year of careful planning the teenagers were not about to fall upon the bed in some unseemly scramble. First a shower and teeth cleaning for Peter followed by a long scented bath for Carol.

For what seemed a lifetime Peter sat on the side of the bed in nervous anticipation then Carol put her head around the corner and announced that she had forgotten her toothbrush. "I'm sure they will spares in reception" he responded and the teenager left to seek out the Receptionist.

Whether the catch on the door was faulty or perhaps it hadn't been properly shut but now the door lay wide open.

Helen, the General Manager was completing her final rounds before retiring for the night. Glancing in to the room she was struck by the forlorn look on the teenager's face.

"Is everything all right?" Helen called from the doorway. The teenager sobbed, but nodded.

Then in a rush it all came out. No, everything was not alright. The whole story was explained to Helen; all the careful planning, the heightened expectations then the coarseness of the sister's boyfriend. This was not how it was meant to be. Tears streamed down the teenager's face and the confession was almost inaudible "I'm not ready. I don't want to do it!"

Helen put her arm gently round the heaving shoulders. "It's alright, it's alright you do not have to do anything you don't want to do. Just say NO!" she advised.

Helen drew the teenager's head onto her shoulder, wrapped her arms all around and repeated over and over "It's alright, it's alright".

That's how they were sitting when Carol re-entered the room.

The Midnight Swimmer

Pat Sweeney kicked off his shoes, undressing quickly he folded the clothes neatly and placed them on the bank of the lough. Seeking about in the moonlight, he found a suitable stone and placed it firmly on top of his clothing.

Smiling grimly as the moon sent a glimmer of golden light across the gently rippling waters, Pat reflected on another who had been equally fastidious about his clothes before slipping into the water. Unlike John Stonehouse MP who had disappeared into the water only to reappear three or four years later in Australia, Pat was certain that he would not be found.

"How had it come to this" he wondered, not for the first time. He looked back towards the Castle where his wife would be fast asleep, having taken her nightly supply of sleeping tablets. Pat had ensured a good night's sleep for her by slipping two or three extra finely ground pills into her cocoa. He had made her nightcap deliberately strong to disguise the taste of the ground pills, thereby risking the sharp edge of her tongue about being unable to do anything right.

He waited until midnight until she was snoring soundly and the hotel sounds had faded for another night before slipping quietly outside. He neither knew nor cared whether or not she would waken in the morning; all that was important was that he would be free.

He stood silently in the shadows watching quietly as light after light went out in the Castle, now all he needed was a cloud to obscure the moon.

As he waited like some wild animal in the shadows he reflected on thirty years of misery in a marriage made in Hell! Trapped by an unwanted pregnancy when he was barely twenty and her twenty four, religious norms demanded a quick wedding.

By the time his son was born, five months post marriage Pat's home life was heading towards destruction. Divorce was out of the question because he and Sheila were 'good' Catholics. Appearances had to be kept up at all costs; attendance at Mass every Sunday with confession and communion once monthly. Traditions must be maintained at all costs, regardless of the soullessness of home. The boy was baptised and named Kevin amongst mush pomp and ceremony. As the priest poured the holy water over the child's head Pat resolved to be there for him, at least until he was an adult.

All forms of normality ended with Sheila's increasing harpishness, marriage had been a mistake, she was too good for a mere painter, she could have done so much better. Pat moved into the spare room becoming father and mother to his son. Sheila's coldness grew with every passing year, together with the sharpness of her voice and her demands for ever more 'housekeeping'. It was beneath her station to have to seek work so Pat worked hard enough for both of them.

When Kevin was five and started school, Pat struck out on his own 'taking on' one apprentice.

On his thirtieth birthday Pat opened his 'first' painters and decorators store while maintaining his own painting skills. The long hours prevented having to have any contact with the harpy who shared his home other than attendance at Mass on Sundays. Long past any attempt at civility or accord Sheila followed her pursuits while Pat worked eighteen to twenty hour days. All of Pat's spare time he devoted to his growing son, indulging him in his every whim. Aged twelve Kevin began to support Manchester United football team, by which time Pat's business was flourishing and he was able to 'cut back' a little. Saturdays were now spent with his son following United all over England. Sunday remained the day for family attendance at Mass, then Kevin got his place on a little team on the Sunday League. Life was almost bearable, only having to 'see' his wife for a couple of hours on a Sunday.

If Pat's heart did not break when Kevin left for University when he was eighteen, then it certainly was badly bruised.

As Kevin found a new life, Pat lost his. Aged forty he opened a superstore with good men and women in place to run the business. Though he no longer needed to 'wield the brushes' Pat continued to do so. With no warmth at home he took to dropping into his local every night after work, rarely going home before closing time.

Betty Finch was a popular hostess, smilingly greeting all her punters as old friends. Betty knew all their little foibles, listened patiently to stories she had heard one hundred times as she pulled their pints. One customer she knew hardly at all, despite the fact that he had been coming into her pub for more than two years. Pat showed no interest in local gossip, avoided the darts and snooker preferring to sit quietly on his own with his 'half-un' and bottle ... a Guinness and a small scotch. She knew he drank too much but, as long as he caused no trouble, that was no business of hers.

It was New Year's Eve and the pub was in full swing with couples clearly enjoying themselves; all except Pat who sat quietly in the corner. Betty believed she could 'feel' his sadness. On the spur of the moment she retrieved left over mistletoe, placed it above Pat's head, claiming a kiss.

As she stepped away Betty was taken by the tears that rolled down Pat's face. "Oh my God" she gasped "what have I done, I did not mean to offend you!"

Great sobs racked through Pat's body "you did not offend me" he replied "that is the first female tenderness that I have experienced in twenty years".

"But you are married" Betty said, more a question than a statement.

97

"I may have a wife" replied Pat bitterly "but I certainly am not married".

"I am so sorry" Betty exclaimed but could do no more as 'business' called her away.

Celebrations did not finish until four in the morning when Betty managed to dispose of the last of the customers. Or rather, the last but one, Pat was lying in a state of drunkenness with his head resting on the table. Realising there was nothing she could do, Betty went upstairs, returning with a blanket which she placed around his shoulders.

When Betty came down to clean up at ten o'clock Pat was still sleeping. Having made a strong coffee she shook him awake. She noticed the fine tremor and the rattle as he returned the cup to the saucer "Won't your wife be looking for you?" Betty asked.

"No" came the empathic reply "my wife never looks for me!"

"Listen" Betty said "come up the stairs and have a shower while I make you a bit of breakfast".

With some shoving and pushing she got him up the stairs and into the bathroom then set about making bacon and eggs.

Betty stood back from Pat as he struggled with his bacon and eggs. "Not half bad-looking" Betty thought as she took in the tousled curls of his hair, the tanned face and the strong workman hands. Over and over he muttered "I am so sorry, so sorry" he kept repeating.

"It doesn't matter" Betty assured him but it did to Pat. Somehow he managed to make it to work and complete twelve hours 'in a trot'. Then he was back in the local, standing rigid with embarrassment holding up a large bouquet of flowers.

"Please accept my apologies" he asked handing over the flowers.

"I have already accepted them" Betty laughed "but red roses are usually only given to loved ones".

She laughed as Pat reddened.

That night Pat left early and sober. Where he went he didn't know, but he knew where he wanted to be!

Pat took his trade elsewhere for a couple of weeks but it wasn't where he wanted to be so he drifted back to Betty's place.

Betty made no comment about the earlier episodes and initially Pat was grateful for it. The he remembered the kiss. Waiting until closing time Pat seized the initiative. Walking, or more correctly, wobbling up to Betty he asked if she would allow him to take her for dinner. Before she could answer he added "you know I have a wife but I really do not have a marriage".

Betty could never explain why she said "Yes!" Perhaps she felt sorry for him, perhaps she was lonely or maybe she remembered the tousled hair as he struggled with his bacon and eggs! Whatever the reason she found herself enjoying dinner the following Sunday night and more importantly enjoying Pat's company.

Quietly and undramatically they drifted into a relationship; a warm loving relationship.

For three years they enjoyed a mutually fulfilling 'love affair' but gradually the rumours leaked out. A word here, a word there and then it reached the W.I. then Sheila heard the story.

Sheila was incandescent. Twenty five years of social climbing had seen her rise through the ranks of the Birgini, Woman's Institute, The Legion of Mary and a myriad of other committees; she would not allow that coarse feckless husband of hers to bring her down. She had always known that it was a mistake to marry beneath herself but she would be damned if she would allow the 'painter' to bring disgrace to her dear son. Kevin was doing so well and his glittering career must not be caused to falter because of the uncontrolled loins of his father.

Sheila had sat in cold fury listening to her 'friends' who thoroughly enjoyed delivering the salacious stories. In response to her questioning they had told her that she must know where he was and who he was with; the woman with whom he spent every evening. After all this time, the only time Sheila knew where Pat was, was when he accompanied her to Sunday Mass; despite everything mother church must be mollified. So they told her about Betty.

Betty and Pat had only been upstairs about ten minutes following closing the bar. They were stretched out on their armchairs enjoyed a well- earned cup of tea when the doorbell rang, incessantly.

Betty dragged herself to her feet claiming "it will be some punter looking for a carry out". Wearily she traipsed downstairs to answer the endless noise. As Betty opened the door, Sheila slammed it backwards, pushed past her and raced upstairs. Pat had jumped upwards when he had heard the fracas downstairs, readying herself to get rid of the offending punter.

Sheila's face was white with cold fury as she lashed out verbally "what are you doing here with this whore?" She demanded. Pat turned to protest that Betty was not a whore, but Sheila was far from finished. Her words were like icicles as she threatened to inform the Parish Priest, Betty's elderly parents and, of course, Kevin must be told. Her words cut into the lovers hearts, but Sheila was not finished; "don't think you will ever get him" she hissed at Betty "I will never give him a divorce". Then she 'changed her tack'. "You hypocrite", the voice was ever icier "I've seen you at Mass and going forward to take the sacraments. I'm sure Father John would love know about this".

Betty wilted beneath the onslaught as the tirade seemed to go on forever; eventually she said "I will give Pat up if you promise to keep Kevin out of this" looking across at her lover, with a look of sheer misery on her face.

Sheila grabbed hold of a Bible from a bookcase "swear it on the Holy Bible" she demanded.

Betty 'took the oath' watching miserably as Sheila and Pat left her home. Driving back to their 'home' Sheila declared "don't think you will have the freedom that you have taken for granted. I shall be watching you from now on".

Then the mental torture began. At every opportunity Betty's name was brought up, despairingly "Who was his whore with now? Was her new man better in bed than he was? He had never done anything for her!" Nothing was too low, too despicable to escape Sheila's vile tongue.

Pat's drinking spiralled out of control. Twice in eighteen months he ended up in hospital with alcohol related liver problems. On the second occasion Pat came near to death, collapsing with jaundice; bedecked with i/v infusions, cardiac monitors and all the paraphernalia of hospitals the Consultant warned Sheila that she must prepare for the worst. Sheila played the distraught wife to perfection.

Following a three week recovery period Pat was on the way home. The abuse started before they had left the hospital grounds "I supposed your whore sneaked into see you" the voice was even nastier than usual.

"No" Pat replied "she is a 'good' Catholic. She gave her word and she will stick to it".

Pat's defence of his ex-lover ignited a torrent of abuse "Not good enough to stay away from a married man" she began, then the 'bile' really developed.

Pat sat quietly all the way home.

The verbal and psychological torture continued for more than a year then Hell worsened for Pat. They were on their way to Mass when Sheila announced, "I see the whore drowned herself" she gloated adding that Betty's body had been recovered from the canal earlier in the week.

"Stop the car" Pat demanded. That's where the serious drinking began. Eleven days later Pat woke with a scream without any idea of where he was. The room stopped spinning and he realised he was at home with no notion of how he got there. Insects, worms, snakes crawled

100

over his body; ants had invaded his arms and legs. Frantically he tore at his arms, drawing blood in an attempt to end the infernal itching. One snake crawled out of his ear ready to strike at Pat's eyes; again he screamed in terror. Perspiration paused from him, yet failed to dislodge the tiny creatures that scuttled about, over and inside him. His scream pierced the walls and Sheila eventually came to mock him.

"Can't stand your loss!" she shrieked "going to join your whore, you weakling?" Then Pat had a massive convulsive seizure. As he threshed around the bed Sheila's disdain turned to disgust as bowel and bladder opened. "He can't even die with dignity" she thought but she did summon am ambulance.

Six weeks in an Alcoholic Unit rehabilitation had followed the detoxification programme and Pat was ready for discharge. His Counsellor had recommended a short break together, where Pat and Sheila could re-establish earlier more positive feelings for each other. Sheila had organised a long weekend at the Grand Castle Hotel, explaining to the Counsellor that the good food, the Atlantic breezes and an opportunity to relearn how to talk would do them both good. The Counsellor had beamed with pride at his great success; others had felt the marriage was irretrievable but he had persisted.

Pat had been confined to bed for three days following his admission to the Unit. Initially in the horrors of delirium tremens he gradually responded to the parentrovite injections, i/v infusions and gentle nursing care. For a further four days Pat sat by his beside, rediscovering his appetite and walking round his bed on shaky legs. At the beginning of his second week in the Clinic Pat joined the Group. The Clinic specialised in talking therapies involving doctors, nurses, social workers, clergy and counsellors.

It was towards the end of his fourth week that Pat 'opened up' confessing to his affair, discussing the dreadful relationship with his wife and the terrible loneliness that was his life.

The Clinical Team decided that Family Therapy was the best way forward for Pat, if only they could get his wife to agree to join him in therapy. Sheila was nothing, if not a great actress, 'outside the house' she was a pillar of society and the epitome of kindness. "Of course she would do anything to have her husband back to the way he once was".

The Team decided that the resident Counsellor would be best to provide the Family Therapy. With ten years' experience of dealing with family issues he was the recognised expert, and had the greatest success rate on the Team.

For eight hours a day over a two week period the Counsellor worked intensively with Pat and Sheila; the affair was addressed together with passive aggression, lack of respect and a host of 'mental mechanisms'. Sheila gradually came to see that she was a factor in Pat's alcoholism while he recognised that his lack of attempts to communicate had contributed to the

101

breakdown. At the Counsellor's urging the holiday had been organised with Pat and Sheila agreeing to attend A.A. and other support groups in their own area.

Together they left from the Clinic to drive directly to the Castle. Sheila pleaded tiredness so Pat drove the two hours journey to the Castle. Sheila slept all the way.

Having booked in and unpacked Pat suggested that they should have afternoon tea, downstairs. Pat was buttering his scone when the diatribe started "I suppose she will be your next floozy" Sheila's voice was laden with scorn. Pat jerked back into chair in astonishment.

"What are you talking about?" he asked.

"That floozy!" Sheila whispered "I saw the way you smiled at her".

"I simply thanked her for the tea" Pat answered.

"Yes, she's more your type, waitresses are about your level, or maybe you would prefer the barmaid?"

Pat groaned inwardly.

"Maybe you could drive her to suicide, like your last whore" she hissed while maintaining a fixed smile for the other guests.

Pat stood up "Excuse me" he said "I am going for a walk".

Pensively Pat plodded around the banks of the great lough, and his plan began to form.

The biting, caustic remarks continued over dinner, quietly enough to ensure the other diners could not hear, but making sure that every word was a dart through his heart. Her final 'dig' before retiring was to gloat about how she had fooled that arrogant Counsellor, then she drank her cocoa.

Pat stepped in to the water, then swam strongly for half an hour. As he swam Pat smiled at his 'act of revenge'. Last week he was examined by his Psychiatrist who gave him a 'clean bill of health'. According to the letter Pat was of sound mind, was neither a danger to himself or others and was perfectly able to manage his affairs. Pat had accepted the letter but smilingly asked for a second opinion. The Consultant expressed his surprise, claiming that he was often asked for a second opinion when he said someone was not of sound mind. This was the first time even that a patient asked for a second opinion when he had been found to be of sound mind. The second Consultant's assessment reflected exactly his colleague's opinion. Then Pat had sent for his Solicitor explaining his desire to make his will. Handing over his two medical letters the Solicitor smiled, suggesting that Pat had some knowledge of Mental

Health Law. Pat did not, but a Barrister in the group did. The Solicitor did as requested and assured Pat that the will was 'watertight'.

"This is it" Pat thought with a grim smile; he had 'willed' half of his fortune to his son, Kevin and the other half to Moira Dougan, the girl who had been his girlfriend when he first met Sheila. "That should set the cat among the pigeons" he thought.

Pat reckoned to himself that he was no John Stonehouse MP, his plan was fool proof.

Then he stopped swimming!

The Inept Adulterer

He could not stand to look at her for another moment; he simply had to get away.

Stepping out into the hallway he spoke quietly and urgently into his cell phone "Can you get away?" he asked.

The answer must have been a question he added "Now".

Then he said "I will think of something. Can you make it?"

The answer must have been in the affirmative because his voice had lightened as he whispered "I will see you in an hour beside the Garden of Remembrance".

He stepped back into the room with the announcement "I have to go, there is a problem with one of the Plants in Kerry. I will be gone for three or four days but I will let you know when I am returning".

"I did not hear the phone ringing" she replied not unreasonably.

"How many times do I have to tell you? These modern phones do not ring, they get your attention by vibrating in your pocket" he replied, trying desperately to keep the irritation out of his voice.

While everything about her irritated him after ten years of marriage, he could not afford to be too critical. She was the one with the REAL money. She had used some of her inheritance from daddy's money to purchase this two million mansion while he was only an engineer. A very good engineer, earning a good salary but not nearly enough to maintain their present lifestyle. Her money and social position had brought many rewards, membership of a gentleman's club, seats on several prestigious Boards, membership of the best golf and rugby clubs ... the list went on and on. He was quite happy with his discreet peccadilloes but he would certainly not give up his lifestyle.

For the past six months he had been 'seeing' Anita, a journalist from the local newspaper. Anita had come to his office to interview him about a new Plant that was being opened in Kildare; by the time she had seated herself on the Queen Anne chair and crossed her long elegant legs he knew that he would seduce her. Anita was 'freelance' with much flexibility in her life. When she had married her editor fifteen years ago he had seemed powerful, exciting and charismatic even though he was twenty five years older than her. Now he was simply old, whinging and annoying, but he still had great contacts. Since going freelance five years ago Anita needed those contacts.
As she crossed her legs in Tom's office having seated herself on an elegant Queen Anne chair she knew she would seduce him.

Over the past six months they had come to realise the perfection of their relationship. Though both were married, neither was tied down by a job that entailed mechanical rota, with flexibility being central to their roles. During the course of their relationship they had been flexible in Dublin, Cork, London, Manchester and Glasgow. Both were aware that this was no 'great love', neither wished to leave their partner nor their exalted lifestyle; this was what it was, lust.

It had taken him less than fifteen minutes to pack and store his 'stuff' in the boot of the Jaguar. Now he was sitting outside the Garden of Remembrance promising himself that he would go in sometime.

Anita stepped into the passenger side, flashing that magnificent smile "Where to?" she asked, tossing her holdall on to the rear seat.

"I hadn't thought" Tom responded "I just had to get away. Any ideas?"

"What about the Grant Castle Hotel near Connemara?" she asked.

"The Castle it is" he replied pressing the accelerator.

Tom had been left the house less than a minute when his wife made the call. "How would you like a weekend away with me?" she laughed, continuing "Tom is off to Kerry, some problem with machinery. He won't be back for three or four days." Sally was just as bored with the marriage as Tom was but she had made her vows. Despite her best intentions she had fallen in love with Jack, their part time gardener and she too had started a clandestine relationship. Though well connected Jack loved the outdoor life with no ambition to spend his lifetime in a stuffy office. When he had been undertaking his degree Jack continued his grass cutting, post- university. Then he opened a little Garden Centre, followed by a Store selling gardening and household equipment. During the summer months Jack continued with his grass cutting and that is how he met Sally. They're shared love of shrubbery, flowers and all things botanical led to a deep and meaningful love for each other. Thanks to Tom's flexible work schedules there were few restrictions on their meetings but Jack wanted more. Within three months he was begging Sally to leave her husband and come to live with him. He assured Sally that his business was doing well and they both could have a good life together. Jack hated those times when Tom was at home and most of all he hated the thought of him being in bed with Sally.

Despite Jack's 'beggings' Sally was adamant that she would not leave Tom. He was not very exciting, could be irritable at times and boring at others but he was her husband. Tom had done nothing to deserve being hurt. Sally assured Jack that she loved him with all her heart but she would not leave Tom, she had made her vows.
Moralists might argue that Sally had broken her vows by getting involved with Jack, but that is not how she saw it. She knew her relationship with Jack was wrong and it did cause her

guilt, but he was the love of her life and she would do her very best not to hurt Tom; that much she promised herself!

She also had one unbreakable rule; she would never allow Jack to make love with her in Tom's bed.

Jack also had one rule; he would never make love in Jack's bed.

"Where to?" Jack asked when he rolled up in his ancient Volvo. "Anywhere, but South" Sally answered.

"Why not just follow the road and see where it takes us?"

They stopped at a little village for dinner, dining in a tiny restaurant by a bridge over the river. Following a series of winding roads they soon got lost. Darkness was falling when Jack spotted the twinkling lights from a little village. "Let's head for there" he suggested, "Someone will know where we can find a hotel".

The first villager they asked laughed heartily and pointed across the road. "Would that one do?" she laughed looking at the huge edifice.

By the time they had got booked in it was too late for an evening meal, but coffee or tea and sandwiches could be provided in their room. "Perfect" responded Jack "we had a meal earlier but sandwiches sound delightful".

As usual Anita was late getting ready for breakfast. Tom had learned early that Anita would not be rushed when it came to hair, nails or make-up. Until she was 'perfect' she would not leave the room. This morning she was having particular difficulty finding perfection so she declared "You go on ahead. I shall join you shortly."

Tom was ravenous and had learned that shortly could be anything up to half an hour.

"Ok" he whispered "try not to be too long".

Walking into the dining room the first couple he spotted, over by the window was his wife and some vaguely familiar man. Tom's first impulse was too rush back to the room to warn Anita but then he stopped himself from doing so. There was plenty of time to deal with the situation before making his exit. The last time he had heard of payouts in Court cases for adultery the 'innocent' party had got one million pounds. This situation could really work to his advantage; if ever there was a case of 'having his cake and eating it' this was it.

As Tom strode purposefully through the dining room Sally was first to see him. "Oh God" she gasped "What is he doing here?" Had he set a trap for her? Was the Kerry thing a mere ruse to lull her into a false sense of security: her mind buzzed.

Spotting Sally's discomfiture Jack asked "What is it?" All she could was indicate with her head before Tom was 'upon' them.

"What the hell is this?" Tom demanded.

Sally sat dumbstruck; Jack reached across and laid his hand on hers in a vague attempt at reassurance.

"I said, what is this?" Tom's voice had risen to a high pitched screech.

The Head Waiter quietly crossed the room and touched Tom on the elbow "You are upsetting the other diners sir, you must be quieter." Then he looked at the ashen faces of Sally and Jack. "Is everything alright Mrs Jones ... Mr Jones?"

The miserable couple could only nod as the Head Waiter turned around to leave; then he stopped and stared at Tom, who stood there like some old fashioned Sergeant Major on parade, "I'm sorry sir, I forgot, Mrs Smith asked me to tell you that she would be down in fifteen minutes, she insists that you should start without her!"

A Cold Room

I was standing in the foyer, flicking through the Irish Times when the reedy voice cut through my deliberations.

"Would you bring in my bag, boy, it's in the back of the BMW that's parked at the door".

Naturally 'prickly' I immediately took offence at the 'boy'.

"If you are looking for the Reception it's over there" I pointed towards the Receptionist; biting my tongue to prevent myself adding 'you decrepit old fogey'.

The old man looked as old as time itself, what flesh remained resembled ancient parchment and a face more creased than the choppy waters of the lake that rose and fell outside the Grand Castle Hotel. The long spindly fingers were topped by talons rather than nails and the mottled hands and wrists bore testament to a hundred falls and accidental collisions.

Good manners obviously played no part in the old man's repertoire; without another word he trotted over to Reception. The final word I heard before leaving was the old man demanding lodgings in Room 123.

Standing immediately before the front door blocking the exit was the oldest BMW that I had ever seen. Like the old man himself, the car had seen better days. Both front wings were dented and long scrapes ran down both sides of the ancient vehicle.

Returning to Reception, I interrupted the old man's dialogue with the Receptionist. As politely as any irritable man could be I asked the old man to move his car in order to allow me to get out.

The old man fumbled through his pockets for several minutes before locating the car keys on the desk before him. "You move it, boy" the words rattled out.

"May I tell you, Sir, I am not a boy and I am a guest in this Hotel" my voice had lowered to an icy coolness.

His shaky hand reached over and he ordered me to park the car as near to the door as possible.

I looked at the Receptionist, whose look told me it was probably easiest just to move the damned thing. Despite my annoyance, I agreed with her.

Moving the BMW was a history lesson in itself. Despite its battered exterior the inside was in pristine condition. The rich smell of old leather pervaded the air, the walnut fascia gleamed and the ancient dials spoke of a time gone bye. After some false starts I eventually managed to move the vehicle and went about my business completely forgetting to return the car keys.

Some hours later when I returned the Receptionist brought my lapse to my attention. I found the old man dozing over tea and cream cakes.

Returning to the Receptionist I dropped the car keys on to the console. The Receptionist seemed keen to talk so I made some comment about the ancient resident. The Receptionist then gave me a blow by blow account of the old man's itinerary. He had left Kent in the South of England several days ago and drove all the way to Cairnryan in Scotland before crossing to Northern Ireland on the ferry. Without stopping to sightsee in Ulster he then drove to the Castle. The old man had had a couple of 'close shaves' on the way. Firstly he had fallen asleep in Cumbria and woke to find himself firmly wedges in a road side ditch; then in Scotland several motorists had 'flashed' him as he was driving up the wrong side of the motorway. It seems that he became confused going round all the roundabouts as he took the ring road around Dumfries. The Receptionist felt it was a miracle that the old man had 'made it' at all. At ninety four years old, his eyesight fading, memory diminishing and suffering from Parkinsonism, he was not safe to be on the road.

"Silly old fool" I said "why did he not simply drive to Holyhead and cross on the Dublin Ferry?"

The Receptionist had no answer but she had more to say.

"It's very strange" she said "he insisted on having Room 123 but most people avoid that room".

"Why is that?" I wondered.

"It's supposed to be haunted" she admitted frankly. "I have never heard or seen anything but we do have to turn the heating up in Room 123. Over the years dozens of guests have rung the Night Porter complaining of the cold: apparently the temperature drops suddenly about two o'clock in the morning".

The scepticism must have shown on my face!

"We have had numerous plumbers, engineers and electricians in to try to find a cause, all without success". She lowered her voice and looked around. When she ascertained that there were no eavesdroppers she whispered "people have heard crying in the room and there are reports of a young woman walking down into the lough". Then her voice took on a conspiratorial tone "a young woman drowned herself in the lough in nineteen forty one and the haunting started almost immediately. Locals claim the young woman is searching for the lover who deserted her".

I've always prided myself on being a logical man so I 'poo-pooed' the haunting idea. "I'm sure there is some logical explanation for the phenomenon" I asserted.

The Receptionist was less certain.

The old man was seated in the dining room when I entered for dinner. At least some of the food was making it into his mouth. I walked over to the old man and asked if he had managed to retrieve his car keys. For several seconds he stared vacantly at me. "I moved your car" I explained. He fumbled in his pocket and retrieved ten pence "Thank you" the trembling voice managed.

"No" I explained "I am a guest here, I am not a Porter".

"Oh, I hope I haven't offended you" he managed with what remained of his Estuary English.

On impulse I asked "do you mind if I join you?"

He signalled towards a chair and I sat down opposite him.

Made uncomfortable by the silence I sought desperately for something to say. Eventually I managed "do you come here often?"

The tremble in the old man's voice worsened as he told me he had been here once before; in nineteen forty one with his girlfriend.

I claimed the area must have changed greatly since then.

"I really don't know" the old man whispered and I detected a great sadness in his voice.

"Were you only here for a short time?" I pressed him.

"It was not so much the time" his voice faltered "it was my motive for coming".

I waited.

"I was a British Soldier based in Northern Ireland and I was a frightful snob. I had 'made' Captain by the age of twenty three and I thought I was God's answer to God. I strutted around the barracks like a vain peacock and 'blasted' the men at will. I was due to be posted to North Africa and fully expected to be blown to pieces by Rommel".

The rheumy eyes filled with water "As well as being a snob, I had the morals of an alley cat, taking my pleasures wherever I could find them. I met Moira on the base where she worked as a Domestic in the Officers Mess; she was as pure and honourable as I was corrupt and debased. I convinced Moira that I was a gentleman and my intentions were strictly honourable so we started walking out together. As far as I was concerned she was merely a distraction, but I said things that made her believe otherwise. Eventually I convinced her of my honour and she got the impression that I was going to marry her".

His voice seemed to forsake him so he raised a glass of water shakily to his lips, again managing to retain some of it.

"How could I have married her?" he challenged me. "I already had a wife and son at home in Kent. Besides I was an Officer and gentleman and she was a Domestic Assistant it would never have worked."

"An Officer maybe but a gentleman, never" I thought.

"What happened next I asked", but he had nodded off to sleep.

I finished my meal and left him sleeping in the dining room. The old man's story fascinated me, so I determined to hear more at the earliest opportunity. I missed him at breakfast so I took the opportunity to walk into the village for a couple of newspapers. On my return I peeped into the lounge and there he was, spilling most of his tea down the front of his shirt and into his saucer.

I plumped myself down beside him and offered him my copy of The Times. 'Jumping right in' I asked about the rest of his story. At first he was confused but I brought him up to date with his monologue. "Ah yes" he said "Moira, I treated her abominably".

"How so?" I asked.

"When she agreed to come with me to the Castle, she probably thought I was going to propose to her?"

"Why would she think that?" after such a short time.

The old man sighed "I may have led her to believe that that was the purpose of our trip". He seemed to have some internal argument with himself as his voice firmed up and he announced "Of course she thought that!" then he added, "In nineteen forty one it was a real challenge and quite an adventure to come over the border. As a British Army Officer I was forbidden to leave the jurisdiction. There was a war on and petrol was rationed and besides I did not have a car". He looked at me imploringly "I wanted her badly, if you know what I mean so I begged, borrowed and stole to achieve my ends".

I certainly did know what he meant but I held my own counsel.

"The roads were poor in those days and there were no motorways so the journey took several hours" the old man's eyes brightened as he remembered the journey. We were not very original" he added "booking in as Mister and Missus Smith, then our bags were carried to our Room 123".

All life seemed to seep out of the old man's body; his skeletal frame appeared to shrink into itself and his faltering voice contained a lifetime of regret. "Then I had my wicked way with her. She was so happy, glowing that she was glad she had saved herself for me. I was left in no doubt that this was the first time for her. To my shame I felt like a conquering cockerel. Then we dined at the window where I sat last night. I made love twice more to her that night. I cannot claim that I made love with Moira, for me it was a simple exercise of power".

The tears were rolling freely down the old man's face. Whatever he had felt in nineteen forty one it was now obvious that he was filled with guilt and remorse ... and something else; was it a longing to turn back the clock?

"What happened next?" I pressed him.

"She was so happy" he claimed I awoke with her kissing my chest. Her laughter was the tinkle of sweet music; she laughed happily all through breakfast and then we returned to Room 123".

"What happened there?" I prompted.

"I put an end to the laughter" his sigh echoed to the heavens.

"What do you mean?" I asked impatiently.

I told her it was all over between her and I. I told her that I would be in North Africa in a couple of weeks. I told her that I had a wife and a son in England.

A great sob burst from the frail 'skeleton'. "I told her that someone like me would never marry someone like her. She was way below me socially and entirely unsuitable. I stood and watched as that poor girl crumpled before me but I was not finished yet, I told her that all she was to me was a receptacle for my sperm; though I wasn't that polite. I left her sobbing on the bed. Not for a moment did I consider how she would get home. She had served her purpose and that was all that mattered".

"You were a despicable b......" I hissed.

"I could argue that there was a war on and different morals prevailed. I could say that everyone was at 'it', his voice tailed off. When he was again able to speak he added "You are right I was a despicable b...... and worse than that."

"What happened then?" I almost shouted.

"I left her there and returned to my base. Two weeks later I was shipped out to North Africa and for four years I traversed many battle zones. I served in Libya, Syria, Palestine and I joined the push into Germany. After the war I served for a further twenty five years and retired as a Brigadier. That's when the nightmares began".

The old man retreated within himself and I knew that there was nothing more forthcoming for the moment. But, I am a patient man and I knew the old man had more to say and he wanted to tell it.

I joined him at dinner and our dialogue continued "for more than forty years Moira had come to him in his dreams. Her dark eyes drilled into his dreams, her stare was accusatory but never hate filled. Over the past six months her presence had changed. She called out to him inviting him to join her, her voice told him that she had forgiven him, she knew that he had suffered and he must come to her. So that is why I am here" he concluded.

"How will you find her after all this time?" I asked "she may not even be alive".

"She never left" he whispered enigmatically.

I awoke with a start at two am with the old man's story obsessing through my head. Despite desperate attempts sleep would not come so I decided to make myself a cup of tea.

As I drank the hot liquid a finger of moonlight filtered through the curtains. I drew back the curtains, marvelling at the majesty of the full moon. As I watched I became aware of two figures walking towards the lough. I could see clearly that one was a young lady barely out of her teens and dressed in old fashion apparel. The other was my dinner companion. The young lady's smile was evident, even in the moonlight as the old man gripped her hand.

Then a cloud scudded across the moon, obscuring my vision. When the light returned the couple were walking on to the lough, rather than into it. I watched entranced as they embraced. Then they vanished!

Miss Mary Martin

Miss Mary Martin first came to the Grand Castle Hotel in the summer of nineteen forty one. Miss Martin had travelled down from Northern Ireland to enjoy a few days' rest, following a year at school. Miss Martin was petite with the sort of looks that defied accurate assessment of age; fellow travellers placed her as being somewhere between eighteen and twenty five. In reality Miss Martin had just turned twenty eight and was Headmistress of a Private School ... or so she claimed.

Miss Martin looked a little old fashioned in her Donegal tweeds, clothes she claimed to have made herself. With her slight frame, youthful appearance, sparkling blue eyes and her tweeds, Miss Martin might be mistaken for a mythical Irish Pixie.

There was something slightly other worldly about her, an innocence, a goodness that oozed from every pore, yet Castle staff were of the opinion that Miss Mary Martin was a harmless fantasist.

They listened with feigned interest as she told them of her life in the North. Daddy had a successful business in Armagh and her brother Bob managed the family farm that lay just outside the city. According to Miss Martin the land would grow anything; fifty acres were given over to orchards where they grew the sweetest apples. There was a further one hundred acres of rich arable land where Bob grew all sorts of things, the final eighty acres was a mixture of scrub, bushes and forestry.

Staff smiled benignly as Miss Martin enthusiastically described her idyllic childhood there.

Then aged eleven, Miss Martin became a boarder in a large Church school near Belfast remaining there until she was eighteen.

As a girl Miss Martin would have been expected to come home when she finished her education. A woman's place was in the home in nineteen thirties Northern Ireland.

Mary had other ideas, becoming one of the first women from Northern Ireland to train as a schoolteacher. She had to go to London to undertake her training, for no facility existed at home for the training of lady teachers.

Staff fought to stifle their scepticism as Miss Martin described her bicycle rides through Hyde Park where the she frequently met and conversed with David, Prince of Wales. In case anyone had been asleep for ten or more years, Miss Martin told how she qualified as a teacher and obtained a job at the famous Roehampton School where she taught for two years.
Generally staff placed their hands over their mouths when Miss Martin described how Daddy had wanted her home. He achieved his wish by buying a Private School for her. Miss Martin

came home and continued her career as Principal. "Principal, indeed" staff agreed Miss Martin was far too young to be anything of the sort. 'More fantasy' was the general view.

Miss Martin spent her holiday resting, reading and 'toddling' about amongst the Castle gardens where she shared her great botanical knowledge with the Gardener and his staff.

Miss Martin was back in nineteen forty two with a large diamond sparkling on the third finger of her left hand. Her fiancé was an Acting Sergeant in the Royal Irish Fusiliers and Miss Martin was most relieved that he had not yet been posted to 'the front' despite being enlisted for two and a half years.

"Another Miss Martin story" smiled the Housekeeper wondering if such a soldier existed or if the diamonds were real. Miss Martin told of her very great joy at finding a boy who should her faith and like her was saved. Catholic staff wondered if 'saved Christians' were all like Miss Martin; fantasists!

Fantasist or not Miss Martin painted an extraordinary picture of her exciting fiancé; six foot, lean, blonde, handsome, brilliant at all sports especially rugby, rowing and boxing. Only the war stopped Alan, for this was his name, achieving an Ulster Cap.

More smiles all round.

Nineteen forty three and Miss Martin is back, still without her fiancé who is now in Wales, having been promoted to second Lieutenant. Miss Martin swells with pride as she informs all and sundry that Alan won the 'Sword of Honour' at Officer Training School and was now preparing for mobilisation. Sotto voce she tells the staff he could not come here, even if he wanted to. British Officers were forbidden to cross the border, besides there was a security risk if he did.

A very convenient story, the staff agreed as they laughed amongst themselves.

Miss Martin kept herself cheerful by pottering among the flowers and spending hours in the glass houses with the under Gardeners. Fantasist she may be, but the garden staff all agreed that she had 'green fingers'. Her work of the past two years had come to fruition, much to the benefit of the Castle's external environs.

Nineteen forty four and Miss Martin is considering selling her school, she is finding it difficult to run the school while she is under so much personal strain. Four years of Miss Martin's stories and the staff approach them with a 'huge helping' of scepticism. It would be dreadful if she was 'caught out' perchance some hotel staff travelled to Armagh. Good manners made them ask about Miss Martin's 'personal difficulties'.

Alan had been captured by the Germans following a horrific battle somewhere in Europe. Alan had fought in North Africa, had been on Malta for most of the siege and had been wounded on one of the Greek Islands. He had been captured just before Christmas nineteen forty three and brought under terrible conditions to a P.O.W. Camp in Germany. With her sense for the dramatic Miss Martin told staff of her feelings when she had received a letter from the War Office informing her that her fiancé was missing, presumed dead. Staff covered their mouths with their hands when Miss Martin told them that he had survived and was being recommended for the Victoria Cross for his bravery.

"Oh yes" thought the staff collectively but next year she will tell us that her fiancé just missed out for his medal.

Mid -June nineteen forty five and Miss Mary Martin is welcomed back to the Castle by the General Manager and the Housekeeper, Miss Martin is clutching a large scrapbook that she plonks on the Receptionist's Console.

"I just had to show you these" she cried "you have all been so good to me and have been such good friends". The General Manager and the Housekeeper cringed with embarrassment.

Miss Martin was too busy opening her 'book of memories' to notice anything. "Look" she said, "here's one of David and I cycling in Hyde Park". The youthful good looks of the abdicated King was unmistakable. "Here we are at lunch" Miss Martin added turning the page. "Oh this was a happy day" she cried as she displayed her graduation photo; "this was Roehampton" she added, having turned another page.

Another page turned, more photographs "I did not sell it" she exclaimed "this is my school." This sign was very distinct Miss Martin's Preparatory School; Miss Martin was being congratulated for some educational achievement by the Prime Minister.

"And this is Alan" Miss Martin pointed to the handsome young soldier in his dress uniform with an array of medals.

"Your fiancé is so handsome" the Housekeeper enthused.

"He's no longer my fiancé" Miss Martin responded.

"Oh" gasped the General Manager "what happened?"

"He's now my husband" Miss Martin laughed "I am now Mrs Andrews".

Right on cue a young man, ramrod straight entered the foyer laden with baggage "car parked and everything present and correct, madam" the young man reported.

Mary laughed and a look of pure love passed between the young couple. 'Amazing' thought the General Manager 'that such a love could grow and flower amidst the vile awfulness of war'.

Alan and Mary paid little attention as they linked arms and laughed all the way to the elevator.

A Band of Brothers

Tim and his new age band of brothers (and sisters) arrived at the Copse in early spring. As his band settled in, Tim began to explore. Deep into the Copse the trees gave way to a dense thicket. Squeezing through the foliage Tim chanced upon the perfect summer lodgings. Completely surrounded by ferns, lichen and gorse the ancient barn was almost invisible. The roof, though collapsed in several places, was protected by branches, bushes, twigs and a hundred years of detritus provided by dozens of kinds of birds. Visible only from where Tim waited the barn had the sort of inviting presence that appealed to his psyche.

Hurrying back to his comrades Tim excitedly communicated his plan. For nearly a year now his band had been driven from village after village and now found themselves on the point of exhaustion. Food stores were low and something needed to be done to restock with reserves of food.

Making as little change as possible Tim and his band would move into the barn, which was large enough to hold all of them. It was highly unlikely that they would be disturbed so should be safe for several months. Nods of agreement all around and soon all were ready to take up their stations. As leader Tim had pick of the best location with others being directed according to seniority and closeness to the Leader.

The decision was made to 'sleep up' during the day, moving out only at night to undertake their nefarious activities. April and May were productive months as the band grew fat from their nightly raids on local farms, orchards and gardens. June, July and August saw winter stores being laid up, while September was a fallow month as the group argued about the need to move to drier quarters for the winter. Cold breezes had begun to blow through the barn as October days saw shortening of sunlight and cold night air. Tim had been scouting for several weeks, keeping well out of the way of the troublesome villagers, when he chanced upon The Grand Castle Hotel. For several nights he watched the movements, sought out quiet areas and looked for open doors and windows; then Eureka, he had it. The old tower that had served as quarters for guards over many centuries now lay empty and unused.

Tim concentrated his attention on the Tower for many nights, noting that nobody went near it. Then he sneaked into the Hotel and learned that there was access from the Castle into the Tower, residents from the Tower could gain entrance into the Hotel. Yet a problem still remained; how could he get his entire band into the Tower without being detected.

Access from the front was impossible, with guests coming and going all the time and a Concierge guarding the front entrance by night and day. No, the only possibility was to gain entrance from the rear, but therein lay a difficulty. The waters of the lough extended right up to the Castle walls with no doorways out on to the water. High up on the walls was a single window, on the second floor, somehow they must get it opened and kept open.

In the dead of night Tim slipped into the Hotel through the window of the negligent guest. Silent as death he made his way through the Hotel to the oldest part of the Castle. Fearful of every creak, rustle or sudden noise Tim slowly made his way to the Tower. Staring at the giant edifice Tim realised that he simply could not get through the heavy door. Staring upward in a mixture of fear of discovery and a driving need to provide for his band Tim sought frantically for an answer. Then he spotted a sliver of light high upon the battlements and realised there must be a flaw in the stonework or perhaps some other means of access. With much difficulty he made his way to the top, finding the answer to his prayers. For some reason an earlier resident of the Tower had made a tiny window opening, perhaps for light or more likely for use to fire arrows outwards. Regardless of prior use, Tim could now 'squeeze through' and open the window above the lough.

For the remainder of October the 'pioneers' moved everything into their new quarters. Tim made the decision that he and his nearest and dearest should have the top floor with the remainder of his acolytes scattered throughout the other three upper floors. When everything was in order the travellers moved in 'en-caravan' on a dark moonless night. Settled in, Tim and his compatriots congratulated themselves on their ideal home; all were warm, safe and comfortable. Winter was a time for eating, resting and sleeping before making any more decisions about next year.

Winter passed as winters do, in slow time with long nights and short days. Hail, rain and snow had no effect whatsoever on the residents of the Tower who remained warm and snug in their winter lodgings.

The days were lengthening with the hint of spring in the air when Tim awoke to the sound of human voices "I suppose we could smoke them out" the Groundsman was declaring. The Estate Manager was less sure "let's send for the Countryside Officer" he directed.

That notary arrived and flashed his light upwards "I'm afraid there will be no smoking, nor anything else to disturb them. Those are mouse eared bats and a protected species. Don't think for a moment about harming them as I will be inspecting them every month. The law says those creatures must not be disturbed.

Tim went back to sleep, secure in the knowledge that he had found their permanent home.

The Snatch

The 'Snatch' had gone so well that she could scarcely believe it could have been this easy. Sister had told her to take the babies back to the nursery and 'put them down' for the night. It was time for mothers to rest and regain their strength.

She had done exactly as Sister instructed, lining the babies up in their designated places. Then she crossed to the baby girl, born earlier today; she was perfect. At five pounds she was lighter than the other babies, but she was in perfect health, if a little small.

This was exactly the 'type' of baby she had been waiting for; when she returned to England she must be able to pass off the newborn as a premature baby.

For more than a year she had planned the snatch from her home in Norwich in the East of England. Unable to have children of her own she had sought to adopt, but Social Services were so unhelpful. With a history like hers she would never be allowed to adopt a child. Drug addiction, alcohol abuse and a long history of violence precluded her from even being granted a child.

First it was necessary to create a new history, which she did by moving to the outskirts of Manchester. Soon she became involved in local activities, joining a gym, a social club and a church debating society. She explained her lack of a partner by claiming that her husband was a soldier, presently based in Afghanistan. To add to her difficulties, she told her new friends, she had just discovered she was pregnant. With an earlier background in amateur dramatics she had been able to obtain several prosthetics which provided her with the necessary 'bumps' as the baby developed. She had carried out extensive research and realised the chances of snatching a baby in England were small. With cameras everywhere, especially throughout the hospitals, security men in abundance and cameras on every street corner she was unlikely to get away with it.

Eventually she decided that Ireland was a safer bet; fewer cameras and hardly any security men.

Over tea following an interesting debate on the 'woman's place in society' she announced that she would not be back for a few months. At almost seven months pregnant; and showing it thanks to the latest prosthesis, she announced that she was travelling over to Dublin to see her Irish relations before the baby was born. She had not seen her 'Nana' for several years and felt she could not leave it any longer.

Her plan was simple; she would get a job in a maternity unit and wait until she found a 'small' baby. Then she would return to Manchester to a readymade support group with her 'premature' baby. Of course, if it all worked out, and she remained in Manchester she may have to have her husband shot in Afghanistan or have him run off with a Qaranc girl. But that was for later.

With her excellent forged references she soon obtained work as a Care Assistant in the maternity unit in Galway City. Her original plan had been to fly to Dublin and seek work in the Capital City. Within a few days she realised that Dublin was as security conscious as Manchester so she had taken the bus to Galway, having already 'shed' her prosthesis.

Galway was perfect. Large enough for a stranger to pass unnoticed and friendly enough to 'fill her in' on the best pubs, restaurants and places to see. Having obtained lodgings in a small guest house she set about bringing her plans to fruition. She was a perfect 'carer' willing to work long hours, flexible, hardworking and possessor of a 'genuine' love of 'newborns'.

She worked hard and waiting patiently for the perfect baby; the right baby had to be small yet healthy. She must be able to pass it off as an 'eight month' baby when she returned to her friends in Manchester.

As she waited her spare time was taken up with sightseeing and shopping. She visited the rugged Cliffs of Moher, but her main interests were the city itself. Window shopping on a rare day off she spotted an unusual ring in a jeweller's window.

The jeweller handed her the unusual Claddagh ring, explaining that it was a 'one off', specially made for a young couple whose relationship had ended. The jeweller pointed out tray after tray of Claddagh rings; most were plain silver or nine carat gold while some contained emeralds embedded in the heart shape at the centre of the ring. The jeweller was charming and helpful pointing out that the 'emeralds' and 'diamonds' were really only made of glass, hence the price of one hundred pounds.

The 'beauty' that she was now holding was very different; the heart consisted entirely of a one carat diamond held in place by 'hands' of eighteen carat gold. It had been meant to represent both an engagement and wedding ring and a love that would last forever. Unfortunately the love lasted less than six months and the jeweller had acquired the ring at less than half its original price. "That" he explained "was how he was able to 'let it go' for a mere two thousand Euros.

She really wanted that ring! Having received his assurance, guarantee and certificate of authenticity she left the shop with the ring on the third finger of her left hand. She smiled to herself as she left the shop, having bartered the price down to one thousand eight hundred Euros. Of course she could not wear it at work as it was imperative that she did not leave any clues to entrap her; and she did want to wear that ring.

The Clinic had been particularly busy with six babies having been born in the space of as many hours. The moment baby Doyle had been wheeled into the ward she had known this was the one. At five pounds weight, with lusty lungs and a 'clean bill of health' the tiny baby girl was perfect.

She had settled the babies for the night and returned to the ward where she wished Sister "Goodnight". Sister had smiled and responded with a "see you tomorrow" as she completed her 'admin'. Hurrying quickly, but not too quickly, she waved her goodbyes to Sister, thinking this really is goodbye. She had returned to the nursery, quickly swooping up baby Doyle and hurried to her locker where she withdrew her bits and pieces and a large carrier bag. Gently placing the baby in the bag she simply walked out the door; all the while expecting alarm bells to go off. No bells sounded.

Walking quickly to the car park she placed the precious bundle in the seat beside her and drove off in her little hire car. Back 'home' she collected the fruits of her many shopping trips; a carry cot, a range of babies clothes, feeding bottles and feeds, nappies and a mixture of lotions, creams and medicines. Moving quickly and quietly she transferred the baby 'stuff' to the boot of her car, placing them alongside the recently purchased baby buggy. Then she hurried back and fetched her own belongings, but not before removing her long blonde wig and bright blue 'stage eyes' and incinerating them in the fireplace.

She had grown so accustomed to her blonde, blue eyed persona that she barely recognised the short cropped brunette with the deep brown eyes. The transformation pleased her; if she did not recognise herself, others would have even more difficulty. Not for the first time she was grateful for the years she had spent in amateur dramatics. One never knew when one had to take on a new persona in real life, as well as the stage.

She had her baby, she had her things, what now? She was all too aware that the Garda would soon be looking for her. They would check the ports and the airports; a blonde, blue eyed thirty something Englishwoman travelling alone with just a baby should not be hard to find.

Well she smiled to herself 'she was no longer a blue eyed blonde' but help was needed. One phone call to George should sort out her next problem.

"Inspector Martin!" the voice was crisp and professional "how can I help you?"

"It's me George, I need your help. I need you to fly over to Ireland to help me solve a little problem" she was deliberately vague.

George instantly sat upright. Her problems were never small and always involved risk to himself "what do you want?" he lowered his voice to prevent being overhead.

"I need you for a day or two. I need you to fly over and spend a day or two with me!" she remained vague.

George realised from the tone of her voice that she was in trouble and trouble for her could mean trouble for him.

"What do you want me to do?" he reiterated.

"George" she was becoming exasperated "I simply want you to drive me back to England".

"Why can't you do that yourself?" he asked.

"I've broken my ankle" she replied adding a little pain to her voice.

"OK" he said resignedly "where shall I meet you?"

"Meet me at The Grand Castle Hotel" she instructed "I will book in as Mr and Mrs Martin!" Then she gave him the timings and directions and added "bring your ID" before ending the call.

She arrived early at the Grand Castle Hotel with her darling baby asleep in the carry cot. "My husband shall be joining us in a few hours" she announced "he has been held up at a meeting in Dublin with the Garda Commissioner. Some case involving international co-operation" she laughed.

The Receptionist had little interest in the Garda or missing husbands but she did love babies. "She is gorgeous" she smiled "what is her name?"

"Naomi" she answered, noticing the Receptionist's name badge.

In her rush to do other things she had completely forgotten to name her baby.

"Gosh" the Receptionist gasped "this is my name" then she added eagerly "may I hold her?"

"Of course" she answered realising that she had made a new friend ... and potential ally if circumstances required it. "She is beautiful" the Receptionist cooed "Such a coincidence we have another new born in the Hotel".

"Oh?" she asked, and the Receptionist was happy to explain.

"We have a young lady staying with us!" she explained "apparently she and her partner were delivering a boat to Limerick when she went into labour two months early". The Receptionist laughed "her seven months baby is a 'bruiser' at least as big at Naomi!"

She filed the information for later use, if necessary.

"Where is her partner now?" she asked.

"We never saw him" the Receptionist replied "apparently he had a tight deadline to meet and went on alone".

"Odd!" she murmured.

"Very odd" the Receptionist agreed.

Right on cue George arrived. "Ah, here's my husband" she announced "I must get him upstairs with Naomi! Darling" she called rushing over to meet her husband "I will explain when we get to our room".

The Receptionist smiled as the loving couple and little Naomi left the foyer, what a lovely coincidence she thought, another Naomi.

"No, no, no" George protested within the privacy of their room. "I'm a Police Officer for heaven's sake. I cannot get involved in the kidnap of a baby. What were you thinking?" he demanded, the poor mother must be demented.

"I will give the child a good home" she protested.

"That is not the point" the Officer shouted "you have committed a crime you could go to jail. I will not become involved in this terrible thing".

"I think you will George" she spoke calmly "and please keep your voice down. I don't want you to waken Naomi or disturb our neighbours".

"Naomi, is it" his question was rhetorical "and why should I help you?"

Her voice took on an icy coldness "may I remind you that I gave you an alibi when you were accused of indecency in a public lavatory!" her voice tailed off "I did keep tapes of our conversations and your promise to be my friend!" She added "I'm sure the tapes would end a brilliant career and what would your wife think and those poor innocent daughters? Tut-tut!"

"What do you want me to do?" he asked brokenly.

"Stay here tonight, then we will drive north tomorrow. I will think of something".

George nodded.

"Swear on your oath" she demanded "that you will never tell anyone".
George swore on the Bible.

George would be a problem for later. She did not doubt for a moment that he would help her carry out her plan but she was equally certain that a police force somewhere in England would receive an anonymous call informing them of the whereabouts of a missing baby. She nodded to herself; she could take care of George at a later time.

"You stay here with the baby" she commanded "I will go down to Reception to get hold of an atlas or a local road map".

In Reception Naomi was chatty as ever, asking how to Mrs Martin came to have her baby in Galway.

"George had a conference to attend and I thought I would accompany him" she replied "I had planned to visit my Nana in Dublin, but things did not work out that way hence the small baby".

Naomi glowed "she is really beautiful" then she added "so is the other lady's but her baby was nearly eight pounds".

"Wow" she responded "what would it have been if it had gone full term?"

Naomi's voice took on a note of concern "you know Mrs Martin, the other lady's baby does not look like a premature baby".

"No?" asked Mrs Martin, "but you must call me Sinead!"

"Well thank you, Sinead" the Receptionist smiled "you really are Irish with a name like Sinead".

She had no idea where 'Sinead' had come from but the name seemed to fit and the Receptionist now had her firmly as her new best friend.

Then Naomi spotted her unique ring. "Not only an Irish name" she declared "an Irish wedding ring as well!"

Then Sinead recounted her lifelong desire to wed wearing an Irish ring. She told how she and George had consulted with the jeweller to design a ring that was totally special; the diamond heart represented their engagement, the gold their marriage and the clasped hands their lifetime commitment to each other.

The Receptionist almost burst into tears at the beauty of their love story. If only someone who love her like that, she wished.

Over a very quiet dinner with George she was delighted to notice that the other mum had blue eyes and long blonde hair.

Next morning on her way to breakfast, her new best friend whispered "Sinead". Telling George who would be with him in a moment she crossed over to Naomi. "Something wrong?" she asked.

The worried look on the Receptionist face confirmed that something was indeed wrong. 'Sinead's' heart skipped a beat. The Receptionist mutely pushed over several morning newspapers. All contained variations on the same headline 'BABY STOLEN FROM GALWAY HOSPTIAL'.

"My God" gasped 'Sinead' "what are you thinking?" her heart was still racing.

"Look at the picture" Naomi instructed "the woman who stole the baby was caught on camera".

'Sinead' felt faint as her legs wobbled and her body threatened to give way on her.

"Sinead" the Receptionist was still talking "look at the photo, I think it is the other mum".

'Sinead's' palpitations eased "there certainly is a resemblance" she agreed "but I am not certain that it is her!"

At that moment the 'other' mum walked past on her way in for breakfast. "Look" the Receptionist demanded "I do think it's her!"

"You may be right" 'Sinead' agreed, a plan forming in her head.

"What should we do?" the Receptionist asked.

'Sinead' noticed the 'we' but let it pass. "Perhaps we should ring the police" she suggested.

"What if we are wrong?" Naomi asked "then I could be in trouble for bringing the Hotel into disrepute" she looked at her new friend. "I couldn't do it" said 'Sinead' "as a new mother myself I could not stand the same if I was mistaken".

126

"Perhaps an anonymous call from a phone box in the village might be best" Sinead thought out loud "but I couldn't do it. I am the only one here with an English accent. It would need to be somebody local; someone who could disguise their voice".

"I could do that" Naomi responded "I would only be doing my civic duty".

"You are right, Naomi; you could slip out at break time; no one would notice that you were gone".

'Sinead' joined her 'husband' at breakfast whispering urgently 'eat up and get ready to leave, we have just had the most marvellous bit of good luck' Leaning across the table 'Sinead' recounted her entire conversation with the Receptionist. "We must go to our room and get packed. We will leave the moment the Garda take the baby snatcher into custody. I think we have a twenty four hour window of opportunity while the police question her. We will drive to Donegal and take a plane to Glasgow from Carrickfinn".

She pointed out the route and the sign for the tiny airport. "How do you know there is a flight today?" George asked "I don't, but Inspector Martin will ring to find out". She answered, with a new confidence in her voice.

As George rang 'Sinead' worked out the timings. I think we can be in Carrickfinn in just over three hours, allowing for a couple of stops to see to the baby. When is the next flight?"

"If we get left here by one o'clock" George estimated "we should be at the airport in plenty of time for the seven thirty pm flight to Glasgow".

"Excellent" 'Sinead' said "no one will be looking for us today. By the time they realise their mistake we could be in Leeds or Birmingham or London. We are home and dry!"

Then she added "and you can return to the bosom of your family, never to see or hear from me again".

"I say Amen to that" George thought.

The Irish Police were more efficient than their English counterparts 'Sinead' thought as she watched three large Gards led their prisoner away before midday.

"Right" 'Sinead' announced to George "we are on our way!"

"I'm sorry to see you go Sinead" the Receptionist seemed genuinely upset to lose her new friend.

"Don't worry" 'Sinead' smiled "we will keep in touch".

127

"Good; and take care of little Naomi!" the Receptionist wished.

"No doubt of that, Naomi" she laughed and embraced her friend.

Then they were off. Without a single hiccup they arrived at Carrickfinn at a minute past three thirty pm.
"You stay here and watch the baby" 'Sinead' instructed as they drew up at the car park of the tiny airport "I will go in and sort out the tickets".

"Everything sorted" she declared on her return. "The lady on the desk said we should return about six thirty pm. She also told me there are excellent restaurants in Gweedore where we would get lunch at a reasonable cost".

Following a simple but tasty meal and with some time to spare 'Sinead' suggested a short drive around the coast. Where she had examined the map last night she had seen an interestingly named promontory "Would you believe there is a place called 'Bloody Foreland?

The day was beautiful and the roads were empty as 'Sinead' sought out the Bloody Foreland. "Here it is" she declared spotting the signpost on a right angle turn. The drive upwards was easy, belying the mighty drop just outside the side of the car. Stopping at the top, she read the little plaque indicating that two teachers had fallen to their death from the very spot some years previously.

Seemingly preoccupied with her own thoughts 'Sinead' ambled over to the highest and most dangerous spot. The view across the Atlantic was stunning, taking in the islands, and a myriad of rocks. In the far distance she could just discern the outline of South Donegal, many miles away. Immediately beneath her feet was drop of several hundred feet.

Still apparently entranced she 'started' when George spoke 'It's incredible, isn't it?"

"Yes, incredible" she agreed coming over to see something far below.

George stepped forward on her left hand side and shuffled in front of her. He too craned over to see what he had been missing.

It took the slightest of pushes with her left hand to launch him into space. She checked again but she was entirely alone.

She watched with satisfaction as George bounced of jagged rocks on his descent to the bottom. Even from the great distance above she could see from the strange angle of his head that he had broken his neck on his downward descent. She stood silently for several minutes at that lonely place. There were no movement below, nobody running to the rescue, only the lapping sound as the Atlantic 'broke' on the rocks. She checked her watch; it was time to catch a flight.

The flight was uneventful and now she was on the train from Glasgow as it hurtled southwards towards Manchester. Soon she and her new baby would be home safe and sound in the bosom of her friends.

She WAS sorry about poor George, but it had to be done. No doubt the East Anglian Police Force would concoct some story as to why a Senior Police Officer was in another jurisdiction, without permission. Undercover work, an unfortunate slip, a medal for valour, the family taken care off. Over the years legends would grow up about his daring exploits, about his fearless approach to danger. 'Sinead' smiled; in a way she had done him a favour.

She dozed peacefully, her daughter beside her.

Meanwhile a Senior Detective from the North Western Crime Squad was poring over the images on his computer. He could clearly see the tall man walk over towards a smaller figure. The tall man had stepped towards the cliff edge and a smaller arm seemed to reach out to embrace the tall man. There seemed to be the slightest of touches, then the tall man disappeared.

"Freeze that" the Detective called to the Technician. "Can you enlarge that frame?" He called to his Assistant.

"Give me a few minutes Sir" the IT God responded.

"There it is" the Detective declared. "It's as clear as day. It's a woman wearing an odd sort of ring! Can you focus in on the ring" the Detective called. Then he smiled. The micro cameras that had recently been embedded in the fence posts had just 'earned their money', "there can't be too many of those in the world" the Detective declared staring at the quite unique Claddagh ring.

The Walking Sticks

Lester Stuart elicited sympathy from the moment he tried to struggle out of the taxi that had stopped on the forecourt of The Grand Castle Hotel.

Taking firm hold of his walking sticks Lester tried desperately to swing into an upright position. Seeing his dilemma the taxi driver rushed round to the passenger side forced his arm under Lester's armpit and heaved upwards. It was several moments before his 'rocking' ceased and he was able to walk to the Castle entrance.

'Walk' is probably the wrong word to describe Lester's perambulations. His progress seemed almost crab like; first he would reach forward with one stick then twist his body forward, then repeat the lunge with the second stick. The doorman rushed over, offering to bring a wheelchair. Lester politely declined, 'he knew it wasn't elegant, but at least he had some degree of independence while he was able to use his sticks'.

Lester smiled wearily at the doorman 'it was only a matter of time until a wheelchair would be necessary but, in the meantime he must soldier on'.

The doorman wiped his eyes with a large white handkerchief then blew his nose to cover his embarrassment. He knew that he could never be so brave as this man, with so many problems to overcome.

Lester almost stumbled as he leaned on one stick and fumbled to get his hand into his pocket. The doorman stepped over, supporting the shaky man.

Lester withdrew a crumpled five Euro note from his pocket and offered it to the doorman.

"No Sir" claimed the doorman "I really couldn't" and for the first time in his life it was true.

Lester made his slow stumbling way to the Receptionist, leaning heavily on the Console to support himself as he signed in.

Eliciting the same response as the doorman, the Receptionist offered him a superior suite on the ground floor, with ensuite, sitting room and a ramp on to a private patio. Lester shook his head "I could not possibly afford it" he claimed weakly.

"It comes at no extra cost" the Receptionist lied, clearing the sudden lump in her throat.

The Receptionist stood transfixed as Lester made his laborious way to his suite "Some people have so much pain, so much hardship" she blessed herself "there but for the grace of God, go I" she thought.

The Porter refused Lester's offer of a tip, as did the Chambermaid, the Waiter and the Barman. It would seem that the finest tradition of 'tipping' had ended the moment that Lester struggled through the doorway.

Lester struggled to the swimming pool, to the massage parlour and to the dining room bringing lumps to throats wherever he ventured.

The General Manager, noted for her kind heart, allocated Rob to act as Lester's Private Escort. Anything Lester wanted; Lester could have, within reason. Lester, the Blessed, wanted nothing, nor wanted for anything.

Over a three day period Rob learned a lot about Lester and his terrible affliction. Lester explained in detail how he was wasting away with a space occupying lesion in his spine. The condition from which Lester suffered would eventually kill him. Lester spoke with such calm acceptance of his fate that Rob could do nothing but be filled with admiration for this man. There was no doubt about it, Lester was a true hero.

The first small 'worm' of doubt entered Rob's head when he accompanied Lester to the swimming pool. As he helped Lester swing his 'dead' legs into the pool he was struck by the musculature that Lester still possessed; "My God" Rob thought "his muscles are as big as mine".

Lester spotted the moment of doubt on Rob's face "What is it?" he asked.

"Your legs are as burly as mine" Rob blurted out.

"Well, why wouldn't they?" Lester retorted "the wastage spreads downwards and it's only the myelin sheath that's affected. The muscle wastage in the legs comes much later".

The note of sadness in Lester's voice left no doubt that that was the end stage 'of his disease; of his life!'

Rob felt ashamed. He knew nothing of anatomy and it was doubtful that he had even heard of Pathology.

Rob's embarrassment must have registered on his face, so Lester declared "don't worry old boy, we all make mistakes. Come and join me" he laughed "the water is divine".

An hour of 'floating' exhausted Lester who declared a desire to return to his room and lie down.
Rob heaved the legs out of the pool and handed Lester a large towel; then he stepped over to hand the walking sticks to Lester. "Wow" he gasped "what are these things made from? They are really heavy!"

"Lead" Lester laughed. "Good old fashioned lead. When you are like me, you are a target for all sorts of muggers and 'near-do-wells'. I had the sticks specially made with heavy lead and painted to look like blackthorn. God, help the thug who tries to mug me!" Again, Lester laughed. "God help them, indeed" Rob thought weighing them in his hands. The sticks must weigh nearly two stones.

Lester tittered all the way to his suite. "I am going to have a doze, old boy" he declared "I won't need you for three or four hours. I tell you what" he added "if you are available about seven thirty pm you might join me for dinner".

"That would be delightful" Rob answered.

At seven thirty pm Rob slipped in through the French doors; that way he would not disturb their guest by rapping on the door. Rob moved silently across the room and touched Lester on the shoulder. Lester was instantly awake.

"Thank you, Rob" Lester said "I wonder if you would fetch my sticks" he added, pointing across the room.

That is strange Rob thought how could the sticks get across the room, unless perhaps the Chambermaid had been in.

Rob decided to check "Have you had your room done, Sir?" he said.

Lester replied that he had no idea as he had been asleep since Rob left him.

Rob picked up the sticks and, unnoticed to Lester scratched as deeply as he could with his thumb nail. As he handed the sticks to Lester he realised that he had managed to remove enough paint to see underneath. The handle of the stick was yellow, or at least, that little uncovered spot was. Rob's suspicions were well and truly roused 'lead was a grey colour, but gold was yellow!'

There was no further time for examination as Rob escorted the guest to dinner. In the dining room Rob suddenly changed him mind about dinner "would you mind awfully, Sir, if I passed on dinner. I had some cake at tea time and now I have a bit of a gippy tummy."

"Not at all, old boy" Lester responded "get an antacid and lie down for an hour or two. It will do the world of good".

"Thank you Sir" Rob smiled "I will come back for you in two hours".
"That would be great old boy" Lester replied "see you then".

It had been Rob's intention to report his suspicions to the General Manager, but hurrying through the open corridor by the guests lounge he spotted the headlines in The Times. Old Major Hughes hands shook from Parkinsonism and fifty years of Gins and Tonics as he struggled with his paper.

Rob stopped as if struck by lightning "do you mind if I have a quick look at your paper, Major?" he gasped taking in the implications of the headlines.

"Not at all" the Major shakily handed over the newspaper. Rob's eyes almost 'popped out' as he read 'a member of staff of the Royal Mint had disappeared along with five bars of gold. It was thought the thief had been disturbed in his attempt to remove the bars as a fully laden trolley had been found abandoned at the rear door. The report added that five bars was probably about all that the thief could manage to carry. All the bars were numbered and hallmarked so could not be passed off in their present form. The report concluded that it was likely that the bars had already been melted down and moved out of the country. The article ended with the claim that the total value of the gold was likely to be almost two million Euros.

"My God" he gasped, realising that the items must be worth four hundred thousand Euros each. "What will I do? His duty was clear but he had grown fond of Lester over the past three days. Rob decided to sleep on it, then report his suspicions to the Manager in the morning. Deep in thought Rob failed to hear someone approach.

"You look like you've seen a ghost, old boy" Lester's voice broke in to his reverie.
"No, no!" Rob assured him "just a little queasy."

"Is there something wrong Sir?" he asked.

"Forgot my glasses!" Lester smiled.

"It's alright Sir" Rob hastened "I shall fetch them for you".

Rob returned with the spectacles and allowed himself to be persuaded to join Lester for dinner. Rob chose his moment carefully. As they enjoyed 'the fruits' of the cheeseboard he casually mentioned the headlines in The Times.

"Apparently" he said "someone managed to get five gold bars out of the Royal Mint. Police think he will have melted down the bars and fled the country, wouldn't it be exciting if we had the thief in the Castle?"

Lester looked at him strangely, but Rob's innocent face told him nothing. "That would be exciting, old boy" Lester's voice had dropped to a whisper.

Suddenly tired, Lester begged Rob's indulgence to help her to his room; he had some calls to make, then he must have an early night.

"Of course Sir" Rob smiled "I will walk with you to your room then I think I too will retire for the night".

Lester smiled.

In the suite Lester lifted the phone, then apparently on impulse, said "I say old boy would you mind going over to the kitchen and making a mug of cocoa for me?"

"Not at all Sir' I'll be back in ten minutes".

"No rush" Lester assured him.

Rob stood in the shadows ten yards from Lester's French door. Well concealed among the rhododendron, he was not in the least surprised when Lester drew his curtains and stepped out on to the patio.

Rob noticed that Lester had a heavy rucksack on his back with his sticks tied behind him, attached to the rucksack. He stood for several moments until a cloud obscured the moonlight..... Then he 'legged it'.

"No sign of paralysis now" Rob thought as Lester sprinted across the lawn, avoiding the shingle laden pathway.

Two things happened almost in unison, first a taxi drew up and Lester increased his pace, then secondly, one of the stick 'bumped out of their mooring'. Not waiting to retrieve the stick Lester ran on, jumped into the taxi and was soon out of sight.

Rob strolled over to where the stick had fallen and nonchalantly picked it up; he looked around carefully and was pleased to see that he was still alone.

Silently whistling Rob ambled round to his car, checked again, then threw the stick into the boot.

Rob had no idea how he would get rid of his windfall, but that was a problem for another day. For now he was safe and sound; if the Police picked up Lester they would never believe that he had lost half of his booty. As for Lester, he would firmly believe that those thieving Policemen would do anything to line their own pockets!

This time Rob whistled out loud.

The Perfect Man

Kris walked into The Grand Castle Hotel and everything stopped. The Receptionist looked over her spectacles and her mouth fell open, her pen stopped mid-sentence as she stared, transfixed. Maura, the cleaner tried unsuccessfully to fight back the words that erupted from her lips "Oh my God" she gasped in utter wonderment "he's perfect". The power seemed to leave her hands and she dropped her mop bucket with a mighty crash. The Supervisor rushed forward, ready to render an immediate rebuke, then she saw the 'vision'. Unconsciously she reached into her uniform pocket, withdrew the tube of lipstick and applied the bright red dye to her already pouting lips.

The 'object' of the staff consternation stood apparently casually unconcerned by the effect he was having on the female staff. Standing six feet tall, the rippling muscles evident beneath the skin tight t-shirt, he presented an image of the ideal 'leading man' in the best love stories. Maura mentally measured him as chest forty four to forty six, waist twenty eight, and hips forty, about fourteen stones weight with charisma that was so palpable that she felt quite faint. With his unfashionably shaven head, the Supervisor immediately marked him down as an American G.I. Not that she had even met a G.I., but she did watch films.

Showing the whitest teeth the Receptionist had ever seen the newcomer spoke with the easy drawl of a man from the Southern States, maybe Alabama, maybe Virginia, maybe ...

"I believe you have a reservation for Kris Montgomery" the voice was mellifluous but the Receptionist merely gaped, open mouthed and slack jawed.

Several seconds passed in stunned silence, then he spoke again "What is the matter, haven't you seen a black man before?" The voice was low, but the tone spoke volumes. The Receptionist gulped, gasped for air and managed "Yes, will actually no, only in films but that's not it. You are so beautiful!"

She had meant to say handsome but somehow 'beautiful' seemed better. Then a moment of sheer delight happened, a moment she would remember forever. He turned those magnificent chocolate brown eyes to her, gazing, it seemed to her, into her very soul. The perfect white teeth were displayed in a smile that was just for her "Thank you, ma'am, I will take that as a very great compliment!"

The Receptionist's face turned bright red, her chest felt crushed as her heart accelerated uncontrollably and she stuttered "you are welcome, Sir".

Her hand shook as she registered his details and she was certain that she would faint as he took her hand in his and thanked her for her help.

For no particular reason the Reception area had filled with staff and female guests who suddenly felt the need to address urgent queries to the Receptionist. Through all the excitement Kris Montgomery stood nonchalantly gazing outwards towards the lough as the Receptionist fumbled to hand over his room key.

About twenty five, the assembled throng guessed as the object of their adoration strode towards the stairs; no need for Porters, no elevator for him. This was a real man, the manifestation of every maiden's dream; and he seemed so unaware of his own power.

In the sanctuary of his room Kris, allowed himself the tiniest of smiles. Of course he had felt the reaction, just as he had had the same responses all across America, Europe and South East Asia. When he thought of Asia the smile turned to a grimace and the liquid chocolate eyes hardened into dark coals of hate. He would never forget Asia.

Kris treated himself to a siesta before descending for dinner. As a result of the cold shower he took just prior to coming down Kris' skin shone over the rippling muscles.

Kris smiled inwardly when he noticed that he had been provided with the best table in the restaurant and staff 'fell over' themselves in their desire to please him.

The new guest took it all in his stride seated as an Emperor on his throne being attended by his acolytes. Waitress after Waitress sought desperately to 'catch his eye' for the Receptionist had been graphic in her description of the 'look'. Kris adopted his 'gentle look', the kindly king bestowed smiles and nods of gratitude for every little kindness. Hardened Waitresses went weak at the knees as he bestowed his blessings on them.

Rising at the end of his meal Kris thanked the chef, the Head Waiter, the waitresses and might well have thanked the Hotel cat, had he known of its presence. Then he retired to his room remaining there for the remainder of the night.

At seven am he was in the gym, trying every piece of equipment. The Sports and Entertainment Instructress stood looking over in silent admiration. Kris' t-shirt was soaked in perspiration, his face fixed in determined effort and the Instructor hoped he would stay forever. This was nineteen seventy five and Irish men had not yet discovered the joys of hard exercise. 'Six packs' were things they brought home from the pub on Saturday nights. Right before her eyes the perfect 'six pack' was revealed as Kris stripped off the sodden shirt.

It was all the poor 'sports lady' could do to prevent herself from gasping at the beauty of this perfect man. Casually Kris 'wiped himself down with the offending t-shirt. His Instructor dreamed of becoming the shirt.

Then he swam; not like any swimmer before, Kris cut through the water like a graceful dolphin causing only the tiniest of ripples. The swim seemed effortless, then he exited from the pool. Rivulets of water ran off the magnificent frame, his breathing had increased only slightly and the Instructor saw 'speedos' for the first time.

She stood riveted to the spot as Kris towelled himself down; the poor girl was transfixed, this was male perfection. Then she noticed Kris search through his sports bag and withdraw a 'patch' that he applied just below the line of his speedos.

Curiosity now aroused the Instructor searched in her memory banks for an explanation; she could find none. Probably some strange American ritual, she thought, and put it out of her mind.

Intercepting him as he was leaving, the Instructor asked if Kris would be back tomorrow. All her dreams came true when he answered "Yes, this evening, tomorrow morning, tomorrow night, that's how it is with me". Mentally she decided to do some overtime!

After breakfast Kris enrolled for the Art Course and Mary, the resident Artist thanked her God for his kindness. Mary immediately resolved to find some way to have her new recruit 'sit' for her and her wishes weren't entirely altruistic.

The first week of the course was spent in the studio/classroom teaching the group about form, shape, light, shade, watercolour, oils, crayons, charcoal, perceptions and a hundred other art 'concepts'. As others scrubbed furiously on note pads Kris sat gazing into the middle distance. On day three Mary could 'stand it no longer', asking Kris if he was bored.

"No, ma'am" he replied back "but I've been through all this in the past". Then he told how he had spent a year in hospital following a tour of duty as a G.I. in Vietnam. Sketchily he told how he had lost the power of his legs and that's when he learned to paint. Mary suggested he join a group who were not beginners.

Now placed in a more suitable group, Kris applied himself with the same enthusiasm that he brought to his work in the gym. His first effort entailed a watercolour of a boat sailing into harbour. Painted almost entirely in black and white with just the merest hint of yellow and green one was left with the impression of an eighteen century Spanish Galleon sailing from light into darkness. By clever use of darkness Kris had created an image of a ship caught in a great cavern where only ruin and devastation lay.

Mary searched the work for flaws and failings but found only one. The work was magnificent, evoking a deep bottomless sadness in the viewer.

Looking into the deep brown eyes she asked "why did you invert the light in the water. You paint the surface impenetrable black, but hint at light below?" Then she added "this is the exact opposite to what you see before you".

Kris answer carried a life of sadness "No, ma'am" he corrected her "the water is the opposite of what 'you' see!"

That was the moment that Mary diagnosed Kris. The deep dark sadness 'obviously' reflected the mind of a man who had been damaged psychologically by the war. Mary surmised that Kris has suffered this new thing she had read about called Post Traumatic Stress Disorder. "Yes, that was it" she decided "there was not a 'mark' on his perfect body so the injury must be inside." With great difficulty she refrained from taking him in her arms and reassuring him that everything would be alright.

By evening everyone knew about the poor lost soul who had suffered so much. With every telling Kris' story became increasingly complex 'he was' special forces driven mad through torture by the enemy. He had been captured on a covert mission deep into enemy territory. Despite a level of torture that would have killed a lesser man Kris refused to tell anything other than name, rank and number. Then he had killed ten of the enemy, then twenty, the numbers multiplied as he made his escape. Back at base, without food or sleep for more than a week the 'hero' collapsed. Overcome with guilt for the slaughter he had perpetrated he lapsed into a terrible depression. Now he was in Ireland to complete his rehabilitation.

And there were many willing ladies, all too ready to help him with his recovery. They buzzed around him like flies offering comfort and solace. Kris simply smiled.

Mary decided that a day spent painting on Inchagoil Island would provide the artists with an opportunity to extend their talents. Mary thought the Island whose name in Irish is Inin na Ghaill (Island of the Foreigner) was particularly appropriate for her poor hurting American hero who was so far from home. With a history dating back to St Patrick the Island provided everything an aspiring artist could want. The mighty Lough Corrib, ruined churches, the burial place of an archbishop and the stone of Lugna all begging to benefit from the artists brush.

The little group worked feverishly all day, contenting themselves with their packed lunches and bottles of water.

As the day progressed Kris appeared to retreat deeper and deeper into himself. Several times he painted furiously, only to wipe the canvas clean again and again. The he muttered to Mary that he was going off to find a new location, he needed peace and he needed solitude.

The cheery team wished him luck, smiled to each other about moody Americans and returned to their tasks.

With the light fading Mary made the decision to return to the Hotel with a view to returning to the Island in the early morning when light was at its best. Before parting the group agreed to meet outside the Hotel entrance at seven thirty am the next morning.

As was his habit Kris woke at six am, showered and 'HIT' the gym. It took him some time to warm up as he had had a very late night. Having borrowed an easel he had worked on his painting until four am when he expressed himself reasonably satisfied with his work. Two hours sleep and now he was back in the gym. As he worked out he wondered to himself if he should forego the pleasure of today's artwork. Then it was back to his room.

The team stomped around, anxious to get going in order to capture the early morning light. Finally Mary announced that she would fetch Kris and follow the 'team' bus in her car: her decision was met by universal cries of agreement. Kris was a lovely man but this sort of light only came along once in a 'blue moon'.

Mary climbed the stairs and walked quietly to Kris' room. Finding the door slightly ajar, she tapped lightly and walked in. Why she remained silent she never knew, but quietly she padded into the bedroom. Just like the front door, the door to the en-suite was lying slightly open.

Mary looked in through the space at the side of the jamb and instantly jumped back, in shock. Desperately biting her lower lip to prevent herself from crying out Mary brought both hands before her lips to stifle the sound of the groan that escaped. Grateful that Kris showed no sign of having heard anything; she stood transfixed staring at the 'perfect man' seated on the lavatory.

Where his manhood should have been, she saw a mangled mass of broken flesh. Trance like she watched as Kris inserted rubber tubing into a hole in the torn flesh. As the urine began to flow her eyes were drawn to the 'bag' that now hung where the patch had been.

Mentally she 'crossed herself' as she realised that she was seeing a colostomy bag. Now it was clear to her that Kris' injuries were very real, not the psychological troubles that she had diagnosed. This was the legacy of Vietnam, probably from some sort of bomb blast. "Oh, you poor man" she thought, then realised the extent of her intrusion.

Turning and tiptoeing away Mary spotted Kris' painting standing in the corner of his living area. She was drawn almost magnetically to the easel.
Yesterday's work had been changed beyond recognition. The remnants of St Patrick's Church on Inchagoil Island had been moved to a lough side location. With clever use of light and shade Kris had created a monochromatic work. Dark threatening clouds descended to meet the black inkiness of the waters of Corrib, while the grey green church stones stood in deep dark silhouette. The work was 'backlit' and Mary's gaze was drawn deep into the blackness of the waters where the tiniest of pin pricks of light gave the impression of light that was beyond and beneath the great lake. Stepping closer Mary detected the tiny hole in the canvas that allowed the illusion to occur.

Then she understood! Mary quietly closed the door and left.

Births, Marriage and Deaths

Hal stared in open mouthed amazement as the young lady struggled up the gangway and on to the Star of the Sea.

Her companion laughed heartily at Hal's embarrassment and obvious discomfiture. "It's alright" he claimed "we are expecting twins and they are not due for another eight weeks." Then he added, "I'm David and this is Sue."

"Hal" murmured Hal weakly. Inwardly he wondered if this is her size at seven months what would she look like at nine months. Wisely he kept his counsel.

Hal was not entirely convinced by David's exhortation that nothing would happen for at least two months and looked around the other passengers to see from where help might come in an emergency. What he saw did not fill him with confidence. With the season almost over passenger numbers had fallen to the point where it was costing money to keep the service going. Today Hal's customers had fallen to single figures. In addition to David and Sue there was a father with two teenage sons, two novice nuns who were guests of the hotel and an elderly couple of indeterminable age.

With some unspoken gut feeling of impending disaster Hal reversed Star of the Sea out from her mooring and turned towards the main body of the Lough.

Then the bad feeling came. Hal had had enough experience of his intuitions to know the feeling should not be ignored. With Star of the Sea facing out into the Lough Hal put the engine in neutral and ambled among his passengers. The old couple seemed fine, ruddy cheeks and well wrapped up. The father and sons were pink with health, then Hal stepped over to his heavily pregnant passenger. The bad feeling intensified to the point of nausea and a sick feeling of dread.

"Are you certain that you are alright for this voyage?" he asked. Then he continued, "It gets very cold and can be choppy out on the Lough."

Sue laughed, "I'm perfectly fine," she said. "Of course she is" David reinforced her wellness. There was nothing else for it, Hal must commence the cruise. How could he possibly explain the gut feeling and the dread that encompassed without seeming like a 'stage' Irishman.

The only seating on the deck of the Star of the Sea was plain, plastic and comfortless. Retreating to the wheelhouse Hal returned with a couple of cushions and a blanket to make the mother-to-be comfortable.

Again Sue laughed, "Stop fussing over me, I am in good health. I'm simply having two babies in two months!"

"Yes, yes," Hal responded and returned to the wheelhouse.

With an increasing feeling of dread Hal engaged the gears and began to move slowly into the great Lough. Half an hour in and Hal was berating himself for his own stupidity. Sue had laughed and cheered at every feature of the Lough. As they had passed Inchagoill Island Hal had explained that the word meant island of the foreigner which Sue found most amusing; she announced to her husband that they must bring their twins here to be christened, given the fact that they were foreigners. Hardly foreigners" David exclaimed "we are from Scotland."

Hal forced his bad feeling aside and laughed, "In this part of the world people from Ulster are strangers, so you are foreigners!"

The cold late October day was glorious; the air clean, the gentle breeze caressing faces and hands and the late autumn sunshine presenting the Lough and all its surroundings in all their glory.

Halfway into the cruise and Hal began to relax. With his natural story telling flair he pointed out the Church of the Saints and told the story of Tommy Nevin the last resident of the island. Hal remonstrated with himself about his stupidity; what could go wrong on a glorious day such as this?

Then nature spoke!

The change commenced with a freshening of the wind, followed rapidly by the worst gale that Hal had ever experienced. A giant wave crashed into the Star, throwing her violently starboard side.

With a sudden roll Sue was thrown from her seat crashing onto the deck. Gingerly she started to push herself upright. Then she let out an unearthly scream. Her face was white as a sheet as she fell back onto the deck. "They are coming" she whispered desperately to David. "Do something" she added "I need to get to hospital."

"Too late for that, I think" the elderly lady passenger stated. "I'm not a midwife but long ago I was a nurse and I am sure your babies are on their way."

Hal fought desperately to turn the Star. "How long have we got?" he shouted.

"I don't know" the elderly lady responded "maybe ten or fifteen minutes."

"Not enough time to get back to harbour" Hal called.

The old nurse shook her head.

"Stay with your wife" Hal called to David "I will seek calmer waters by Inchagoill Island." Then he spoke to the nurse, "Can you deliver the babies?" The old lady shook her head; her voice was filled with sadness, "I will help but the young lady is on her own."

With herculean effort Hal forced the Star through the rough waters. "Take the children down below" he called to the dumbstruck father. "I'll help" the old man said taking the arm of one of the boys.

The old man was back in minutes, carrying blankets and cushions from the lower deck. "Hurry" the old nurse called "one baby is coming!"

Hal sought frantically for the old pier at the Island. A piercing cry split the air as Sue struggled desperately to deliver her baby.

"Can you bring help?" the old man called to Hal "a helicopter or something?"

Hal nodded reaching for the phone.

"Push, push" the elderly lady spoke in soothing tones.

In the midst of the mayhem a healthy female child entered the world. Training from years ago kicked in as the elderly nurse took the infant, cut the umbilical cord and slapped her back. The tiny cry seemed to revive Sue.

The old nurse whispered to David, "Take care of your wife and I will go and clean the little one." Then she stepped into the wheelhouse.

The moment the nurse and the infant entered Hal knew that something was wrong.

"The baby?" he asked.

"The baby is fine but the mother is losing a lot of blood. Have you managed to call up a helicopter?"

Hal nodded, "The chopper will be here in fifteen minutes."

"I hope that is soon enough!" the old lady whispered. But the doubt in her voice told a different story.

"I must go" she whispered to Hal.

Back on deck her husband had erected a wind shield and David held his wife in his arms. Gently the nurse placed the baby in Sue's chest announcing, "You have a beautiful daughter."

Eleven minutes later the second twin tried to make it into the world. By now Sue was weak from blood loss, then the nurse detected potential disaster. And disaster it was as the second child fought to be born with the umbilical cord wrapped tightly around its neck.

The nurse knew that she was fighting a losing battle. "Help me" she called to one of the transfixed nuns, "The child will die if we do not do something."

No one could tell how they delivered the baby but it was obvious that the child had lost an impossible fight. "Baptise my children" David cried. "What is your name?" he looked at the old woman.

"Eve" she whispered. "And his?" he looked to the old man.

"Henry"

"Then so be it. Eve and Henry." He looked to the two novice nuns.

Eve and Henry were baptised using still water bottled in the wilds of Connemara.

"Oh my God" the nurse's gasp was audible only to David "she is slipping away."

David leapt to his feet and strode to the wheel house. "Marry us" he shouted "Ships Captains can marry passengers and I want you to marry Sue and me."

"I am not a ship's captain" Hal explained.

"It doesn't matter" David's voice was frantic with fear, "Marry us."

That was the moment that Hall knew why he had always carried his grandfather's bible when he went out on the Lough. Many earlier passengers and friends had scoffed at his superstition accusing him of having no confidence in the Star.

Hal lifted the old bible and knelt beside the 'happy couple'. "Do you David take this woman Sue as your lawful wedded wife?"

He was going to continue with 'for richer or poorer' but the nurse gasped, "No time."

Hal turned to Sue, "Do you take this man David to be your lawful wedded husband?" Hal's voice was drowned out by the clatter of the helicopter as it landed by the shore.

David's cheeks were wet with tears.

He looked across to the Island of foreigners, then he whispered in his wife's ear, "Take good care of Henry and I can assure you that Eve will never be a foreigner in Connemara!

Johnathan Charles Montgomery IV

The die was cast; there could be no going back, Johnny was going to marry Marion no matter what obstacles were placed in his way. From the moment he had set eyes on her Johnny was hopelessly, helplessly lost in a maelstrom of hot emotions.

Of course there had been other earlier crushes but Johnny had soon come to see them for what they had been; childish crushes dressed up as love. In the brilliance of his new love he could only wonder at how he could have been content with the earlier lights that had burned so dim.

Johnny's heart rate increased exponentially with each new memory. How could mere words capture this feeling that had possessed him? Yes he could explain the rapid heartbeat, the dry mouth, butterflies in his stomach but nothing existed to describe the exquisite feeling that must be heaven itself.

He could barely believe that it was only eight days since he caught his first glimpse of Maria as she exited the door of the Viceroy suite; the suite that he and his parents would occupy for the coming two weeks.

In her smart new uniform, with her hair pinned up beneath her tiny cap she epitomised everything that was beauty. Her hair was fine, brunette, with a tiny wisp escaping over her left eyebrow, her deep blue eyes sparkled and she smiled shyly as she wished him welcome and hoped that he would enjoy his stay.

From that moment Johnny knew he would enjoy the holiday that he had been resisting form the previous three months: he had argued cogently that Martha's Vineyard was so much more fun in August or California or Florida might make a pleasant change. Johnny had no wish to leave the United States but father was adamant. If he was going to follow in his father's footsteps it was time to start seeing the world. Father was Vice President and Chief Executive of a major conglomerate whose tentacles reached out into five continents and Johnny must learn about everything.

As his father claimed, Johnny would be the fourth member of the family to head up the company founded by his great grandfather in the nineteenth century. Or, as his father put it, Johnathan Charles Montgomery IV would have his brass plate over the shop.

It was more than one hundred years since great grandfather had started the first general store which had expanded into electronics, banking and a host of other (very successful) ventures. Doubtless the Grand Castle had been chosen for its reputation as one of the world leaders' in the field with endless facilities for the guests. Equally however, John Charles III felt that it was time for Johnny to meet the Taoiseach of this funny little country, together with the great and the grand of Irish society.

Johnny would much rather have spent his vacation kicking a ball along the golden sand but he had learned early that father was not a man to be crossed. And therein lay the problem! Father had to be told about Maria.

Johnny's blood ran cold at the thought of his father's reaction when he was told of his plans. Like every aspect of Johnny's life father would have already have made a list of suitable candidates to join the family. He could hear his father's booming voice extolling the virtues of marrying 'one of their own', the daughter of a Duke (or Dook as father pronounced it), and English Princess or perhaps a Rothschild or a Kennedy.

Well, this time Johnny was having none of it; he was going to marry Maria. Not that Maria knew anything of his plans, apart from a few shy glances and single sentence exchanges they barely knew each other: But Johnny knew she was interested; knew that her heart jumped as much as his own when they met. All that was needed was to find a way of moving the romance to the next stage and that would not be easy.

He could not confide in his own mother about something as important as the rest of his life. Naturally mother would tell father and the cat would be out of the bag.

There was only one thing for it, he must stand up to his father. The thought of facing his father made Johnny feel quite faint, knowing how his father reacted when he was crossed. Nevertheless it had to be done!

At this time of day father would be in his study in his part of the grand suite with the door firmly shut. The closed door was a signal to family and staff that he must not be interrupted under any circumstances. Well today he was going to be interrupted!

Walking firstly on rubbery legs to the kitchenette Johnny filled a large glass with water which he quaffed in one go. Still his mouth was dry and his heart was pounding.

Another glass, drunk more slowly, was some help so he quietly approached his father's closed door.

Several times he turned away without knocking or turning the handle. Furiously he upbraided himself, 'what sort of a husband would he be for Maria if he could not talk to his own father.'

Finally he straightened up and marched purposefully to the door. Johnny rapped firmly on the door and entered the room without waiting for an invitation.

As usual his Father was seated behind a bank of computers with phones all round him. The slightest look of irritation crossed his brow as he looked over and muttered, "Well what is so vitally important that it cannot wait until I finish my lunch?"

Johnny's words poured out with a squeaky yelp, "I am going to marry Maria" he said and then gulped and more deeply announced, "I am going to marry Maria!"

The look on his Father's face screamed silently, 'you interrupted me for this' but what he said was "Maria?"

"Yes Maria" Johnny's confidence grew.

"Maria who?" Father asked with more than a little of his attention directed towards the host of figures on the computer screen.

"Maria, the chambermaid" Johnny elucidated "I love her".

"The chambermaid?" Father's voice rose several octaves.

'Here it comes' Johnny thought 'the great family, the need to marry your own or more specifically not beneath yourself. Without doubt a hotel chambermaid did not count as one of your own.'

"The chambermaid?" Father repeated, "Why she is about fifteen or sixteen years old." Then his tone changed, "Has anything happened between you?"

"Of course not!" Johnny answered.

Father's eyes bored into Johnny's head, his eyes took on a cold pitiless look. He punched a button on one of his gadgets summoning his wife to the room.

Almost before Johnny's mother had entered the room Father's cold icy voice cut into the atmosphere, "Summon the maids and tell them to pack our things, we are leaving now!"

Mother was familiar with this tone and knew that an argument was useless. Softly Mother spoke to reception, informing them that something had come up and they had to leave immediately.

Johnny stood frozen as Father began to dismantle his computers. Following several minutes of hateful silence Father instructed, "Get packed, we will be out of here in thirty minutes. We will be back in America in time for tea."

That was the moment that Johnny knew he hated his father.

"Yes Sir," he whispered, returned to his room and began to pack.

Through misty eyes and owning a broken heart Johnny knew he would not always be eight years old.

And one day he would return!

Lady Mary Fitzwilliam-Howard

Lady Mary or Maria as she was known to family and friends was a born rebel, existing only to torture family, staff and friends.

To the house staff and the estate workers Lady Mary had a well-earned reputation as an impish whirlwind who caused havoc wherever she went.

When she was only six years old Lady Mary glued Simpson, the butler's cup to the saucer. Standing quietly in the background of the servants' kitchen she suddenly cackled manically when Simpson drenched his stiffly starched shirt, losing much of his dignity before the kitchen maids.

On another occasion Maria decided to wash the kittens in the dishwasher, much to the Countess's chagrin. At ten years old Maria announced that she was forsaking her private tutor to attend the local primary school, a decision the doting Earl was happy to facilitate. A retinue of tutors had informed the Earl that Lady Mary was uneducable; a diagnosis the Earl dismissed with a great harrumph! Maria was the baby and her father's little pet; in truth Maria reminded him of himself when he was a boy.

Maria had been a little afterthought or 'accident' when the Earl and Countess were both forty six and had their children raised; or so they thought! The Earl's eldest son. Viscount Richard was twenty three when Maria was born, Lord David, 'the spare' was twenty.

Rather than settling peacefully into late middle age the Earl and the Countess found themselves as parents in a 'new age' that neither of them understood. Nearing sixty with a wild child daughter who was utterly spoiled by her mother and older brothers, the Earl was the only disciplinarian in her life. Had anyone asked, he would have been hard pressed to remember a time when he had to discipline his bewitching daughter. If truth were told the Earl was the most indulgent of all Maria's family and staff!

Much to the surprise of all Lady Mary 'shone' at primary school, bringing a self-discipline to her work that no one thought she possessed.

Post primary, Maria moved to a local comprehensive school with her 'mates', outshining all of them in academic achievement. At fourteen Her Ladyship could clearly see her future; she would study hospitality management, then set up her own catering and entertainment business in the Castle's grounds. The Earl smiled indulgently.

That is how Maria found herself on work experience at the Grand Castle Hotel as a chambermaid for the duration of her summer holidays.

Simpson, the butler, muttered to the Earl about such work, which was beneath Lady Mary's dignity. Cook claimed that no good would come of it and the head gardener thanked his God that he would have some peace for the summer.

Daddy 'pulled strings' and Maria found herself under the tutelage of the housekeeper; a legend within the hotel.

Maria took to her work as a duck takes to water. With only four weeks experience she felt able to advise her mentor about housekeeping practices. The housekeeper smiled, thought about the new suggestions and then implemented them. Maria was summoned to the housekeeper's office and told about the imminent arrival of very important guests. Jonathan Charles Montgomery was a very important client whose good opinion could lead to many further bookings. Conspiratorially the housekeeper whispered that Mr Montgomery was a personal friend of the Taoiseach.

Maria stared at the housekeeper with a total lack of ignorance. What was the strange word 'Taoiseach', she thought, there were none of them in England. The housekeeper explained that Taoiseach was the Irish name for Prime Minister; she sat back waiting for Maria's expression to register shock. Nothing happened.

The Earl was a close friend of Royalty, gentry, Prime Ministers and politicians so it would take more to shock Maria than this announcement.

The housekeeper concluded her speech by announcing that Maria would be responsible for the care of the Montgomery's and nothing must go wrong.

On the day of the impending visit Maria had just finished her final check of the Viceroy suite and was closing the door when she became aware of two large brown eyes staring at her. With a smile she stood back opened the door and bade the family welcome.

As she exited the suite she could feel the deep brown eyes boring into her back. She imagined the little boy was nine or ten and thought to herself that one day he would be a heart breaker; he was so beautiful.

Maria smiled some more, wishing the boy could be five or six years older!

For ten days Maria 'gave it her all' in pursuit of excellence for her VIPs; she paid attention to every little detail and always retained a special smile for Johnny whom she found endearing. Then they were gone!

Life moved on, with Maria returning to England to finish her studies but returning each August to gain further experience in the Grand Castle Hotel.

M.A. followed her B.A. (Hons) and after two years gaining management experience Maria 'struck out' on her own.

Nearing seventy now the Earl was happy to let Maria take increasing roles in managing the Castle and the Estates. The Earl smiled indulgently when 'his baby' branched out into 'Premier Catering', Countryside Fayre and locally sourced jams, pickles preserves and country clothing. As Maria increased her business so also did the house visiting benefit everyone's satisfaction.

On her thirtieth birthday Maria started to franchise her brand 'Lady M' confectionary; the list grew with each passing month; then the Grand Castle Hotel expressed an interest in her products.

What could be better, Maria thought than August in the West of Ireland so she booked into the Victoria Suite in readiness for the promotion.

It was sheer coincidence that Jonathan Charles Montgomery IV was booked into the Viceroy Suite at the same time.

Helen, the general manager had really 'laid it on' providing a space for the Lady M display. The banqueting hall was redolent with fragrance from a thousand flowers grown in the hotel gardens.

Helen looked round the setting with pride in a job well done for a young woman she considered her protégé. In the twenty years since Maria first came to the Grand Castle Hotel she had grown to become a beautiful and elegant young lady. Despite her growing success and social elevation Maria had returned each year during the month of August to learn more from Helen. Helen smiled to herself knowingly; both 'girls' knew that August was a social rather than a professional event but neither 'were talking'.

Maria and Helen spent the final hours preparing screens, IT and laid out their stalls. Both smiled quietly to themselves that everything that could be done was done. Now it was time for Maria to sell herself to the assembled businessmen and women.

Everything was going well, the audience was alert and interested, occasionally asking questions and smiling at Lady Maria's anecdotes and especially at her profit projections. Almost three quarters way through her speech Maria became aware of a tall, well dressed young man standing just inside the door that was half way down the hall.

Even though he was several feet away Maria could feel his eyes staring fixedly at her. The final ten minutes of her presentation became incredibly difficult as Maria's awareness of the young man's stare increased.

Maria was standing still accepting the applause from her audience when once more she glanced across towards the young man. As she did so a wisp of hair fell across her left eyebrow; she flicked the recalcitrant hair and that was when the young man smiled.

For the next hour Maria was inundated by questions and comments from her potential customers but through it all she became increasingly aware of the deep brown eyes that were fixated upon her.

Eventually only Maria, Helen and the young man were left in the hall.

Without any introduction or any attempt at small talk the young man declared, "You are Maria, aren't you?"

Non-plussed Maria nodded, a look of confusion in her eyes.

"I am Johnny" the young man introduced himself. There was still no recognition.

The young man rushed on, as only Americans can, "Twenty years ago you took care of me and my parents in the Viceroy Suite." He waited expectantly but the penny failed to drop. "You were designated to look after us, which you did admirably but then Dad rushed us home."

Vague memories stirred in Maria's soul, "Oh yes, you were the little boy with the beautiful eyes."

Maria and Johnny both blushed before Maria added, "Not so little now."

"No" the young man insisted. Helen slipped away leaving them to their memories.

Then it was time to go their separate ways but Johnny was not going to miss another opportunity, "I suppose you would not care to dine with me tonight?" Maria laughed, "Are you asking me to dinner or are you asking me not to dine?" Her laugh lilt up her face. Johnny blushed again, "I would be honoured if you would dine with me" he stuttered.

"I would love to" Maria answered, "the Elizabethan dining room at eight o'clock?"

"Great" Johnny practically whooped "I will arrange it."

Since developing her business Maria was always known for her elegance and gracefulness but this evening she spent more time than usual in preparing for her 'date'.

Johnny spent the waiting time in a tizzy of showers, checking and rechecking his appearance and eventually it was time. Johnny had been in the guests' lounge when Maria 'floated in'. He immediately leapt to his feet, well aware that every guest in the room had their eyes firmly fixed on Maria.

Taking courage Johnny met his 'date' with a light kiss on the cheek. The subtle expensive perfume wafted over him as he took Maria's hand and led her to the dining room.

As the head waiter guided them to their table Johnny thanked the Lord that his fifty euro tip had worked its magic. Seated in the bay of the window their privacy was total, the view across the lawns to the mighty lake illuminated by subtle lighting. A soft breeze played with the bushes while the fragrance from the gardens carried the diners to a magical place.

The meal was perfect, the service subtle and unobtrusive and the small talk during the entrée was replaced with something else. Perhaps it was the romantic music provided by the distant harpist, maybe it was the magic of the moonlight or maybe it was love. Whatever it was the 'chemistry' grew and intensified, augmented by accidental touches of hands or knees beneath the table, Johnny's brown eyes were drawn inexorably into the 'pools of blue' across the table. Far from causing embarrassment Maria responded with an intensity that she had never before experienced. Words became extraneous as Johnny reached over and clasped Maria's hands in his.

Following minutes of rapturous silence Johnny burst out, "When I was eight years old I told my father that I was going to marry you; that was why we were rushed home." Johnny's voice held more than a little regret as staccato like he spat out his defiance, "You see you were only a chambermaid and not good enough for me!" Then he added, "If only he could see you now!"

A deep well of sadness echoed across the years as Maria told Johnny that back then she was Lady Mary, the daughter of an Earl.

Johnny's voice bitterly castigated his father, "He would have loved that, his little son married into British nobility." Maria smiled wistfully but the moment was gone.

Try as they might the chemistry was gone replaced with feelings of regret and opportunities missed. Reluctantly Maria announced, "I must go; I have an early start tomorrow."

"Of course" Johnny replied standing to escort her out of the dining room.

He simply could not let it end like this; taking both Maria's hands in his he declared, "I have loved you for more than twenty years. Tonight has made me love you even more." Despairingly he added, "Can I have any hope for the future?"

Maria's voice was tiny, "I am Her Grace Mary Duchess of ----" the name was lost by the babble of diners.

The look of sadness emanated from her soul as she whispered, "I am married with two sons. The Duke is a good man and I would not do anything to hurt him."

Rising on tiptoe Maria kissed Johnny on the cheek and whispered, "Goodbye."

Johnny stood watching as she walked the length of the corridor. Looking skyward he silently whispered, "Thanks Dad!" with more than a trace of irony.

Part 3

The Staff

Mrs Hughes

Mrs Hughes came to work in The Grand Castle Hotel at the beginning of March nineteen forty seven. Despite being a mere twenty four years old Mrs Hughes had travelled all the way from London for the post of Housekeeper.

Three of the interviewers expressed grave reservations that one so young could manage such a responsible job in the recently refurbished Hotel. Tom Duggan the new owner saw something the others had missed; yes they were all impressed by Mrs Hughes qualifications and experience in a large London Hotel and her references were excellent but Tom detected a quiet self- sufficiency and a determination to succeed. Following discussions with the Board Members he suggested a compromise; a three month trial period at the end of which each party could decide to end the contract.

When Tom relayed the news to Mrs Hughes she visibly relaxed causing Tom his first moment of concern "Oh Thank you" Mrs Hughes gasped "I am most grateful".

Tom noticed the 'cut glass' English accent, thinking it might cause problems for Mrs Hughes here in Ireland. In Connaught nineteen forty seven there was little love lost between Irish and English people but Tom was prepared to follow his 'gut instinct'.

Two months into the job and Mrs Hughes had reduced wastage by twenty percent and staff costs were down by twelve percent. Training schemes had been initiated for all staff with Mrs Hughes providing the expert input.

Each day on his arrival at the Hotel Tom could not help but notice that Mrs Hughes had already been there for some considerable time, had concluded her correspondence, revised the rotas and begun her rounds of the Castle.

Tom had a quiet word with his Directors and offered the job on a permanent basis a full month before the end of the trial period.

Mrs Hughes hesitated "there is something you should know Sir, I have a daughter. Her name is Susan and she is ten months old and I would wish to bring her over to Ireland if my job is to be permanent."

Tom's second moment of concern 'kicked in'. There had been no mention of a child at interview nor during the past two months. Now that she had a permanent post the baby 'appears'. Now Tom was a 'fair-minded' man and, of course Mrs Hughes had no legal reason to inform him of the presence of a child. All that was important was her ability to 'do the job'.

Tom responded "and Mr Hughes will he be coming over?" Mrs Hughes voice carried sadness "there is no Mr Hughes, he is dead!" Her tone of voice prevented any further questioning about her husband.

"How will you manage with a job and a little baby?" Tom asked, more than a little concerned about his Castle.

"I supposed like so many others after this dreadful war I shall have to 'muddle through'. I have rented a house in the village and my mother has promised to join us. She will help with Susan".

Fifteen years later and Tom had never regretted his decision. As far as Tom was concerned Mrs Hughes was a Godsend. On numerous occasions he had offered her promotion, all of which she simply declined. As Housekeeper in the Hotel and as a single parent she believed that she had found a near perfect balance. Promotions would bring more promotions and more responsibilities would mean less time for her beloved daughter. Susan was two years old when Mrs Hughes first brought her to a gala that had been organised in the grounds of the Hotel. If ever a child captivated an audience it was Susan. With a head of blonde curls, sparkly blue eyes, a perpetual smile and the ability to chatter to everybody she met Susan stole everybody's heart. She certainly stole Tom's heart and he stole hers. When Mrs Hughes introduced Susan to her 'Boss' she reached out her arms and was rewarded with a swing through the air. The Boss was rewarded with a squeal of delight and a cry of 'more'.

The apartments were built about the time when Susan started school. One block was designed to provide a member of staff with accommodation, ostensibly to facilitate 'sleep overs' but in reality to maintain order in that area. Tom assured Mrs Hughes that she would be the ideal tenant. The 'town house' contained three good sized bedrooms, a living room, kitchen, bathroom and a study where Susan could work or play. An additional benefit was a good sized private garden at the rear of the property.

Ms Hughes still had reservations "What would happen to her if she was fired or someone else took over the running of the Hotel?"

Tom dismissed her concerns with a laugh "I'm not selling, I'm not going to sack you and the tenancy is rent free. Effectively you are getting a substantial rise to your income". Tom went on to point out with Susan at school there would be added costs, so any extra money would be very useful.

Mrs Hughes had to agree so next day she and Susan moved into their 'turnkey' town house. On the first evening of her residency Tom dropped in to see if 'everything was ok?"

Mrs Hughes was having a cup of drinking chocolate prior to retiring for the night. The rich chocolatey aroma accosted Tom's nostrils, provoking a memory from childhood. "You know Mrs Hughes, my mother used to make drinking chocolate for me every night before I went to bed!" He stood gazing into the past "I do miss her and I haven't had drinking chocolate since she died."

How could she not offer a cup of the amazing 'elixir'? As they sat together sharing their bed time drink Mrs Hughes asked her first personal question in five years. "It's easy to make" she claimed "why don't you have it now?"

Tom's laugh was more than a little embarrassed "Nobody to make it for me and I'm too lazy to bother myself!"

Mrs Hughes blushed prettily, Tom thought, "I'm sorry for prying, I was not trying to be nosy" she said.

"I know" Tom laughed now more at ease.

Having finished his cup Tom rose to leave "I think I will invite myself around for a nightcap more often. That was lovely and it was a joy talking with you."

"Anytime" Mrs Hughes responded.

For ten years Tom dropped in for his cocoa, then to help Susan with her homework, then to give advice about the garden. Throughout it all their professional relationship never wavered; though Tom became 'Uncle Tom' to Susan he was always 'Sir' to Mrs Hughes and she was 'Mrs Hughes' to him.

Staff soon learned about the Boss, Housekeeper relationship but not one person suspected that it was anything more than friendship. And friendship was all it was. Both would have been shocked if anyone considered that there was anything illicit about their friendship.

In late autumn of nineteen sixty two Tom dropped his bombshell over their usual Friday night 'cocoa'. "I've had an offer for the Castle" he announced.

"Oh!" Mrs Hughes pretended not to be perturbed. In reality her heart was racing and what would happen to her little tete a tete, she looked forward to them so much. No doubt Tom would leave the area and the thought depressed her more than she thought possible.

"An American Consortium have made a fantastic offer" Tom added "and I not getting any younger!"

In their fifteen years together Mrs Hughes had never discussed age or anything like that, but now she 'had' to know. "What age are you?" she asked.

"I will be fifty next month" he smiled "a nice ago to retire don't you think?"

"Not at all" Mrs Hughes protested "you are far too young to sit and do nothing!"

"I hadn't planned on doing 'nothing'" Tom protested "I have my eyes on a property at the upper end of the lough. It comes with forty acres of good arable land and has fishing rights on the lough. I thought I might try my hand at market gardening and mixed farming in a small way". On impulse Tom added "would you like to come with me to view the property?"

In fifteen years Tom had never invited her to anything, not even dinner in the Castle restaurant, she could barely believe that he was inviting her to see his potential new home. Somewhat demurely Mrs Hughes said "I would like that".

"Then I will arrange a visit" Tom smiled.

Three days later a bemused Castle staff watched open-mouthed as Mrs Hughes stepped into the Boss's Jaguar and they drove off together.

All the way to the 'new' property Tom 'gabbled' excitably about the new house and his plans for the garden centre. Mrs Hughes was struck by the fact that she had never seen him this animated about the Castle and told him so.

"The Castle is my business" Tom responded "but the land is my love. I was raised on a farm and I have always dreamed about going back to that way of life".

Mrs Hughes got quite a shock when she saw the 'new' home. Though substantial and evidently grand at some point it was now dishevelled and severely run down. Built over three floors Tom announced excitably that it was more than three hundred years old and some of the outhouses were even older.

"It looks every day of it" Mrs Hughes thought.

Tom's state of excitement mounted as he showed Mrs Hughes over the property. Words fell from his lips like shell fire as he outlined plan after plan.

Despite the decrepit state of the house Mr Hughes loved the location and told Tom so. Tom responded like a grateful child beaming from ear to ear at her approval. As they drove home Tom spoke quietly "I am going to make an offer on the property".

For many months things returned to normal. Cocoa on Friday nights, impromptu 'call ins' to help Susan with her homework then Tom announced his intentions. The Hotel was sold and his new property had been completely restored. All he needed was advice and 'a woman's touch to turn the house into a home.

Again they drove to the 'new' house. Mrs Hughes could hardly believe the difference; it gleamed line a new pin in the summer sun. Inside was even better and yes, it did need a woman's touch. Tom ran excitedly in front of her pointing out things that she could clearly see for herself.

"You like it?" he asked anxiously. "I love it" Mrs Hughes responded "you should be very happy here".

Tom looked straight into her eyes "Would you come?" he asked. Mrs Hughes hesitated then demurred "Thank you for the offer, but I am very happy in my job at the Castle and I don't think I would leave it for any other job" Mrs Hughes voice contained a little sorrow.

"I'm not offering you a job Mrs Hughes, I'm asking you to marry me" Tom declared.

Mrs Hughes shock was palpable "Marry you, marry you, are you sure?" she asked.

"I'm very sure" Tom declared.

"Then I have to share a secret with you and it may affect how you feel" Mrs Hughes voice dropped to a whisper. "There is no Mr Hughes; there never was a Mr Hughes. Susan was conceived as a result of a drunken escapade with an American Airman on V.E. night. Two firsts in one night" she added somewhat shamefacedly "I had never tasted alcohol until that night and as for ..." she left the sentence hanging. Then she brightened "not that I have ever regretted having Susan, she is the best thing that ever happened for me!" Mrs Hughes waited just a moment then added "you may now wish to retract your proposal!"

Tom's voice was steady "then perhaps I should let you into my secret. I've known the truth about you and Susan since a very few weeks following the start of your employment at the Castle. The Hotel and catering industry is a very incestuous world filled with gossip and rumour, everybody knows everybody else. A girl who worked with you in London is a cousin of one of the Chambermaids who got great delight in telling me about 'the fallen woman'.

"So everybody knows about me?" Mrs Hughes interjected.

"No one knows about you" Tom assured her "I swore the Chambermaid to secrecy. I also know some salacious material about her that she could not afford to have in the public domain. So you see, your secret is safe".

"I do hope it might be a case of third time lucky" Tom smiled nervously "Will you marry me Mrs Hughes?"

Mrs Hughes smiled "Then yes, I would be proud to be your wife."

Tom had one more thing to say, "Do you mind if I call you Margaret, Mrs Hughes?"

They both laughed.

Helen

Helen lived all of her life in the shadow of the Castle. As a child she would play along the river following its course to the great edifice. Helen would sit for hours inventing love stories, murders, kidnapping and skulduggery around the grandeur of the ancient Castle. She would create imaginings about dangerous escapes across the lough, hunts on the magnificent estate or romance on the river to Galway.

The Castle was central to Helen's life from the moment she was born in a tiny back room of a terraced house in a village abutting the Castle grounds. Primary school was just across the road from the main Castle entrance and big school was less than a mile away.

While others beavered feverishly for academic achievements, Helen paid little or no attention to her studies, her only ambition to spend her lifetime working in the glamour of the Castle.

Leaving school in nineteen fifty eight without a single qualification Helen soon discovered the need for evidence of self-discipline and education. Knuckling down to evening classes she spent the next two years gaining the requisite five subjects. Helen presented herself back at the Castle, grasping her five 'bare' passes and carrying dreams of a management position.

The owner of the Hotel, a kindly man, brought Helen into the real world! Management trainees came armed with degrees and were often undertaking 'Masters'. The disappointment on Helen's face 'told its own story'. "What would you be prepared to work at?" the owner asked. "The only job I can offer you is as cleaner" the owner explained but, perhaps if you apply yourself, there would be a promotion for you in the future".

Helen's life 'turned' on that sentence "Oh yes" she would apply herself "she would be the best cleaner the Castle ever had. She would show them!"

Back at home when she told her mother that she was starting working the following Monday as a Cleaner at the Castle, mother was less than impressed "you have qualifications" she declared "why would you want to be a Cleaner?

"I won't always be a cleaner I can assure you" Helen's determination caused her mother to look up "but dear you have never really applied yourself to anything". Mother detected the hurt "I am not criticising" she added hurriedly "but you have always been a dreamer, living in your own world".

Helen did not bother to explain that that world was the Castle, the lough and the estate.

First day at work and the determined Helen set about her work with a new found fervour. She may only be a cleaner but she was going to be the best cleaner in the world. She may
157

not quite have achieved that ambition but she certainly was the best cleaner in the Castle! She came in early, worked late, often worked through lunch breaks and took pride in the fact that her area shone. During times of staff shortages Helen gained experience in the kitchens, cleaning, helping to cook and prepare and present food; in the dining room she learned the skills of good 'waiting' and was, by far, the most efficient Chambermaid when she was in that role. Mrs Hughes, the Housekeeper admired the new recruit's application to work, her warmth, flexibility and willingness to go the extra mile. One year into the job and Mrs Hughes appointed Helen to the position of Supervisor. Though it meant only one shilling an hour's increase in wages Helen's pleasure was untold;' she was on her way.

For the following year Helen was Mrs Hughes' eyes and ears. Not only had she introduced new shift patterns, altered or amended inefficient practices and 'took up the cudgel' when staff failed to appear on duty, in many ways she emulated the great Mrs Hughes. Nearing the end of her second year of employment in the Castle Helen was summoned to Mrs Hughes' office. Mrs Hughes dropped her bombshell "the Castle was being sold and she was going to marry Tom and move with him to their farm, some miles away".

Helen stood 'mouth agape' "I didn't know about you and the Boss" she eventually managed to gasp.

"Neither did I" laughed Mrs Hughes "but the fact is I shall be leaving and I've recommended you for the job of Housekeeper".

Helen could hardly believe her ears, "but I'm only nineteen, well nearly twenty" she gasped.

"I was not much older than that when I first came here" Mrs Hughes reminded her. "I believe you are the person to carry on the traditions that I have established. I have already spoken to Tom about it" she added "and he has related my recommendation to the new owners; they have agreed subject to a six month's trial period".

Mrs Hughes wasn't finished yet "I want you to shadow me, starting next Monday. In the meantime shed that uniform, we are going into the city to purchase your new clothes."

Helen could barely wait to tell her mother. The moment her duty finished she rushed home, bursting in and yelling her amazing news. Mother, being more pragmatic asked "does it mean more money?" Helen had forgotten to ask!

Five years as Housekeeper and the new owners recognised her talents by funding Helen to undertake a degree in Hospitality Management, followed by a Masters in Management. So, 'hooked' on academia Helen then funded herself to undertake an MBA.

As she stood waiting her turn to walk across the stage Helen believed that all her dreams had come true "just imagine" she thought "MA MBA BA her teachers would never believe it"!

As she stood in the queue to return her rented cap and gown she received a tap on the shoulder. "Congratulations" grinned Tony a fellow student through four years and two 'Masters'. "You, too" returned Helen "it's a great relief to be finished with study!"

"Not entirely" Tony responded "I shall miss seeing you". Helen stared in complete surprise "why would you miss me when you have never spoken to me in four years?"

Tony blushed "I never felt able to pluck up the courage!"

"The courage to do what?" Helen asked, bemused.

"To ask you out on a date" came Tony's sheepish reply.

"A date?" Helen reiterated.

"Yes, a date! Am I that ugly that you could not consider that?"

"Not at all" Helen replied "it's just that I've never been on a date. I wouldn't know what to do!"

"You've never been on a date!" Tony's voice was shock filled.

"No. I've always been too busy with my work!" Helen answered.

"Well, you're not busy now and I would love to take you out on a date" Tony asserted.

"A date" Helen repeated "a date to do what?"

"Well we could start with dinner and see how it goes" Tony smiled.

"Ok" said Helen "anywhere but the Castle".

"Why not the Castle?" Tony asked.

"Because I work there". It was Helen's turn to laugh.

Much to her surprise Helen enjoyed her date immensely. Tony was great company, funny, articulate, obviously well- educated but most of all a great listener. Helen poured out the intricacies of her job and her ambitions for the future, while Tony listened intently. Dinner finished Tony asked if he could drive her home, a not unpleasant idea to Helen. Outside her apartment Helen shook Tony's hand and thanked him for a wonderful evening: he sat bemused for several moments even after she had shut her front door.

On her return to work the General Manager sent for Helen, congratulated her on another fine achievement and made her an offer she could not refuse. The owners were keen to show their gratitude for Helen's endeavours and were prepared to create a new position for her. Doubtless Helen had developed a vast knowledge of hotel management but now, it was felt she should extend her talents. The owners would create a new post of Estate Manager with equal status and salary to that of the Hotel Manager. Helen would be charged with turning the outside environment from a place of beauty to a place of beauty and profit. All the outside staff would be accountable to Helen and she would report directly to the General Manager.

Initially daunted by her lack of experience Helen sought guidance from the Head Gardener; his concerns related only to preventing his prize gardens being destroyed. So Helen struck out blindly! She spent two weeks walking over every inch of the twenty thousand acre estate, then she examined the lough. "Such assets" Helen thought "and so underused". For an entire month she put the theories she had learned to good use, finally producing her 'business plan'.

Initial plans included development of a golf course for residents and outsiders, a riding school that would include pony trekking, gymkhana and dressage. Helen felt the lough was very underused and proposed the purchase of a boat to carry guests around the islands, perhaps providing picnics, angling and sightseeing. Windsurfing, banana boating and a sectioned off kiddies area figured in her plans.

As she sat in the General Manager's office outlining her ideas, her boss began to wonder what had been unleashed upon them. "I suppose you don't happen to have costed these plans?" the General Manager asked.

Helen had, and when she placed the figures before him his face turned a deathly white. "I will bring these to the Board" he promised, without much confidence in his voice. Much to his great surprise the Board immediately approved the plans and Helen set to work.

Three years in and the Estate Manager returned her first annual profit. Two further years and the ever extending outside business produced much greater returns than the Grand Castle Hotel. At end of year Helen allowed herself a glass of champagne in celebration.

Working her way through her in-tray, Helen discovered an invitation to the five year reunion dinner and dance for her MBA Course. "Oh dear" she wondered "where had the years gone and what ever happened to that nice man, Tony?" She supposed he was married with a family. For several moments Helen reflected on what might have been, but then he had never asked her out again!

On impulse Helen decided to attend the event which was being held in the city. Over the weeks Helen vacillated, first she was too busy, then she wondered about the others but finally she admitted to herself that she would like to see Tony again.

Through dinner and the speeches Helen upbraided herself for wasting her time by coming to the reunion. She could remember neither lecturers nor fellow students, besides she was far too busy. The speeches became increasingly boring and Helen made the decision to 'slip away' before the dancing started.

Helen was on her way to the cloakroom to collect her coat when the familiar voice interrupted her passage "So you decided to come!" Tony declared "I had a bet with myself that you would be too busy!"

"Why would I be too busy?" Helen asked a trifle crossly.

"Well, you were always too busy to return my calls." Tony's voice held more than a little sarcasm and lack of belief.

"Your calls" Helen asked, looking confused.

"Yes, my calls, your Receptionist left me in no doubt that you did not appreciate my attention". Tony's voice held disappointment.

"But you never called!" Helen was adamant.

"I rang every day for a month" Tony assured her "but you were always out. After a month I finally got the message!"

Then Helen remembered "I was out, I had just been given a new job and I spent more than a month walking over the estate, holding meetings and visiting other facilities."

Making a mental note to rebuke a Receptionist for a five year old lapse Helen said "Had I known you were ringing I would have returned your calls."

"Would you really?" Tony asked.

"Yes, really" Helen responded.

"Then perhaps you would dance with me?" Tony asked. Helen looked directly into his eyes and declared "actually I was on way to collect my coat and go back to my hotel", then she noticed his disappointed look "but I think I will change my mind. Yes I would like to dance with you!"

Helen felt good in Tony's arms and as the night progressed, she allowed her head to rest on his shoulder. A feeling of warmth, comfort, companionship and something more embraced Helen who had a growing awareness of the colour rising in her cheeks. The band stopped, the late night chatter faded and Tony asked if he might escort Helen to her hotel?

161

Helen was pleased beyond words. Back at the hotel Helen asked if Tony would like to come in for a drink. Tony would like and together they walked to Helen's room where she raided the mini bar. When Helen was returning to the mini bar to refresh Tony's drink he intercepted her, took her in his arms and kissed her passionately.

Tony paused, seeking tacit approval to go further when Helen rather breathlessly whispered "thirty seven and I have just had my first kiss."

Tony stepped back in stunned amazement "what do you mean, your first kiss?"

"Just that" Helen responded "that was my first kiss!"

"But you are beautiful Helen, dozens of men must have wanted you!" Tony's voice still contained shock and some disbelief.

"Nevertheless it is absolutely true and I am glad it was with you" Helen said blushing furiously.

If Tony had harboured any lustful intentions, Helen's words had ended them. Again taking her in his arms he kissed her lightly on the lips and said "goodnight". Then added "I will ring, perhaps you will tell your Receptionist to allow Tony's calls to go 'through'."

Helen sat gazing at herself in the bedroom mirror, everything was changed yet she looked the same. Her feelings had changed yet she was the only one to notice.

Tony did ring and then he rang again. They had a proper date in the middle of the second week following the reunion dinner. By the end of three months Helen decided that she and Tony were a couple and three months later she realised that she was in love.

Eight months into the relationship Helen and Tony were dining quietly in the village. As usual the food was delicious, the barman charming and the waitress most helpful. Towards the end of the meal Helen noticed that Tony was unusually quiet, not joking or making the usual quips about her excessive workload. "Is something wrong, Tony?" Helen asked.

"Yes Helen, something is very wrong" Tony answered through gritted teeth "do you know how many times you cancelled this meal?" Before Helen could speak Tony answered his own query "Five times you have had to pull out at the last minute!" Then he added "and how many times has the Castle paged you since you came out? Three" he said bitterly "three times you have to interrupt the meal to go and ring work!"

Tony's bitterness and frustration roared up "have you any idea of the number of times you have cancelled our dates?" Helen looked blank. "No, I didn't think so".

Tony spat the number out "forty eight times in eight months I have had to make other arrangements".

"It cannot be that many!" Helen's tone was apologetic.

"You know what the problem is?" Tony asked, standing up "in your drive to be a career woman you forgot how to be a woman".

Helen had no answer, she had no reassurances that she could give, every word that Tony uttered was true.

"Goodbye Helen" Tony whispered dropping several large denomination euro notes on the table.

The barman had overheard the exchange and placed a glass, well filled with brandy into her hand.

Helen sat there staring into nowhere for ages, then she laid down her drink and left.

Perhaps that is when Helen made the decision that she would dedicate her life to her career. There would never be another Tony!

In nineteen eighty four Helen celebrated a major milestone in her life. At just over forty one years old Helen was appointed as General Manager for the Hotel and Estate with a substantial raise of salary and numerous subtle 'perks'.

Helen ran the Hotel with clerical efficiency couple with positive people skills, adding an indoor swimming pool, spa, beauty salon and inviting businesses to 'franchise' within the complex. With the onset of the nineteen nineties and the computer/IT era Helen 'moved with the times' 'selling' her product to a world-wide audience.

Nineteen ninety five was the first time that Bob came to the Hotel. He was everything that Tony was not. Where Tony was tall, handsome with a shock of reddish hair, Bob was little taller than Helen herself. At five feet seven inches tall Bob was never going to be seen as a John Wayne figure; the fact that he was plump, balding and plain meant that he would never be a 'leading man'. What he did have though was endless optimism, a cheerfulness that belied the sufferings and loss he had experienced and a 'happiness' that transferred to everything he touched.

Bob represented a large brewing company and he sought Helen's agreement for exclusively for his products. In return the Castle could sell their beers, ciders and lagers for twenty per cent less than their rivals.

Helen wasn't sure, considering the customers' tastes to be more important than profit margins in this instance.

"Look", Bob insisted" let me take you for dinner and I will convince you of the sense in my proposal."

Much to the surprise of the staff Helen agreed to dinner. As she recounted her outing to her Manager she was clearly tickled pink. "I don't think I have laughed so much in years, I have never met such a genuinely funny man". Helen enthused. Her Deputy was too kind to point out that no one had seen Helen laugh for years.

Over a second dinner with Bob, Helen let him down gently. What he was proposing was a great business idea but she would not be following it up.

Bob laughed out loud "You don't have to sound so worried" he laughed "I will work on you until you agree to my proposal".

And work he did! Twice a year Bob turned up at the Castle with his 'business proposal', and twice a year Helen turned it down, usually over hilarious dinners. The millennium and Bob had a new proposal; he had won a cruise around the Norwegian Fjords and would be pleased if Helen would accompany him. Bob had made his proposal over afternoon tea and the shock was enough to make Helen splutter over her creamed scone.

"What exactly are you asking?" Helen queried.

"I am well aware that the best I can hope for is your friendship and that is all I ask!"

Helen had not been on a holiday for five years and she did enjoy the company of this jolly, little man. "Separate cabins and friendship only?" Helen asked.

Bob nodded.

Ten days in the Fjords were idyllic with Helen visibly relaxing with every passing day. On the final night of their cruise Bob and Helen sat on deck enjoying the stillness and the majesty of the stars. Then Helen detected something she had never seen before, with Bob ... sadness!

"Something wrong?" she asked.

"Not wrong, exactly" Bob answered, "it's just that I hate going home to an empty house. The only reason I 'stay on the road' is to assuage the loneliness, God knows, I don't need the money." Helen raised her eyebrows quizzically.

"My wife and daughter were killed in a car accident nearly fifteen years ago and my life ended. Every year since then has only been existence."

"But you are always so funny, cracking jokes and making everyone around you happy" Helen offered.

Bob's voice had an ocean of sadness "the tears of the clown, the tears of the clown!"

Spontaneously Helen reached out and gripped Bob's hand declaring "you will always have me!"

"Yes" responded Bob "but only as a friend! I never wanted anyone else since Molly died, but you changed all that. I suppose you wouldn't marry me out of pity" Bob laughed sadly.

"I'm sorry Bob." Helen answered. And she really was!

The cruise created a precedent. For ten years the friends had bi-annual holidays together; to Egypt, Turkey, The Bahamas, France, Spain, Italy and once to Australia.

On every single occasion Bob asked Helen to marry him; on every single occasion Helen's answer was the same. "I'm sorry Bob, just friendship".

In two thousand and ten the staff of The Grand Castle Hotel together with the 'outside' staff planned a surprise party. For weeks there were secret meetings behind closed doors, whisperings that ceased if Helen appeared. Had Helen been in any way paranoid, she would have believed the staff were plotting against her.

But nothing could be further from the truth. The great day arrived and the Hotel Manager rang Helen to tell her there was a problem in the banqueting hall. Mildly irritated about being called away from the accounts Helen entered the hall to be met with a thunderous refrain "For she's a jolly good fellow, for she's a jolly good fellow" the staff clapped and cheered. "What is all this?" Helen asked, having genuinely forgotten that this was her fiftieth anniversary at the Castle. Bob led the queue with the largest bouquet of red roses that she had ever seen "typical of him" she thought "totally flamboyant". The tributes seemed to go on forever. Then dinner was served with Helen and Bob as guests of honour.

Helen smiled indulgently at her 'boys and girls'. Looking over the collective assembly she realised that she had handpicked every last one of them. The room crackled with excitement, joy and appreciation of a great leader.

It started off with a tightness in her abdomen. Indigestion thought Helen. At least it can't be a heart attack, Helen thought, no central gripping pain nor no pain going down her left arm. I must have listened to something on those first aid courses. Then the pain crashed in!

Bob looked almost as pale as Helen felt "Oh God" he gasped "don't let this happen. Send for an ambulance. Now" he shouted.

The paramedics arrived to find Helen seated with Bob holding her hand; they did their observations and inserted an i/v infusion.

"I'm going with you to the hospital" Bob announced. Bob held her hand all the way to Galway. As they bounced over the roads Bob leaned over and kissed Helen on the forehead, "I love you, you know and I really do want to marry you" he managed through his tears.

"Don't be silly, I'll be fine in a day or two!" Helen whispered wearily. "Did you ever count the number of times you proposed? No. I suppose not, twenty nine, you silly old fool."

Bob knelt down beside her in the ambulance "Ok" he said "for the thirtieth time will you marry me?"

Helen smiled.

At the hospital Helen was placed on a trolley and rushed to the intensive care unit. Bloods were taken, lines were attached and the Surgeon announced the need for an angiogram. He explained the procedure to her and assured her that he had performed the procedures many times. One of the Nurses administered an intra muscular injection and began to wheel Helen into the operating suite.

Just prior to entry Helen called out "Stop, I must speak to Bob."

The Nurse reassured her that she would see Bob in less than an hour; but Helen was insistent, "she must see Bob, now!"

Reluctantly the Nurse rang Reception and Bob was accompanied to the theatre entrance. Taking Helen's hand Bob announced "I'm here, Helen!"

"Yes, Bob" Helen smiled "the answer is Yes!"

Bob's smile creased his face, "I shall be waiting for you!"

Bob was pacing in the waiting room when the Surgeon rushed through the rubberised doorway. In forty minutes Bob's emotions had changed from exhilaration to frantic worry. After more than ten years she had finally said "Yes". Dare he hope for a better future?

The Surgeon's face told Bob another story "I'm sorry Sir, we lost her just as we commenced the angiogram!"

Sean and Billy

Sean grew up in a Catholic ghetto in West Belfast. The son of a notorious hard man, Sean was everything his father was not; soft, gentle, kind and ... homosexual. Naturally he could never 'come out' as he was all too aware of his father's feelings about 'queers'. Over the years Sean had witnessed gay and lesbian people being beaten, tarred and feathered and knee capped because of their orientation. In his early teens Sean had fought desperately against his nascent homosexual urges, joining gangs and indulging in 'queer bashing'. There was nothing effeminate about Sean; daily he attended the local gym, also played football, joined the boxing club, had his hair cut short and had his arms decorated with bizarre tattoos. As the son of a 'hard man' Sean was afforded a great deal of respect and had real kudos in the community. At sixteen years old he managed to have 'a relationship' with a nice enough girl from school. When she finally ended it Sean was less than heartbroken. Now twenty one and a heavy drinker, like his father, Sean had never again had a girlfriend. In truth, all through his teenage years Sean wrestled with his inner feelings, at first denying them, then despising them before finally accepting that this was who he was.

Plucking up all his courage Sean confessed his terrible secret to his mother. At first all his mother could gasp was "does your father know?"

Sean admitted that he could not bring himself to tell his father. "Thank heavens for that" his poor distressed mother wailed. "Your father would kill you, if he knew." She went on to say that such an admission would have an adverse effect on his father's position 'on the street'.

Not once did his mother seek explanation or comfort him. It seemed to Sean that all that mattered was his father's reputation. His mother looked Sean in the eye "You don't look like a queer, have you done the filthy action?"

Sean reeled back in shock at his mother's revulsion. "Only a small minority of gays are camp" he answered "and no I have never had a gay experience!"

"Then how do you know you are queer?" his mother demanded. "I just know" Sean responded.

His mother's final words made his decision for him. "Never tell your father, nor anyone else around here" she hissed.

Sean left home the following morning without so much as leaving a note of goodbye.

Billy came to work in East Belfast when he was sixteen years old. Raised in the 'Bible belt of Northern Ireland' growing up had been a misery for him. By the time he was twelve years old Billy knew that he was 'different'. He had no desire to play rugby, football or gymnastics, preferring to indulge in more artistic matters. Teased mercilessly by his schoolmates, Billy soon learned that he was a 'queer'. The teasing turned to bullying and four miserable years at secondary school left Billy traumatised and totally lacking in self-confidence. Billy did not deliberately become increasingly feminine. If he was 'camp' he simply did not know it. It was the way he walked and maybe he did exaggerate his hand movements when he wanted to make a point, but so what, that was just Him!

At Church each Sunday Billy soon learned that he would roast in hell as he now knew that he was homosexual. He was an abomination, a product of Sodom and Gomorrah and doomed to an eternity in hell. Every family in Billy's area was some shade of Presbyterianism, his own family being members of the right wing Free Presbyterian Church. The views of the charismatic President of the Church filtered through every ordained minister; 'He' was a God of retribution, sinners must repent or be destroyed, Billy was on the path to hell.

Taking his leave just as soon as he finished school Billy headed for the 'liberalism' of Belfast. During his first week in Belfast Billy learned about peace walls to separate Protestants and Catholic communities. There he was instructed in the finer arts of them and us; taigs and prods! Billy was a fast learner; he would seek lodgings and work amongst his 'own'.

East Belfast was a mere mile or so away from West Belfast but it might just as well have been on a separate planet. Where West Belfast was bedecked with tricolours, Catholic Churches, 'Fenians' and IRA men, the East was 'pure' loyalist. Kerbstones painted red, white and blue, union flags at every window not a 'Fenian' in sight and Protestant Churches everywhere. Like the West, East Belfast had its hard men and one of them offered the 'camp' Billy a job in his pub. A month later the hard man offered a different position in his bed. For three years Billy fancied himself in love. Maybe his boyfriend did beat him up occasionally but that was only because he was jealous and besides, it showed Billy just how much he loved him. Besides there were many compensations in being the boyfriend of a hard man; nobody teased, scoffed, nor insulted, nor laid a hand on him in anger, Billy thought, he had must for which to be thankful.

Then his lover 'put him in hospital'. Billy woke from surgery, aching all over. With a fractured jaw, three broken ribs, damaged kidneys and two severely blackened eyes Billy knew it was time to move on.

By coincidence Sean and Billy travelled together on the 'Enterprise', the Belfast to Dublin express train. The coincidences continued as they caught the same bus to Galway.

Billy was soon 'snapped up' for his bar skills in The Grand Castle Hotel while Sean 'bummed' around Galway.

Sean was sitting reading the evening paper at the rear of a riverside pub in the City when he heard the 'gay-baiting'. A young man, minding his own business, was being taunted by two skin head thugs. Though it was none of his business, Sean stood up and ambled over to the 'gay baiting'.

"I think my friend would like you to leave" he informed the skin heads. One of the punks began to bluster but the other held him back with a firm hand on his elbow. One look at Sean with his 'boxer's' frame and six foot of muscle had convinced the punk that the fun was over.

"Only teasing!" he claimed.

"My friend would like you to apologise". Sean told the punks. Heads downcast, apologies were muttered.

Billy beamed "would you care to join me for a drink?" he asked.

"Don't mind if I do" responded Sean.

One drink led to two, to three to four ...

Eventually Sean slurred "have you any place to stay?"

Billy had forgotten all about getting home.

"You can sleep on my settee, if you wish!" Sean offered.

Over breakfast Sean learned that Billy worked at the Castle. He also learned that the Castle were looking for waiters and outdoor staff. Sean laughed "I can't see me in a uniform in a dining room?"

"I don't know" Billy returned the laugh "maybe you would clean up all right". Besides it would be nice to have another 'Northerner' at the Hotel, Billy added.

"Even if it was a 'taig' from West Belfast?" Sean asked. It makes no difference, Billy was adamant.

Though Billy was 'the only queer in the village' like the TV show claimed he was popular with everyone. Besides, if there were any homophobes Sean was always there to take care of his friend.

At the end of the 'season' both men were asked to stay one and become permanent members of staff. Both men were happy to say yes. With new permanent jobs Billy got 'digs' in the Castle apartments while Sean was quartered in one of the converted labourer's cottages. Living in luxury, as Sean put it.

For two years Sean and Billy plied their trades in their tranquil surroundings, increasingly enjoying each other's company inside and outside of work. Billy was absolutely sure that he loved Sean and Sean was absolutely sure that he loved Billy. They just did not know how the other felt.

In May two thousand and fifteen the Republic of Ireland voted **yes** to legalise marriage for same sex couples as Sean and Billy shared a pint in the Hotel lounge. "Now you two guys can get married" the barmaid called across.

Sean was immediately on the defensive "did she say guys or gays?" he asked his companion.

"It doesn't really matter" Billy responded reaching out and taking Sean's hand!

Charlotte & Simone

Eve brought Charlotte and Simone in as 'Ambassadors' soon after she had purchased The Grand Castle Hotel. In a feeble attempt at a joke Eva told her senior staff not to worry Charlotte and Simone's expenses would not come out of their budgets. As they would report directly to her both Charlotte and Simone would be paid from Eva's personal account.

The two ladies sat impervious to such mundane matters as money. If it were possible to be anymore imperial than the glacier, haughty Proprietress then Charlotte and Simone achieved it without any effort on their part. As they sat enthroned on classic Queen Ann chairs on either side of Eva they exuded an air of cold menace, aloof imperialism and a total indifference to the minions seated before them. Rather unnecessarily Eva introduced the ladies as identical twins; a fact that was readily apparent to anyone with half an eye. Everything about then was identical size, hair, eye colouring, the same haughty look. In short they presented an image of a formidable pair.

Soon all sorts of rumours began to circulate about the ladies; Eva had brought them in to 'clean up' a new acquisition in Thailand, they were really spies for Eva, reporting everything back as required, they were part of this new Health and Safety thing that was causing so much trouble for everybody, the stories grew with every passing week.

Two things did emerge with the passage of time; one no matter how hard staff tried to be friendly or to provide tasty indictments the twins totally ignored them. Then, on Eva's return they would be inside her office within fifteen minutes, doubtlessly being catty about all and sundry. Secondly, despite outward appearances of togetherness Charlotte and Simone loathed each other. Their hatred of each other was such that they refused to dine together, nor would they share the same quarters. To most staff it seemed that they tried to sleep as far apart as possible.

As the years rolled onwards the ladies took on more and more responsibilities, without recourse to anyone. Neither General Manager, Manager nor Housekeeper ever challenged the twins, assuming they had the 'ear' of the Proprietress and no one wished to displease her.

With never so much as a nod to management staff, Charlotte and Simone poked their elegant noses into the deepest, darkest, murkiest parts of the Castle, ignoring even disparaging remarks from guests and visitors. This was their realm; everyone else was a mere minion in the ladies kingdom.

For their own purposes the ladies then reorganised their work schedules. Charlotte continued to prioritise the inner working of the Castle while Simone spent increasing amounts of time outside. Causing great chagrin with gardening staff, Simone left markers all around the estate, demanding immediate attention. Despite Charles, the Head Gardener's protest to the Manager about Simone's behaviour, no rebuke was brought to her attention. The Manager was an ambitious young man with ideas of further promotion across the water to

London; there was no way he was going to alienate Eva because of the concerns of a few gardeners.

With the passage of time Charlotte grew fat and lazy yet Eva never intervened nor disciplined her for her lack of activity. Staff were not blind, seeing Eva's indulgence as a carte blanche to do as the fat twin pleased. Such favouritism inevitably led to petty jealousies and muttered threats against the pair but the imperious ladies remained aloof, showing not one iota of concern about such underlings.

Then one morning 'fat' Charlotte failed to arrive for breakfast. The Housekeeper despatched one of the Waitresses to wake the lazy lady. The Waitress was only seventeen years old and had never seen a dead body before; the scream had escaped her lips before she could suppress it. Chef and the Housekeeper came running, fearing some foul deed had been committed. Chef recovered first. "Someone should check on Simone, I've heard that twins often die within hours of each other."

The Housekeeper took one look at the trembling Waitress and announced "Not you dear, you've already had too much shock, I will go."

Just as the Chef had claimed Simone was also found dead in her bed.

The Housekeeper hurried to the General Manager's office. No doubt Eva would have to be told and perhaps, the Garda in case there had been a crime committed. The Manager knelt by the electric socket while the General Manager was fiddling with some knobs on a strange looking machine. "Charlotte and Simone are dead" gasped the Housekeeper.

"What an odd coincidence" the General Manager remarked "we have just been experimenting with those new- fangled electrical devises that will kill rodents more humanely than our recently deceased Siamese twins!" Thankfully there will be no further need for cats!

Pierre's Pickle

Pierre was a man who was capable of great love. He loved all mankind; he especially loved all womankind; he loved making food but most of all he loved himself. Pierre came highly recommended as Head Chef to The Grand Castle Hotel. At twenty nine years old Pierre was one of the youngest chef's in the world to hold two Michelin Stars for his creations. In Pierre's view the Castle was lucky to have him.

There was no doubt that Pierre had enhanced the reputation of the Castle with clientele coming from all over the world to sample his cuisine. The whole 'Pierre experience' was not limited to simple dining; on several occasions Pierre deigned to converse with his adoring customers.

With his dark curly hair, easy Gallic charm and boyish good looks Pierre was particularly popular with the wives of many middle aged diners.

Perhaps it was jealousy among junior chefs and other kitchen staff that led to rumours that Pierre had a mirror placed strategically in his domain to ensure that he always presented the right image; curly hair just a tiny fraction too long with one strand astray over his left eye.

Eminent Psychologists and Management Strategists have written tomes about the most effective and efficient means of management and leadership but Pierre had his own method for getting the best out of his team. He simply seduced all of his female staff, always delicately and with finesse making them feel special;, most important of all to each member he whispered with devilish Gallic charm "this is our secret, no one else must know that you are my special one!" As with his skills with cuisine Pierre conducted his affairs of the heart with great skill and utmost confidentially.

Ann and Bev were lifelong friends and deadly rivals. Born within minutes of each other, the competition began when the babies were placed beside each other in the nursery. Competing for 'coochie-coos' set the pattern for a lifetime of rivalry. It was always a 'close run thing between the' bright bubbly blonde outgoing Bev and the dark, polite, beguiling Ann. Kindergarten, nursery and primary school and the rivalry continued. There was never any doubt who would be first and second in class; the only speculation would be 'who will win this time'. Nothing changed through secondary school; Bev was first to become a Prefect but Ann pipped her to become Head Girl. Academically the competition continued as both girls gained ten A Stars at 'O' Levels and competed fiercely for who would 'win' at 'A' Levels. For the first time in the history of Education the two girls attained identical scores in each of their four 'A' levels; topping the class, naturally.

Rather than going to Uni, the girls opted for the Army, where they beat the boys at their own game. Graduating from Officer Cadet Training School Bev won the Sword of Honour for best student, with Ann as reserve.

Five years of army experiences and nothing changed; promoted to First Lieutenant on the same day, then attaining their Captaincies together. Just for the hell of it Ann and Bev continued their competitiveness 'pulling' Majors and Colonels, but Ann, with bad grace had to admit defeat when Bev pulled a 'Brigadier General'. Unheard of!

As they stood at ease before their Commanding Officer the girls listened passively as he outlined their achievements and their prospects. If they were to enrol for a further nine years there was no doubt they would attain their Majority within three years and then become Lieutenant Colonels. "Thank you Sir" they replied in unison "this is very kind but we have decided to take a year out, then re-join."

More than a little disappointed (for he had slept with both) the Colonel pointed out that they would lose their seniority and drop down the pecking order; better if they stayed in.

But the girls were determined and one month later, rather than being Senior Captains they were unemployed hitch hikers.

They hiked round England, Wales and Scotland then took the ferry to Belfast. In Ireland they hitched from the North, down the East Coast as far as the South Coast then turned northwards to enjoy the famous West Coast. In Galway city and almost out of money a fellow drinker told them that there were jobs available in The Grand Castle Hotel. Naturally, they hitch hiked and soon obtained positions in the kitchens of the Castle.

Ann was first to 'fall under' Pierre's lascivious eyes. With her dark elegance she could almost pass for French, Pierre thought as he brought his legendary skills to bear. By a strange co-incidence Pierre was already in Pat Carney's bar when Ann walked in. Wednesday evening was her only time off during the week and she valued her time away from the Castle. By closing time she was dancing closely with Pierre, laughing at his jokes and thrilling at his fingers running through her hair. As they stumbled back to Pierre's rooms, Ann assured him that this would be their little secret and nobody else would know; not even Bev. Pierre laughed and called her his 'Wednesday girl'.

Friday was Bev's turn and she 'fell' as easily as Ann had. She felt special to be described as his 'Friday girl'. Miraculously Pierre was still able to carry on his clandestine relations with both girls for more than three months without one knowing about the other, or indeed knowing about any of his other little peccadillos.

On a rare weekend off the friends decided to go into Galway for some little mementos and postcards to send home. Having finished their shopping Ann and Bev were enjoying coffees as they waited for their bus to carry them back to the Castle. They spotted him at the same moment "the cheating b.....d" they cried out in unison as Pierre came out from the cinema, arms around a Waitress from the Hotel. Then a second realisation struck "You too?" they asked simultaneously. Both nodded. Then they plotted their revenge.

174

Back at work on Monday morning both girls behaved with total normality. Unaware that he had been seen Pierre flirted with both at every opportunity, but as always, with the utmost discretion. The day passed as normal with its share of crises, words of congratulations and periods of rest. Back in his rooms, he opened a bottle of fine claret in his kitchenette and strolled into the lounge, throwing himself on to the settee. He immediately leapt to his feet, disgust registering across his handsome face. "What on earth is this?" he muttered, his disgust deepening as the foul odour seeped into everything. No matter where he went the horrible stench followed. He found the first 'parcel' of offal stuffed down the back of the settee, rotten fish sewn into the curtains and excrement smeared in his bathroom. Several hours and hard scrubbing later he showered and retired to bed. No matter how hard he tried he could not get rid of the awful stench that had accosted his nostrils.

Next morning the girls grinned as they noticed the dark rings beneath his eyes and the tired stoop of his body. "More to come" they whispered to each other. That night, the stench was worse but this time he could not track it down. All he could do was open all the windows and pray for a cleansing breeze. No breeze came. First he thought of reporting the matter to Helen; the General Manager always knew what to do. Then he realised that there was no one he would tell; it could be any one of the kitchen staff, or their boyfriends or husbands. When his nefarious activities came to light his reputation would be ruined. He would be out of work and unemployable; not only that, he would be the joke of the entire industry all across Europe. The realisation came early and with emphasis; he could not report this to Helen or the Garda or anyone else. He must solve this problem himself.

Punch drunk with lack of sleep he returned to work the next day. He would solve this venomous attack upon him, it must be one of the staff! Marie, one of his Waitress 'friends' mentioned to him that Ann and Bev had been in Galway the previous weekend; the same weekend he was in the City. "This was it" he thought "it has to be either Ann or Bev but which one?" Now he had his suspects!

No matter how closely he observed them Ann and Bev behaved in their normally friendly manner. The stench in his rooms was getting worse.

On Wednesday Ann had her day off and that evening Pierre discovered that all his designer clothes had been shredded. Now he had his suspect. It could not be Bev as she had been in his company all day. Now he would keep a very close eye on Ann.

Friday was Bev's day off and that evening Pierre discovered the long scratch marks on both sides of his beloved Alfa Romeo. Pierre's theory 'went out the window' by his process of reasoning the culprit could not be Ann or Bev, someone else must hate him! His rooms were uninhabitable so he booked into a guest house in the village. For the first time in almost a week he had a good night's sleep. Having eliminated Ann and Bev from the investigations he now confided in them; separately, of course and in the strictest confidence. He installed hidden cameras in his still putrid rooms and in the kitchens and naturally he told Ann and Bev.

The torture continued; his Cartier watch disappeared, his credit cards were cut into tiny pieces and still he was no nearer the truth.

Pierre was worked to a standstill, he missed his morning break and his lunch. By three pm he was on the point of collapse and desperately in need of sustenance. Nodding to Bev he asked her to make him a sandwich and get him a glass of milk. Together Ann and Bev made up a delicious chicken salad, buttered some bread, placed them on a tray with a glass of milk and Bev carried the treat across to Pierre. "Thanks" he whispered as Bev returned to her work. Pierre, a 2 star Michelin Chef of world renown lifted the chicken leg in his fingers and raised it to his mouth. The chicken was delicious as were the tiny tomatoes, the greens and the boiled egg. As he reached for the glass of milk the hotel cat brushed against his leg. Carrying his milk to the outer door, Pierre lowered the glass and poured the milk into the cat's dish.

Returning to his station Pierre placed the half full glass on a work top and lifted the final piece of egg. As he reached to 'finish off' his milk he noticed the cat lying at the door in a strange position. Returning to the milk dish he saw immediately that all the milk was gone and the cat was dead. Realisation dawned and he began to run back to his station, just catching Ann rinsing out his milk glass. He looked across at Bev and she smiled back, Ann was also smiling.

Frantically he ran to his rooms, threw his clothes in bags and rushed out to his badly scratched car. Maybe he could get a job in Kerry, he had heard that a hotel in Kenmore was looking for a first class chef. He sped away.

Ann and Bev took a few minutes to go to Pierre's room and remove the mattress from his bed. Struggling to carry the awkward mattress they managed to get it to the dump where they dowsed it with petrol and set it on fire. In minutes the mattress with the prawns and fish heads sew in was reduced to ashes. Ann and Bev took just long enough to pack their rucksacks, collect their pays and left.

As they headed out of the estate Bev mentioned that Pierre had spoken about moving to Kerry.

The girls started to hitchhike south!

Wee Hughie

Eva was on one of her 'efficiency' drives. Efficiencies to Eva meant 'economies' which was a polite word for savings. The easiest way to achieve 'efficiencies' was by reducing the number of staff while maintaining the same standards of service.

Eva was well aware that, over time, all Managers went native; falling for a sob story here, a hard luck tale there and recruitment increased ... without any discernible rise in standards.

Eva had situated herself in Helen, the General Manager's office and together they studied the Employment Registers.

Eva had already examined the Registrars for the hotel and for the estate services and was now scrutinising 'other services and miscellaneous'. She scanned down the page, then her eyes lit upon Hugh Fitzwilliam, two hundred Euros per week.

"Who is this Hugh Fitzwilliam?" Eva demanded.

For a moment Helen was 'stumped'; then it came to her.

"That's wee Hughie" she replied brightly.

"Who is wee Hughie?" Eva asked "and what does he do?"

"Ah" Helen smiled "Wee Hughie is simply Wee Hughie, he carries clients baggage to their rooms when they arrive and returns them to their cars when they leave."

"For two hundred Euros?" Eva was flabbergasted.

"Ah" Helen was still smiling "Wee Hughie does much more than that, he does all sorts of things."

"Things?" Eva's question contained oodles of cynicisms.

"Things!" Helen repeated.

"I must meet this Mister Hugh Fitzwilliam" Eva declared.

Eva decided that she would spend the following week conducting a 'work study' on Wee Hughie's activities.

"Helen" she declared "have Mr Fitzwilliam meet me in the foyer when he starts work; by the way at what time does the gentlemen start?"

"Usually about seven am" Helen smiled.

"Usually?" Helen frowned.

"Sometimes he comes in earlier, but I will have him meet you in the foyer at 7 am" Helen was still smiling.

Hugh Patrick Fitzwilliam or Wee Hughie as he was universally known left his special school at sixteen years old with a modicum of language, many domestic skills and the most pleasing personality. Loved by peers and teachers alike, Wee Hughie seemed destined for a lifetime of 'nothingness'; for this was 'backward' Ireland and Wee Hughie had Down's Syndrome. It would be wrong to say Wee Hughie suffered from Down's Syndrome as that implied pain and distress, and Hughie was endlessly cheerful, helpful and smiling. In his own inimitable way Wee Hughie walked into the foyer of The Grand Castle Hotel seeking employment and walked out having been appointed as a 'handyman'. Within days Wee Hughie had become an indispensable feature of the Castle, charming all and sundry with his winning ways.

Eva stepped into the foyer at the dot of seven where Hughie had been waiting for some time. "Mr Fitzwilliam" Eva queried. "Me" Hughie smiled that disarming smile, stepped forward and shook Eva's hand, with more vigour than she would have wished.

No one had told her that Hughie was Down's syndrome nor that his vocabulary was very limited.

Eva was unaware that her voice was patronising and insulting as she deliberately spoke slowly and staccato "I will be with you all day" she slowly enunciated her speech.

"Goody" Wee Hughie rubbed his hands in glee at having a companion.

As Helen had explained Wee Hughie hefted heavy baggage to and from the Hotel. He also ran messages for staff and guests, helped the maintenance men, got involved with the cleaning, went to the village to collect the Hotel's newspapers, swept the driveway until it was pristine and washed the Hotel 'limo'. Following a fifteen minute lunch break he cut grass for Charles the Head Gardener and carried away the cuttings, he escorted guests down to the pier, helped clean out the stables and escorted the children to the banana boat. Then it was back inside to unload supplies for the Housekeeper and later for the Kitchen Staff. Hughie disposed of soiled laundry, replenished stocks of linen and detergents for the Housekeeper and eventually went home at ten pm, having not had a break since one o'clock.

Eva tottered on her Jimmy Choo shoes to her private suite, before kicking of the torturous footwear and cooling her aching feet in the bath. She decided to have one small glass of Glenlivet before she took her shower. She poured the nectar and sat on 'her' chair. At four am she woke cold, stiff and sore and staggered over to her bed. Fully dressed she collapsed on to the bed where she drew the duvet about her.

Eva groaned as her alarm roused her, two and a half hours later. A quick shower, a coffee, dressed in flat shoes Eva was back in the foyer at seven am. Hughie was already busying himself, tidying chairs, emptying bins and smiling all the while.

Tuesday was even busier than the day before, with Hughie completing his chores on the run. Today it was almost midnight when Hughie left for home. Eva abandoned all conventions of hygiene, walking straight to her bedroom and falling fast asleep on top of the duvet.

Wednesday morning and a Chambermaid was sent to rouse Eva at seven thirty am; clearly she had slept in. At noon she forsook all hope of 'keeping up' with Hughie and abandoned the management exercise. Wee Hughie smiled throughout it all.

Eva returned to her suite, had a long bath and decided to 'lie down' for an hour. She crawled into bed au-natural and promptly fell asleep. Eva woke briefly around seven then immediately returned to the 'land of nod'.

Finally refreshed Eva met with Helen in her office on Thursday morning "How many hours does Hughie work each week?" she asked.

"I have no idea" Helen replied "Hughie just comes and goes but I would imagine it must be around one hundred hours".

"One hundred hours" Eva gasped "and we pay him two hundred Euros per week, we must be breaking a dozen European rules!"

"Not at all" Helen smiled, as she always did when she spoke of Wee Hughie "he is employed for thirty hours per week; the rest if entirely voluntary!"

"But Helen" Eva insisted "we could be accused of exploiting a Down's syndrome child!"

"Nobody exploits Hughie" Helen was still smiling "and I very much doubt that anyone sees him as a child". Then she went on to tell her boss how Hughie was the recipient of more than half the tips received by staff, always topped the guests satisfaction ratings and was the most popular person among all the employees.

The Management Guru who started off by considering making Wee Hughie redundant raised his salary to three hundred Euros per week and slipped away to Switzerland.

Wee Hughie continued with his cheerful chores.

Helen was having her afternoon tea when Wee Hughie rushed into her office, grasped her by the hand and firmly guided her out into the small lounge. Alone in the lounge was an elderly couple with a daughter who was clearly 'Down's Syndrome'. Hughie steered Helen over to the guests and declared "My Girl" smiling inanely at the young woman.

Helen was more than a little non-plussed. The elderly gentleman stood up and assured her that everything was fine; it seemed their daughter Lily had found a soulmate.

Hughie and Lily beamed at each other.

Assuming that Helen was Hughie's mother the elderly gentleman invited her and Hughie to join them. Following explanations of Helen's role, Lily's parents informed Helen (and Hughie) that they were seeking to rent a home in the village and were staying at the Castle until such times as they were successful. If it were possible Hughie's beam grew brighter.

Lily and her parents were soon successful in their quest, moving to the village within a fortnight. Then they started what was to become a 'tradition'. Every Tuesday afternoon they 'dropped in' to the Castle for cream teas. Hughie continued to be in the vicinity for the entirety of their stay.

Unannounced and without anyone's approval Lily joined Hughie in his voluntary work in the hotel; they were inseparable with guests and staff alike, beguiled by their innocent smile and obvious love for each other. As General Manager, Helen turned a blind eye to the blatant breach of employment law. For some time now Helen looked upon Hughie more like an 'adopted son' than an employee and she loved to see how happy Lily's presence made him.

As Hughie interrupted her afternoon tea once more, Helen resolved to keep her door locked during her break. Hughie was not to be deterred "Come" he ordered.

Seated in the lounge was Hughie's elderly father, elderly mother engrossed in conversation with Lily's parents. "Come on" Hughie urged Helen over to the parents. Hughie's mother elected herself as bearer of the news "Hughie and Lily want to get married" she announced.

"How lovely" thought Helen but she was well accustomed to hiding her feelings. "What do you think of that?" she asked. Hughie's father's voice was old, tired and tremulous. "Twenty years ago I would not have considered it, but I am dying and his mother is not getting any younger!" he did not really answer the question.

"What do you think?" asked Lily's mother, for she had seen her closeness to Hughie. "How would they cope? Where would they live? What if they had children?" mother's questions ran onwards.

Hughie had been standing, quietly listening. Now he gripped Helen's hand "Come" he insisted and marched outside. Determinedly he marched along the riverbank firmly grasping Helen's hand until they arrived at what had been the original farm house and outbuildings. Now the main house stood derelict, the labourers cottages unpainted and the animal houses in terminal decline. Hughie marched Helen over the property until they reached the end cottage. Nestled beside the river the cottage must have been a lovely home a long time ago, but now it was 'a mess' containing 'stuff' dumped from the Hotel. Hughie's smile grew as she steered Helen through the two bedded cottage "Lily and Me" he announced.

"You want to live here?" Helen asked. Hughie nodded.

"But everything is in ruins!" Helen protested.

"Not!" Hughie insisted leading her outside. He pointed to the other cottages, "people" then to various buildings where he announced "ducks, hens, goats, rabbits".

Helen jumped with delighted "A children's farm?" she asked.

Hughie nodded furiously.

"You are genius Hughie" Helen smiled "what a great idea and you could be Boss!"

"Me, boss" Hughie cheered.

Back at the Hotel Helen outlined Hughie's plan, adding "I believe that someone who can see that potential for development would cope admirably in a controlled environment."

"So you think they should marry?" Hughie's father asked.

"It's not for me to say" Helen suggested "but they are very happy together".

"OK" Lily's father interjected "let's see if he can turn his dreams into reality. If he can make a success of this venture he can marry Lily!" All eyes turned to Hughie. "Can" he grinned and went off, whistling.

Helen set the wheels in motion and left Hughie to 'get on with it'. Hughie still worked his thirty hours per week in the Hotel but then disappeared down the roadway to the farm. Each week he informed Helen that 'farm good' and, as she was very busy, she left it at that.

Three months passed, then Hughie marched into the Hotel grabbed Helen's hand and announced "ready". Hand in hand they walked down by the river to the old farm yard. As they rounded the corner Helen stopped short in amazement. The farmyard gleamed white in the sunlight; liberal quantities of whitewash had restored the tired old buildings. Roof tiles had been replaced, weeds rooted out, rubbish removed and the insides of the cottages painted. "Mine" Hughie insisted leading Helen to the cottage by the river. Gleaming whiter than all the rest due to Hughie's obsessive cleaning and painting; the windows sparkled brightly, the frames painted an emerald green, the garden pristine and the new fence did much to 'set off' the property.

"Inside" Hughie insisted leading Helen indoors "My God" she thought "it's White O'Morn from the Quiet Man". It may well have been, but it was White O'Morn with electric lights, running water, too fully furnished bedrooms, a bathroom and a handmade kitchen.

"How on earth did you manage all this?" Helen asked.

"Savings" Hughie managed, with difficulty.

"It is so beautiful, Hughie, Lily will love this!" Helen's response elicited an even bigger smile.

"Outside" Hughie commanded leading her to pens for goats and sheep, a diverted section of the river for ducks, a hen run, rabbit hutches and a paddock for ponies.

Helen's amazement tickled Hughie's sense of humour.

"Not finished yet" he announced. Then he added "want to marry Lily?" "Does Lily want to marry you?" Helen asked. Hughie nodded furiously.

When the parents saw what Hughie and several workmen had achieved they agreed to the wedding, with some reservations.

The event was held in the Castle with presents coming for the happy couple from all over the world.

The 'farm' still had to be stocked and final preparations made. Helen allocated a 'Frontsperson' to help Hughie with communications and administration and Lily was an enthusiastic volunteer but Hughie was in charge. And Helen let him get on with it.

Over several months Helen received written reports of the farm's progress from the 'Frontsperson', but Hughie's cheerful presence was no longer felt at the Castle. From time to time Helen noticed school and tour buses making their way down to the farm but the 'official' opening was yet to occur.

On impulse Helen decided to visit the farm on the week prior to the gala opening. Entering the farm, she could not believe her eyes, several buses were parked up on the newly laid car and bus park and individual cars were linked up in their parking lanes. The entire area was a buzz of activity with the first point of entry being the restored farmhouse. Helen failed to recognise the 'Frontsperson' seated behind her counter, laptop and phones at the ready. Hard copy detailing the activities and sights rested on the console, tables and attached to shelves on the wall. A finger post pointed upstairs where artefacts and historical documents from the Castle were on display. Schoolchildren babbled excitedly at one thousand years of history. Six of the cottages had already been let out with the parents and children enjoying the farming experience.

"How wonderful of Hughie" thought Helen "being able to see that holidaymakers would actually pay to do farm work". Four Fallabella ponies were being led around their pasture, by excited schoolchildren and equally excited teachers. Ducks quacked happily on the pond, accepting duck treats that children had been sold in reception. Children played with rabbits, goats and sheep and there, happily cuddling day old fluffy golden chicklets, sat Hughie, displaying his usual happy grin.

"Boss, Boss" he cried passing the chicklets to some lucky children and running to greet his friend.

"Come, come" he said having carefully closed the gate to the hens' enclosure.

Every step provided Helen with a new surprise, but Hughie obviously had a destination in mind. "Surprise" he announced pushing open the half door and entering the cottage beside his own new home.

The entire 'innards' of the cottage had been removed and converted into a coffee/tearoom. Standing beaming behind the counter stood Lily surveying her realm; the tearoom was full to overflowing but Lily coped admirably with the aid of several helpers. Hughie attempted 'volunteers' but the word was beyond him. "All volunteers" Helen asked.

Hughie nodded, happily.

"Tea?" Hughie asked.

"Yes, please" Helen responded. The hug mug of steaming tea was very different to her normal porcelain cup, but the contents tasted so good ... and the scone, butter, jam and cream was delicious.

Helen smiled all the way back to her office thinking how important it was to not look for a person's limitations but rather to see what their capabilities were.

The Mysterious Michael

The intrigue began at the moment Jim signed the register. The receptionist looked at the names, looked up and stared straight into the faces of Jim and Beth. The stare continued for several seconds until the new guests began to feel slightly uncomfortable.

"Is there a problem?" Beth asked already suspecting that their telephone booking had not been registered; or perhaps there had been a problem with her credit card.

Of a nervous disposition, Jim's voice took on a note of alarm. "Well is there a problem?"

The receptionist blushed and stammered, "Not at all, it is just that I noticed your surname is Urr."

"And?" Jim demanded impatiently.

"Well we have a waiter here whose name is Michael Urr and the name is unusual." She went on to explain that like the newcomers Michael was from the North of Ireland and she thought that there may be a connection.

Beth put on her best placatory voice, mainly to calm Jim down who could be impulsive when confronted with anything. "Where does Michael come from?" she asked with a winning smile.

"Belfast" the receptionist replied.

Jim interjected with, "Belfast has a population of seven hundred thousand people and we live in a part of Co. Down that is twenty miles from the capital."

"Oh!" the receptionist responded, completed the booking and directed Jim and Beth to their room.

The baggage handler was forthright, "Are you related to Michael?"

"No" Jim snorted, handing over a tip and guided the young man out of the door.

Stomping his feet impatiently at the entrance to the banqueting hall Jim asked sarcastically, "Do you think one of the staff will see us?" Beth demurred.

Then a very tall, very erect, very self-assured gentleman appeared, "Room number please?" he requested in a German/Austrian accent.

Beth smiled and provided the number. Immediately the tall man's demeanour changed; he smiled and said, "Ah Mr and Mrs Urr, did you know your namesake works for me?"

Jim began to say something but Beth interjected, "yes we have heard that you have a waiter named Michael Urr who comes from Northern Ireland."

Jim smiled through gritted teeth s the tall man introduced himself as Konrad, the manager and added that Michael was a very popular member of staff.

Jim's impatience was beginning to show so Beth smiled, "We look forward to meeting him!" The smile worked as Konrad preceded them to a table with a magnificent view across the lough and assured them of first class service.

Following a superb meal the sated couple returned to their room where they found the chambermaid turning down their bed. "Mr and Mrs Urr" she exclaimed, "I am so pleased to meet you, did you know that we have a Michael Urr working in the hotel?"

Only Beth detected the slightest note of irritation in Jim's voice as he responded, "So we have heard" then sotto voce, "numerous times!"

For three days the ghost of Michael Urr haunted Jim and Beth wherever they went and whoever they met. Beth's reaction was always a winning smile; Jim's was somewhat different.

At breakfast on their fourth morning Jim finally lost his patience when Breige (the latest waitress) asked the usual question. Staccato voiced Jim 'spat out', "For God's sake bring the mysterious Michael to meet us!"

Breige seemed hurt, "I can't do that" she responded "Michael has not come into work for the last four days. Probably flooding" she added "his home is remote and the rain has been torrential."

Again Beth saved the day, with her usual sunny smile when she proclaimed, "We are really looking forward to meeting Michael!"

Jim's face was thunderous!

Then it was their final night. The banquet was superb, the after dinner pianist sublime and the final nightcap tasted like nectar from the Gods.

As usual Beth was gently snoring within minutes of her head 'hitting the pillow'. Equally, as usual Jim paced the room unable to control the buzzing in his head; it was ever thus, Jim worked himself into a state on the night before his return from a holiday.

Eventually he could 'stick it no longer' so sock soled Jim tiptoed down the corridors and into the snooker room.

Turning on the light above the table Jim 'racked up' the balls, collected and chalked the cue and walked to the baulk end of the table.

Before he had struck the white ball a soft voice whispered out of the darkness, "Would you like to make a game of it?"

"Sure" responded Jim when he got over the shock of having a companion in the darkness.

"One euro per frame?" the newcomer asked.

"One euro" Jim agreed.

The games ebbed and flowed until it was four games all. Over the course of nearly three hours Jim learned all about the mysterious Michael. He left Belfast at the height of the 'Troubles', disgusted by the behaviour of his countrymen. One day he took a bus without knowing where he was going. With all his worldly possessions on his back Michael kept riding the buses until he ran out of money in Galway. Jobs were easy to come by and he laboured in various jobs for six years before getting a post in the Grand Castle Hotel. Within days Michael knew that he had found his spiritual home so he decided to put down roots. With limited money he put a deposit down on a dilapidated cottage and moved in without water or homely comforts. For ten years he worked in the hotel earning good wages and better tips and friends urged him to buy a better house. But Michael loved the remoteness of his home which now had electricity, running water and a plentiful supply of turf to keep him warm.

Michael's soft voice, with just a trace of the 'North' still in it was beguiling, painting a picture of a rural idyll.

Then it was time for the final frame. Michael reminded Jim that it was after four in the morning and work started at seven.

Then he laughed, "Let's make the last frame a good one. We could up the ante for some excitement."

'Here it comes' Jim thought 'the hustler is going to suggest a final frame for big money. This is how he made his money' the thought seared in Jim's head. 'Would it be fifty euros, a hundred or more?'

Michael was still laughing, "Well" he asked.

"How much?" Jim asked determined to prevent a hustle.

185

"How about two euros?" Michael asked.

Jim relaxed but it did not help him as Michael won the final frame.

"Time for bed" Michael announced as he commenced the clearing up.

"Time indeed" Jim responded "see you at breakfast."

"Perhaps" Michael smiled.

Beth was still snoring when Jim crept into bed. In minutes he too was fast asleep.

Standing waiting for service at the entrance to the dining room Jim began to recount the previous night's experience with Beth, only to be met by Konrad the dining room manager.

Konrad epitomised Teutonic efficiency, "Good morning Mr and Mrs Urr, your table is prepared."

Jim could not hold back a smile, "Well Konrad, I finally met the mysterious Michael."

Konrad's expression froze, "You did, are you sure?"

Jim pointed to the framed photograph of staff receiving an award for the best hotel, "That is my new best friend Michael Joseph Urr, snooker champion extraordinaire!"

Konrad glanced at the figure at which Jim pointed. With a solemn face he opened the local newspaper at page six, handing it silently to Jim. The headlines could not have been more explicit.

LOCAL MAN DIES IN FLOODED RIVER.

Beneath the headline was a recent photograph of Michael with a report from the pathologist where she estimated that the body had been in the river for at least three days!

Jane

Helen's heart was swollen with compassion or was it pity? Sitting on the other side of Helen's desk was a young woman who might have been twenty years old; or forty if one concentrated on the pain etched on her scarred face.

The young woman 'dived' into her briefcase and extracted a sheaf of cards; she shuffled through the pack and finally held one up. It read, "I do not want your pity, I want a job." Helen could have bitten off her own tongue following her most insensitive if unintended utterance, "Are you unable to speak?"

Realising the discomfiture, Helen apologised, "I'm sorry, I should have been more sensitive."

The young lady smiled and her face 'lit up' momentarily disguising the jagged scar that ran from her right eye all the way down to her chin.

The young woman extracted another card, "I was caught in an explosion in Belfast five years ago that took my right eye and my voice box in addition to leaving me almost completely deaf.

Helen began to speak but was interrupted by another card, 'I can read your lips.'

Helen nodded, "What can you do?"

A look of bitterness flickered across the young woman's face. Dramatically she scribbled on a card then held it aloft, 'Don't see what I cannot do, look for what I can do' was etched on the card.

"Fair enough" Helen replied "but there are many jobs that you cannot do; for example you could not be a telephonist, nor could you deal with queries from our guests."

Tears trickled down the young woman's cheeks as she pushed herself upright.

Helen was not psychic but she could 'read' the young woman's thoughts 'another rejection, another manager not prepared to give me a chance'.

As the young woman was half turned away from her Helen gestured to her indicating that she should sit down.

The young woman retook her seat.

"Alright" Helen said "I shall conduct this interview as near as possible as I conduct all others."

The young woman smiled in gratitude.

"Let's begin with your name."

The young woman spelled out Jane in sign language then reached for her cards.

"That is fine," Helen stated "I have a basic knowledge of sign language. Next why do you want a job?"

Jane scribbled furiously, covering three full cards. Her mother was taken ill and would require nursing home care. Jane had little money but she loved her mother who had always cared for her. She had written of the love her mother had shared when Jane lay shattered in hospital, how she had coaxed and cajoled when the blackness of depression had overwhelmed her. Not sparing herself Jane wrote how her mother had discovered her semi-conscious following an overdose of sedatives and her arm hacked with by a razor blade, never judging, always encouraging and reassuring Jane that she was still beautiful. The final line of script was written in bold letters 'I MUST KEEP HER AT HOME. I CANNOT LET HER GO INTO A HOME.

Helen looked up and Jane showed another card 'I have to get enough money to pay for care in our own home.

Helen lowered her eyes and whispered, "I understand!" Jane was writing again, "not something given out of pity if I get anything it must be a real job!"

Helen nodded, then rose to her feet "Let's walk around inside and outside and see what is available." She added, "I am not promising anything but let's just see."

As they walked Helen was struck by the grace of Jane's demeanour. Despite her handicap Jane could be mistaken for a model by anyone walking behind her; her long black hair shone and played with her shoulders, her dress was immaculate and Helen found herself wishing that Jane could speak.

As they perambulated Helen could feel her mood darkening; there were so many things Jane could not do and Helen began to despair.

As they wandered towards the new wing Helen suggested that they stop for coffee; at which point she could obtain a list of every job in the complex. Rather than examining everything, Helen suggested they could discard all the impossible and prioritise the possible.

Jane was writing again, 'A real job, no pity no poor Jane. I must get a job on merit.'

Helen's heart sank further, "I know" thinking, if I had a daughter I would like one with Jane's spirit.

Coffee over, Helen suggested a spot of sightseeing in the new sports complex. Recently installed the complex had everything required by a first class gymnasium. It also had saunas, massage parlours, beauty therapies and best of all an Olympic sized swimming pool.

Helen described to Jane how proud she was of the new complex which had been her brain child and had taken many months to come to fruition.

Jane's face lit up as they passed from room to room, then they were standing beside Helen's pride and joy – her Olympic sized swimming pool. She could not help herself; Helen was puffed up with pride. As the pair gazed around the magnificent edifice a young child, perhaps two or maybe three years old ran out from one of the changing rooms, slipped and skidded into the deep end.

Jane kicked off her shoes and dived fully clothed into the fifty metre pool. As Helen stood transfixed Jane streaked through the water with the speed and grace of a porpoise. Helen began to run.

Without pausing Jane dived down into the depths of the deep end, emerging several seconds later with a spluttering little boy. Helen arrived beside them, taking the child from Jane's arms.

Only then did the mother emerge from the changing room totally unaware of the drama that had just unfolded. Thanks to the miracle of mobile phones the hotel doctor was with them in minutes, proclaiming the 'casualty' to be fine if somewhat frightened.

When the doctor, mother and son had left Helen reached down and removed a blank card from Jane's briefcase. She wrote rapidly and handed the card to Jane. On it she had written, 'I saw what you could do, you have got a job as a lifeguard, swimming instructor and anything else I can think of!'

Both ladies smiled!

The Laundress's Lapse AKA The Great Conspiracy

Lady Heatherington-Smythe was not the most popular guest in the minds of the staff of The Grand Castle Hotel. She did not so much arrive as 'descend' upon the Hotel, honouring it with her presence. Her husband, Sir George had never been at the Castle but her ladyship provided plenty of examples of his existence. Dispersed 'casually' around her suite, copies of Home and Country, Horse and Hound and Tatler lay opened at pages showing Sir George opening a fete, Sir George speaking at an illustrious convention, Sir George greeting several minor Royals. On one notable occasion the Times had run a full page spread which found its way into the residents lounge; not brought there by her Ladyship, of course.

Some of the more catty members of staff, familiar with the workings of google reported gleefully that she was only the third Lady Heatherington-Smythe. Google reported that her Ladyship was previously known as plain Mary Brown, but there was nothing plain about her now. Even cattier acquaintances claimed Sir George had found her in a cat house ... whatever that was!

Regardless of the truth of her origins her Ladyship took to gentrification much as a duck takes to water. She took elocution lessons, developed a cut glass accent; attended courses on fine wines, cuisine and haute couture and was an expert on all things cultural before Sir George launched her 'on the scene'. Twenty years on she was the 'centre of the universe' with her peers deferring to her great elegance and grace.

Sir George's family had made their money in the West Indies, growing tobacco and cotton and exploiting the slave trade. One hundred years later the slave trade was 'written out' of their history as the family had moved up the social scale.

Unlike most of their contemporaries the family not only held on to their wealth, they expanded it. Despite, two costly divorces Sir George, now in his seventies, was still a millionaire, many times over. His 'trophy' bride was nearing forty and nowhere near as alluring as she had once been. But her Ladyship was no fool, she had seen the way that Sir George looked at that skinny hussy, Cush-Andrews and it was now time to take action.

The hunt ball was being held in Galway city this year and the cream of society would be there, including the skeletal Cush-Andrews. Her Ladyship had prepared well for the coming battle, booking into The Grand Castle Hotel three weeks before the big event. Her Ladyship swam twice daily, attended the gym every day, hiring her own Personal Trainer and walked for miles in order to get fit. Nearing the big night she was delighted when the scales told her that she had lost seven pounds weight. Massages, spas, manicures and hair treatments followed again hiring her own personal Beauty Therapist. Her Ladyship looked great ... and she knew it. With fake tan and professionally made up on the night she would outshine that hussy especially when she introduced her piece de resistance. At vast expense she had flown to Paris and purchased her Versace creation. It was perfect, clinging in all the right places, revealing where necessary. At a touch under ten thousand Euros it was worth every penny, especially when she learned it was the only one like it in the world.

Now all that was required was to have the 'creation' freshened up by the Laundress. Her Ladyship's directions were crisp and simple. "A fine spray of delicately scented aerosol must be followed by the lightest touch with a cool iron". The Laundress was suitably deferential, carrying the delicate creation down to her domain. Reassured that the dress would be returned within the hour, her Ladyship turned to the Beauty Therapist.

The Laundress could never explain how the setting on the iron got turned to hot rather than cool. As she gingerly started her delicate task the Laundresses face turned to a look of horror as the flimsy material attached itself to the iron. Immediately realising the disaster that was happening she switched off the power and began the process of detaching the gown from the iron. Now separated, the Laundress gazed in horror at her error. A tiny triangular burn was clearly marked along the bottom of the gown. The Laundress burst into tears. "Anyone but her Ladyship" she thought, running for the Supervisor. Back in the steam room both ladies conducted an intense examination. Both arrived at the same conclusion it could not be turned up, the burn mark could not be hidden, there was nothing for it but tell her Ladyship. Then there would be hell to pay. As the Supervisor and Laundress stood holding the damaged gown up by the light Marie, a Chambermaid, entered seeking pillow slips "I have a dress just like that" she announced. "Really?" asked the Supervisor. "Yes" laughed Marie "they were marked as GENUINE FAKES in a flea market in Bodrum in Turkey. I bought one for one hundred YTL."

"Exactly like it?" asked the supervisor.

"I think so" she said examining the material. "Yes, exactly like it" she pronounced "when I got it home I didn't even like it!"

The Laundress explained the problem. The Supervisor wondered if Marie would like to run home and bring in her 'genuine fake'. If it could be used to repair the damaged Versace the Laundress would refund her money.

Marie was only too happy to oblige but she lived fifteen minutes away from the Castle and time was pressing.

"Don't worry about that" stated the Supervisor "I'll ring her Ladyship and explain that we have a problem with the electrics, but her dress would be with her with plenty of time to spare".

Meanwhile the Housekeeper, who had been passing when this disclosure was taking place stood silently 'taking it all in'. The Housekeeper slipped away before Marie rushed out and jumped in her car.

The Supervisor was very supportive as the Laundress raised her eyes to heaven praying for a miracle.

Forty minutes later Marie was back with her 'genuine fake'. All three scrutinised the gowns; the materials looked the same, felt the same, the cut and style was identical, nor could they see any differences in the colours. The Supervisor made the momentous decision "I think if we changed the labels, putting the genuine label on the fake we might get away with it" she claimed. "It's just possible that the real labels may have a code, so we had better change them".

As before, the Housekeeper stood outside hearing the whole conspiracy unfold and just as before, she silently slipped away.

The labels changed, the freshening complete, the Supervisor returned the dress to Her Ladyship. Her Ladyship scrutinised the gown from top to bottom, searching for creases or unwanted folds, eventually expressing herself to be satisfied. So happy with the product was her Ladyship that she slipped a twenty Euro note into the Supervisor's hand. Feeling rather guilty, she accepted the note and slipped away.

The great moment approached, the fake tan gave her skin a golden glow, then it was the turn of the Hairdresser and the Beautician to work their magic.

Deciding to forego a bra, her Ladyship slipped on her specially purchased flesh coloured thong and reached for the Versace. A smile of pure pleasure crossed Her Ladyship's face as she gazed at her reflection in the full length mirror. The dress was worth every Euro that she had spent. Her smile spread, she would show that mongrel Cush-Andrews how a real lady looked. She slipped on her Christian Louboutins and moved the door. Holding the door slightly ajar she checked that all her acolytes were already gathered in the foyer. Making just enough noise to attract their attention she moved to the top of the grand staircase where she paused, long enough to allow her coterie to gather at the bottom.

To a chorus of "oohs and aahs" Her Ladyship glided down the stairs. She paused again at the bottom to allow for further compliments.

The acolytes moved closer and the Housekeeper stood silently, partly obscured by a pillar. "May we touch?" someone asked, "It is perfect" another whispered, "I'm told it cost fifteen thousand Euros" one whispered to another "I heard twenty thousand Euros" the other replied. "Class will always out" the first remarked.

Her Ladyship stood serene and graceful accepting her dues than led her minions out to the limousine.

The Housekeeper smiled and padded silently back to her office!

The Managing Director

The new Managing Director of The Grand Castle Hotel was under no illusions; it was highly unlikely that she could hold this prestigious position if she had not been the daughter of Eva the Proprietor and Chief Executive.

Despite the scepticism and reservations of others, Harriet was determined to do a very good job. She would be a success despite who her mother was, rather than because of who her mother was.

Harriet knew that she had other hurdles to overcome; not only was her mother the Proprietor, she had also taken over the job of Helen, the late lamented General Manager. Helen had given fifty years of her life to the Castle and the Estate gaining 'legendary' status in the process. She had been universally loved by staff and guests with many claiming that she was irreplaceable.

Harriet knew that others on the sidelines were waiting to see her fail; not least the Hotel and Estate Managers who had strong claims on the position. Between them the Hotel Manager had given over sixty years service to the Company and were now accountable to a twenty six year old woman who had 'done nothing'.

The woman who had 'done nothing' had competed through a series of interviews against the other Managers. Even though the interviewing panel was independent of Eva, it was hard to escape the conclusion that Harriet had been appointed on name rather than ability. Staff who might resent her appointment would never be allowed to see the findings of the interviewers, nor unearth the many failings that the Managers had displayed during the series of interviews.

Following her appointment, Harriet had been advised by the Board of Directors about the limitations of the two people who would now be accountable to her and made the recommendation that they should be offered early retirement in order to let Harriet get on with her job. It was firmly believed, unanimously, by the Board that it would be easiest and best if Harriet appointed her own people to the senior positions.

Harriet had not hesitated; she would work with the present staff to the best of her ability.

Harriet had spent four years at an Ivy League University in America, graduating with Distinction in Management Studies. Two further years specialising in Hospitality, Personnel and Financial Management followed before a further two years working in one of the greatest Hospitality companies in the world. In those two years she had further developed her knowledge of Financial, Human and Material Management but taking over The Grand Castle Hotel and Estates would be a challenge even for her.

America had taught her so much, not just about Management Theories and Practices but also about different mores, values and customs. The U.S. a much 'younger' country than the first world European nations with their fixed attitudes, Americans valued hard work, drive, ambition and achievement in a way that European cultures did not. In America it was not vulgar to speak of wealth, express naked ambitions or chase the mighty dollar. The repressed, stiff upper lipped, gentry led values of Europe held no sway in the young vibrant America. It may well be an American Myth that every child, potentially, had a General's baton in his armoury or that the poorest 'son of the soil' could become President but it was indeed, a meritocracy ... or so Harriet believed.

Harriet had worked hard to achieve her American dream, but not to the exclusion of a social life. Young, free, beautiful and single she was a 'prize' to be sought by the young man of her faculty ... and by those farther afield. Harriet actually learned to like this 'brash hits' made by her male contemporaries. No subtly, no 'beating about the bush', rather a direct challenge almost when the men sought dates. It was the same in 'the bedroom department' where males simply stated their intentions to have 'their way' with her.

At first Harriet had been insulted, then she was amused and, by her third year, she was ingrained in the American way.

But Ireland was not America and Harriet was well aware that she would have to proceed with caution. While cautious she was determined to do things her way. She just did not yet know what her way was!

Harriet started as she meant to go on. There would be no apology to the Managers for gaining a position they thought of as theirs nor would she leave them with the impression that things would simply go on as before. For three hours she listened quietly as they explained their roles and the extent of the enterprise. It was only when Harriet asked for their vision of the way forward that they became strangely quiet. At lunch time she ended the meeting; telling them that she would be spending the remainder of the week orienting herself into the business. Before they left she quietly and politely asked the Managers to be available to her at all times.

Then she made her first major decision, she totally redesigned and redecorated her office. For the previous thirty years Helen, the General Manager had turned her office into a home from home. A style that worked well for her but Harriet had just spent eight years in America.

In came a Management Design Consultant, a Colourist and a Fen Chu expert. The 'new' office was open plan, well lighted with modern furniture and the latest in Communication Systems. Harriet expressed herself to be well pleased.

Then she sent for the Hotel and Estates managers. Fighting losing battles to disguise their contempt for the new office layout they offered their oligeanious praises for the modern concept. Harriet did not believe in wasting time so she instructed them to sit down and began her observations. Quietly she told them that she had been going through the staff rotas, but could find none for them. Then she introduced the 'dagger through their hearts'. "I'm told that you do not 'cover for each other'; nor do you keep each other informed about leave taking, days off and holidays".

Spluttering in unison they declared that there was no need for such measures as 'Helen was always there".

Harriet's voice took on a steeliness "Helen is not here now, I am and I most certainly will not be here all the time".

Her subordinates began to speak, but Harriet was not yet finished. From this moment onwards there will be once weekly, minuted meetings among us three. In the event of you being absent you will send a deputy together with your position regarding all items on the agenda. In addition I want you to commence monthly meetings with your team with all minutes coming to me. Finally, she stated, we will introduce a 'job swap' arrangement for three months so that each of you are familiar with the other's job starting next month.

The oily smiles were back "Great idea Harriet, we could not agree more".

As they rose to leave Harriet made her position clear "While we are in the workplace you will address me as Miss Henry".

"Of course, Miss Henry" the smiles were weaker but the voices still as oligeanious.

On the following Monday the Hotel Manager sent the Housekeeper to the first senior meeting, while the Estate Manager sent the Head Gardener. Controlling her fury Harriet asked after the whereabouts of the Managers. The Housekeeper spoke first "My Manager is hosting a reception". Harriet interjected "Is his presence totally necessary, or could you stand in?" "Anyone could do it" the Housekeeper said, hating her own disloyalty "it's a little presentation to one of the Waiters, who is leaving after ten years!"

Harriet looked perplexed "Monday is a strange day to leave, I thought most people left at the weekend" she looked towards the Housekeeper.

Clearly embarrassed the Housekeeper responded "Oh, he's not leaving until Friday. It was a 'spur of the moment decision by the Manager".

"Was it?" Harriet murmured then looked to the Head Gardener. "I don't suppose there is anyone leaving the Estate?"

"No Miss!" the Head Gardener responded "my Manager is testing the grass on the Golf Course!"

194

"Is he now?" Harriet rang for her newly appointed P.A.

"Come with me" she announced to the three staff members and walked to the presentation. She congratulated the waiter on his service and invited the Hotel Manager to join her.

"Which grass?" she asked of the Head Gardener.

"I'd imagine the sixth hole, by now" came the response.

"Right" she asked "where is the sixth hole?"

The Hotel Manager pointed in the general direction "Into my car" Harriet tensely commanded and setting off at breakneck speed she hurtled round the narrow road then swung the BMW on to the golf course.

"You can't do that" the Hotel Manager shrieked.

"I just did!" Harriet retorted "and I think you will discover that I can do almost anything I wish".

The Manager sat white faced in the back of the car.

The Estates Manager was at the top of his swing when the car hurtled into view "What sort of an idiot is this?" he screamed to his playing partner.

Harriet screeched to a halt, causing huge ruts in the playing surface. Grimly she thought "I won't be very popular with the Greenkeeper" but she had more pressing matters on hand.

"I believe we have a meeting" she directed her vision towards the Manager. The Manager and his partner stood white faced, open-mouthed and speechless.

"A meeting!" Harriet repeated.

The Estates Manager looked at the ruined fairway; he looked at Harriet then wisely decided to say nothing.

Harriet kept them standing in the sun for two hours as she conducted her meeting. Only the P.A. had shelter, as she took notes seated sidewise in the passenger's seat, feet out the side of the car.

Declaring the meeting over Harriet informed the Managers that they would contribute a half days salary to a local charity.

The Hotel Manager interjected "You can't make us do that!" "Once more, I think you will find I can. Of course, the choice is yours. You can make the donation or have a verbal warning placed on your record!"

The P.A. smiled as she recorded the decision.

Returning to her office, Harriet stared at the door. "Replace the nameplate" she instructed. She scribbled on a scrap of paper "change the wording to this."

The P.A. smiled as she read "Miss Harriet Henry, Managing Director." "In gold letters?" she enquired.

"Excellent idea" Harriet smiled for the first time that day.

Having failed with a 'frontal attack' the Managers resorted to more underhand measures to 'bring down' their boss. All failed and they failed for simple reasons; the Managers were not as well liked as they thought and Miss Henry's people centred approach, coupled with a warm personality and a strong sense of fairness had made her very popular. Consequently, Harriet got to hear of the latest schemes almost before the Managers had thought of them.

Having been thwarted at every turn the Hotel Manager retired four months into Harriet's tenure. Isolated and without support the Estate Manager left six weeks later.

Harriet smiled to herself; the Board had got their wish without having the expense of redundancy payments, Lawyer's fees and golden handshakes.

Harriet immediately appointed the popular and efficient Housekeeper to the position of Hotel Manager and 'brought in' a proven winner to take over the running of the Estate.

Harriet had been in post for more than a year and could afford to relax a little, allowing herself time for dreaming and for nostalgia. As she sat in her modern chair in her modern office her thoughts turned to an earlier time, when she was 'Harriet Smythe'. She often wondered what had become of Jack, the Medical Student, who would love her forever. "Probably married with three children" she thought. By now he must be a Registrar or a Surgeon or a G.P.; definitely not a Pathologist she thought.

A wistfulness swept over her as she considered her loss; they had been so young but she did love him then, she knew that now. There had been other men in her life, in America, but none 'matched up' to the lovely Jack. "What a shame" she thought that they had been so young. He had so much to do and she had been so driven to be a success, like her mother.

Over the course of several months Harriet set aside 'Jack time'. For fifteen minutes each day she would switch off her phone, tell her P.A. that she was not to be disturbed. Harriet was totally aware that the scenarios she created were pure fiction and reality could never live up the dreams she created. She did find though that her 'dreams' helped her to relax and enable her to face the remainder of the day refreshed and with renewed energy.

Harriet was in the middle of her 'Jack time' on the day of her twenty eighth birthday when the P.A. interrupted her reverie. Her P.A. knew that she must never impinge on this time as Harriet's voice was a little sharp as she asked "What?"

There is a young man in the waiting room looking for a Miss Harriet Smythe, who he claims worked here some years ago." The P.A. like all good P.A.s had long since learned of Harriet's subterfuge when she had kept secret her relationship to the Proprietor.

"What is he like?" Harriet whispered.

The P.A. gave his description adding "he is very handsome". Harriet decided on a little prying "Find out where he has been for the past four years, subtly of course."

The P.A. walked to the waiting room declaring that the Managing Director was searching through her files for Miss Smythe. It would take some time as Miss Smythe had only been at the Hotel for a short time and may not have left a forwarding address. The P.A. offered coffee and within ten minutes had extracted a 'life history' of the young man.s

Back in her own office she excitedly informed Harriet that the young man had been working in Africa on a World Health Organisation Project and had only just arrived back in Ireland.

"Bring him into your office" Harriet instructed and put you phone on 'conference', so I can hear your conversation".

"You wicked thing" the P.A. smiled.

Harriet rang back "Would you ask the gentleman to describe Miss Smythe" she teased "it appears there have been two Harriet Smythe's in our employment".

The P.A. knew there was 'nothing of the sort' but entered into the spirit of Miss Henry's teasing.

Harriet could hear clearly as the P.A. described the dilemma. "Perhaps you could describe 'Your' Miss Smythe" the P.A. smiled.

"Oh yes" the young man answered. "She was eighteen and that was ten years ago. As a matter of fact today is her birthday. She was neither tall nor small, with long glassy black hair that was like satin to the touch. She had the deepest, darkest brown eyes that you have ever seen. A beautiful face and a lovely figure and skin as smooth as silk. Her skin felt that it was permanently kissed by sunshine. She was perfect."

Harriet glanced in the mirror, regretting the fact that she had had her hair cut short. "He certainly has become more eloquent" she thought.

Harriet softly opened the connecting door, standing still for a moment to watch the recognition dawn on the face of Doctor Jack Pearson.

Printed in Great Britain
by Amazon

35534525R00118